CARTOON NETWORK

BEN 10

THE TRUTH IS OUT THERE

kaboom!

BEN 10: THE TRUTH IS OUT THERE, March 2019. Published by KaBOOM!, a division of Boom Entertainment, Inc. Ben 10, CARTOON NETWORK, the logos, and all related characters and elements are trademarks of and © Cartoon Network. A WarnerMedia Company. All rights reserved. (S19). KaBOOM!™ and the KaBOOM! logo are trademarks of Boom Entertainment, Inc., registered in various countries and categories. All characters, events, and institutions depicted herein are fictional. Any similarity between any of the names, characters, persons, events, and/or institutions in this publication to actual names, characters, and persons, whether living or dead, events, and/or institutions is unintended and purely coincidental. KaBOOM! does not read or accept unsolicited submissions of ideas, stories, or artwork.

For information regarding the CPSIA on this printed material, call: (203) 595-3636 and provide reference #RICH – 830078.

BOOM! Studios, 5670 Wilshire Boulevard, Suite 400, Los Angeles, CA 90036-5679.

Printed in USA. First Printing.

ISBN: 978-1-68415-319-0,
eISBN: 978-1-64144-172-8

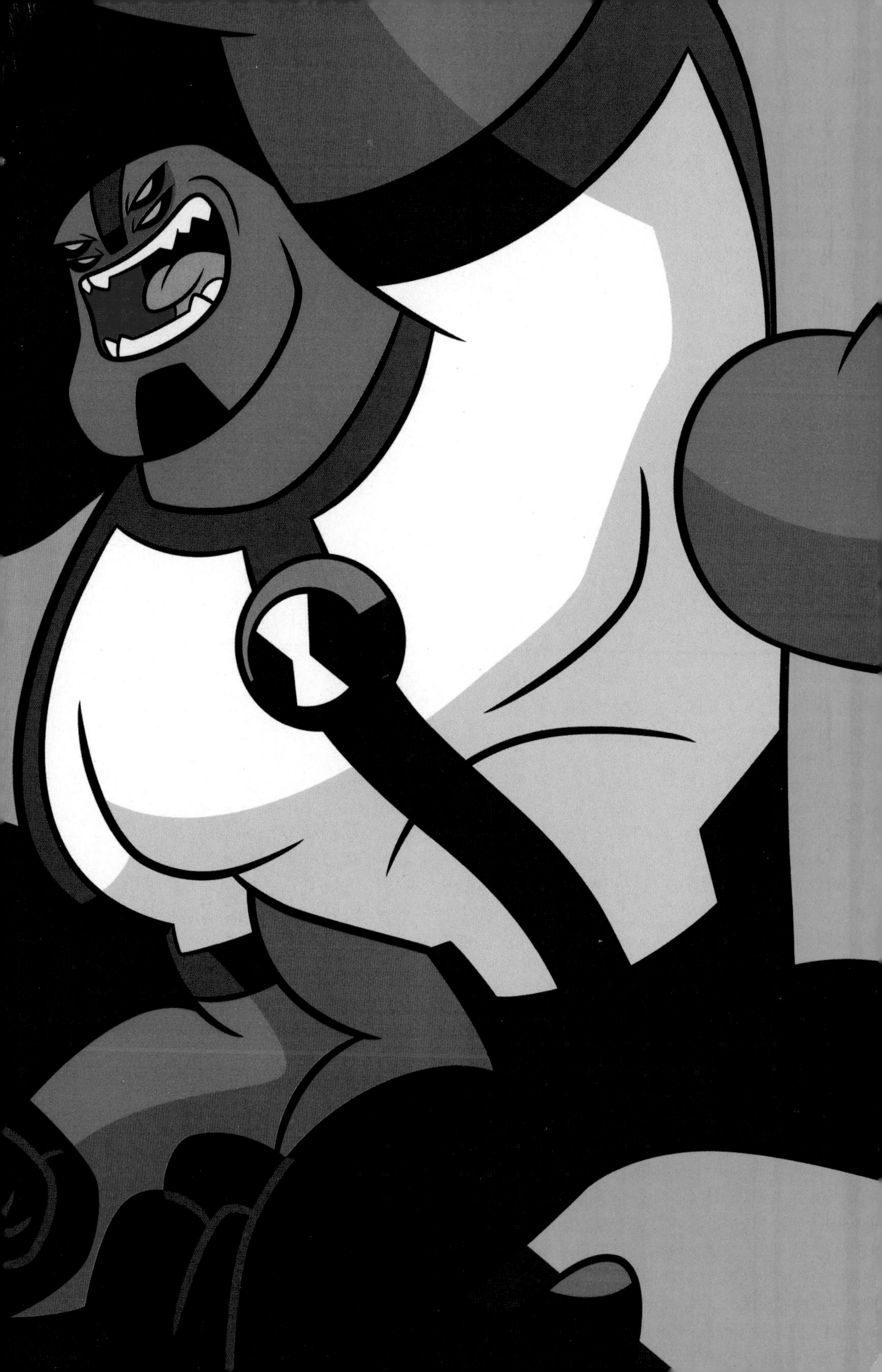

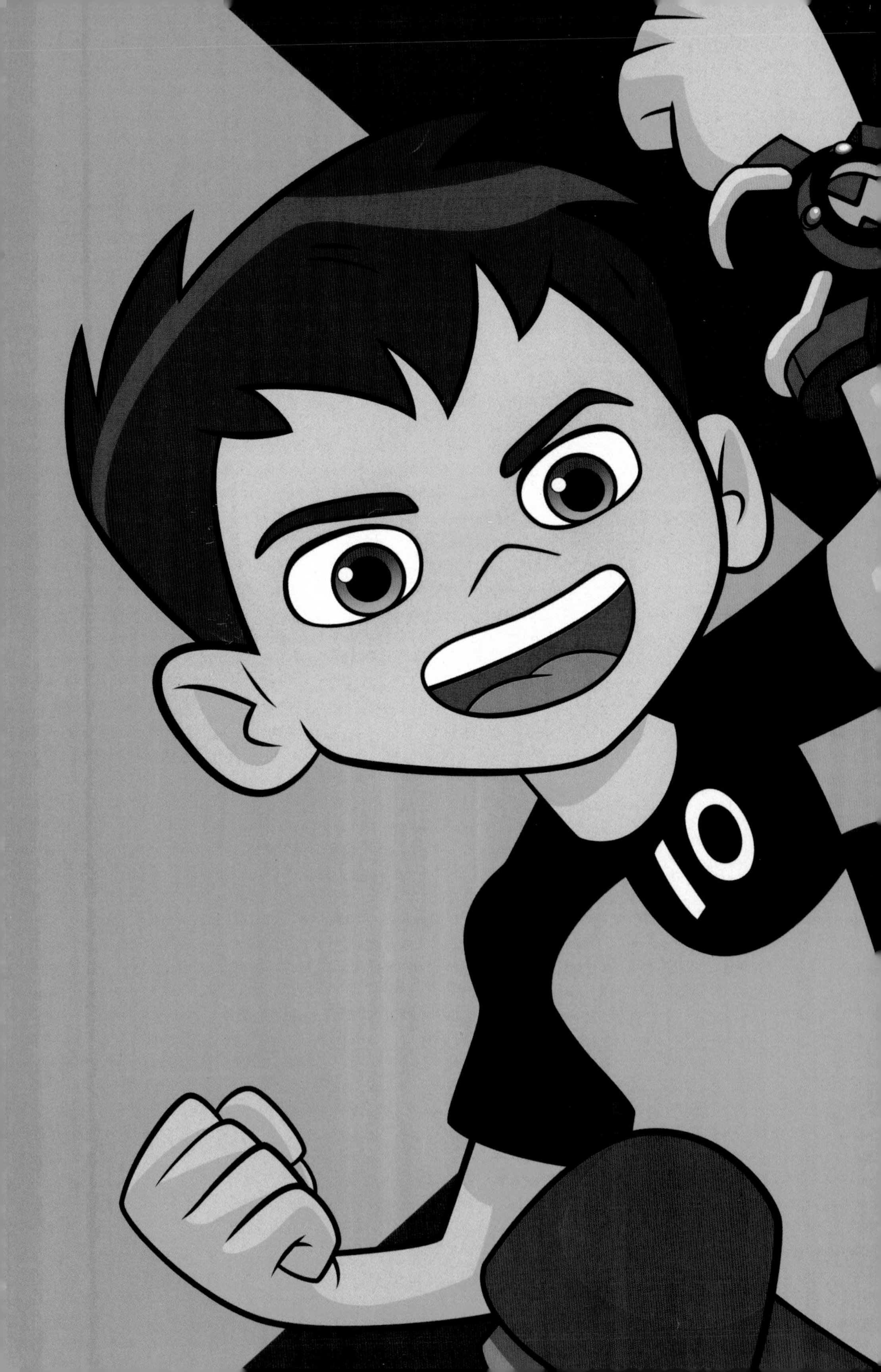

BEN TENNYSON IN...

THE TRUTH IS OUT THERE

WRITTEN BY
C.B. LEE

ILLUSTRATED BY
LIDAN CHEN

COLORED BY
MEG CASEY

LETTERED BY
WARREN MONTGOMERY

COVER BY
MATTIA DI MEO
WITH **LING CHEN**

DESIGNER
JILLIAN CRAB

ASSISTANT EDITOR
MICHAEL MOCCIO

EDITOR
MATTHEW LEVINE

WITH SPECIAL THANKS TO
WHITNEY LEOPARD AND **CAMERON CHITTOCK**

AND VERY SPECIAL THANKS TO
**MARISA MARIONAKIS, JANET NO,
BECKY M. YANG, TRAMM WIGZELL,
KEITH FAY, SHAREENA CARLSON,**
AND THE WONDERFUL FOLKS AT
CARTOON NETWORK.

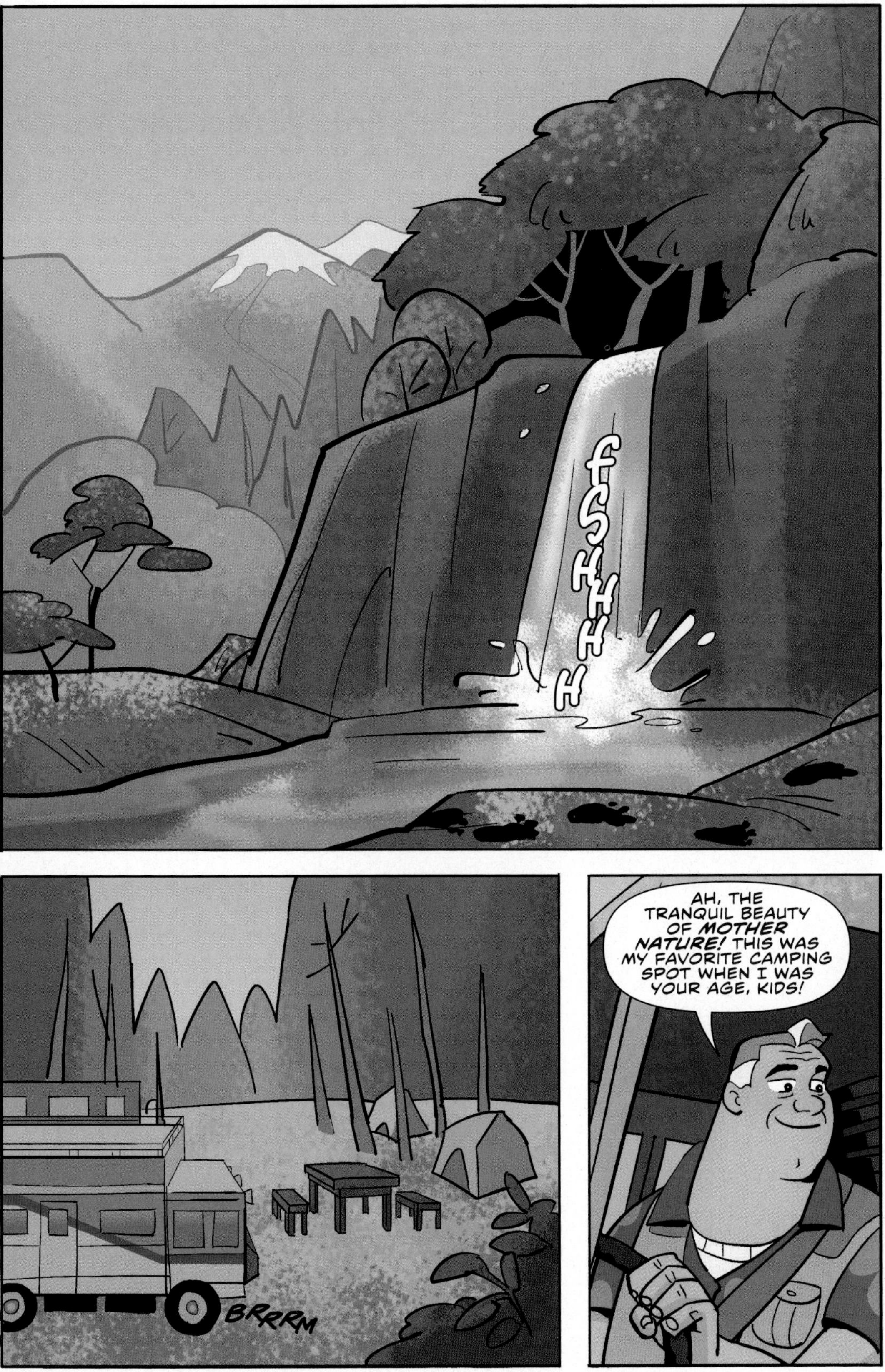
FSHHHHH
BRRRM
AH, THE TRANQUIL BEAUTY OF MOTHER NATURE! THIS WAS MY FAVORITE CAMPING SPOT WHEN I WAS YOUR AGE, KIDS!

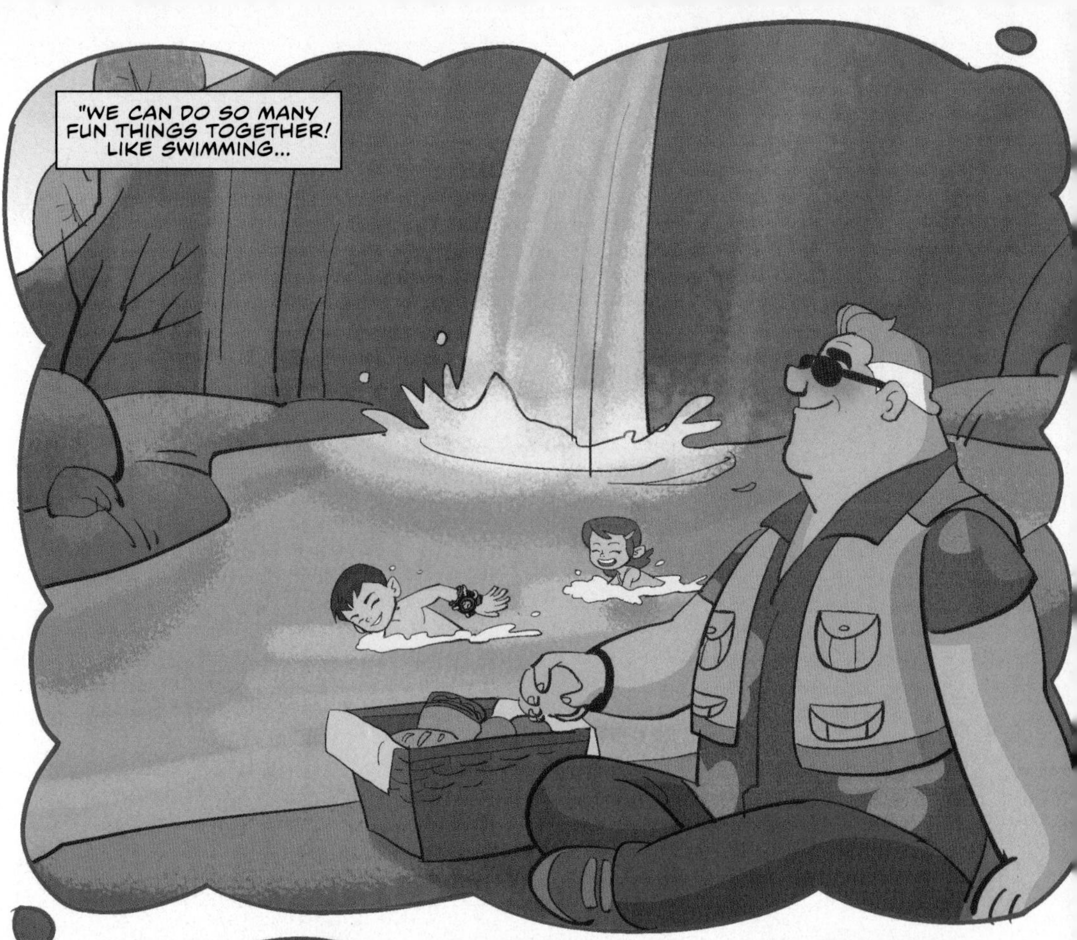
"WE CAN DO SO MANY FUN THINGS TOGETHER! LIKE SWIMMING...

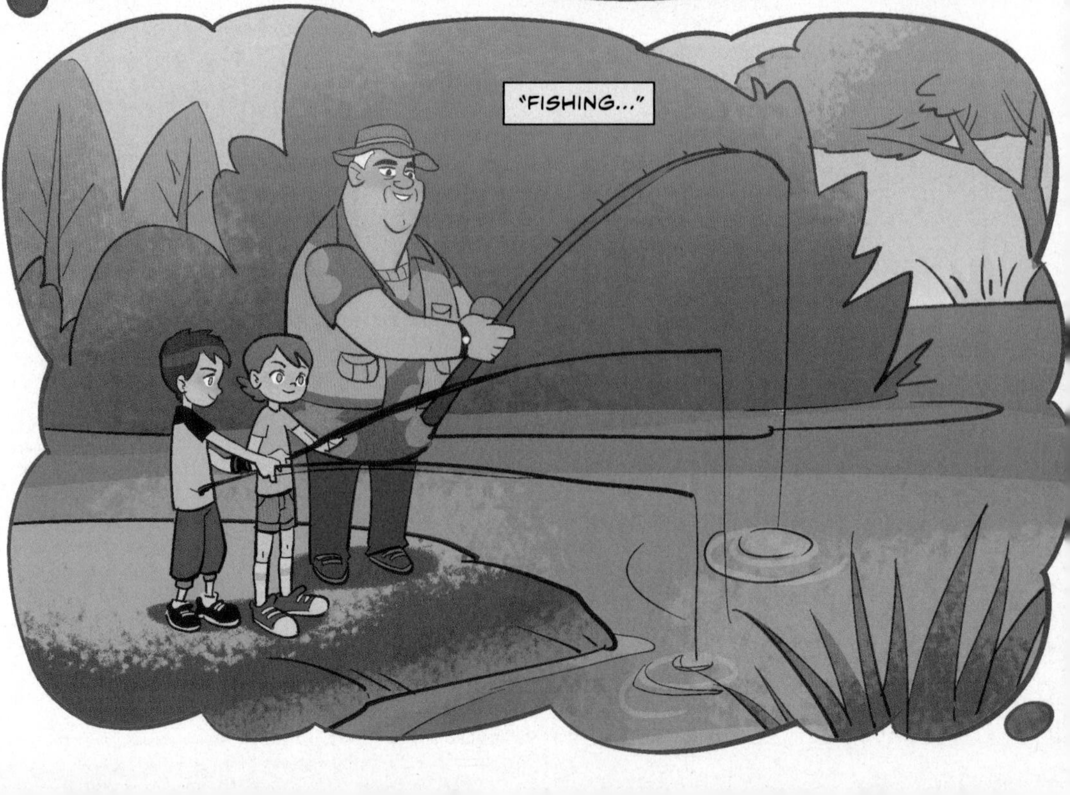
"FISHING..."

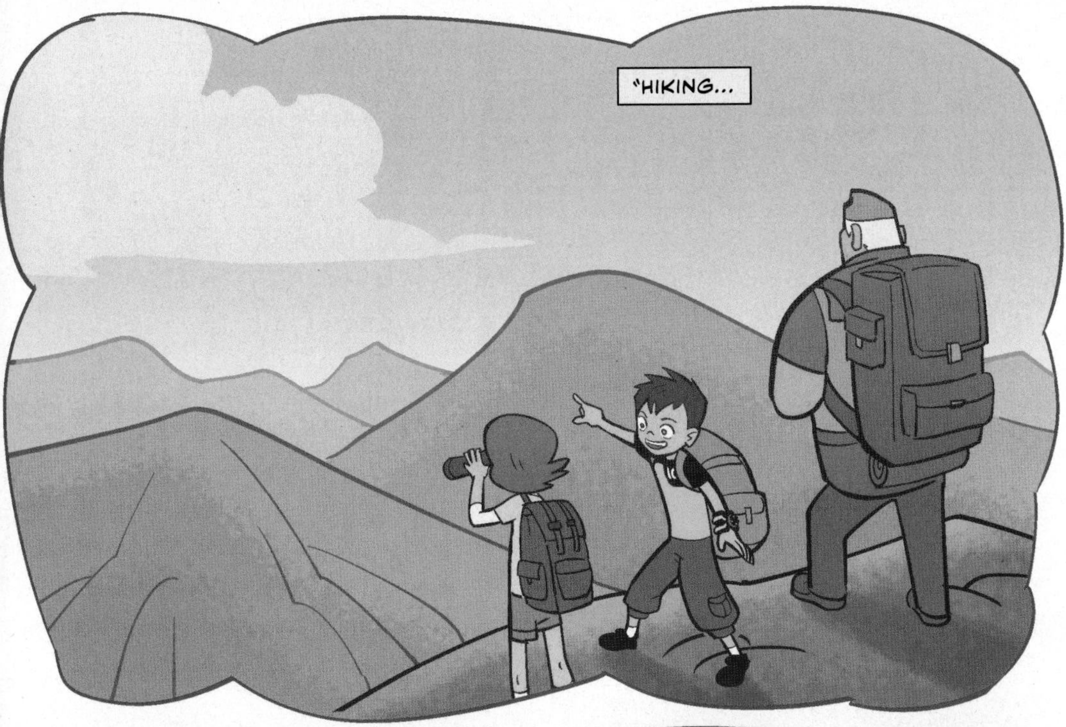
"HIKING...

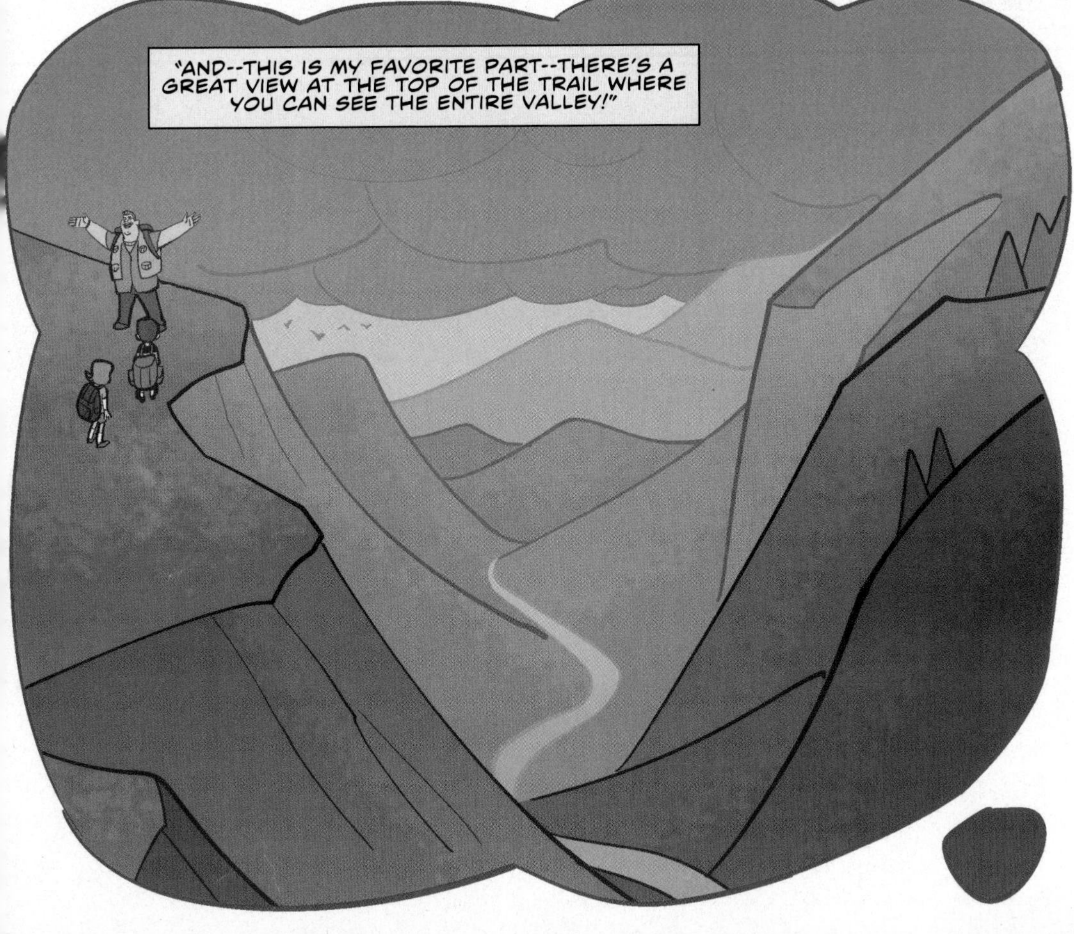
"AND--THIS IS MY FAVORITE PART--THERE'S A GREAT VIEW AT THE TOP OF THE TRAIL WHERE YOU CAN SEE THE ENTIRE VALLEY!"

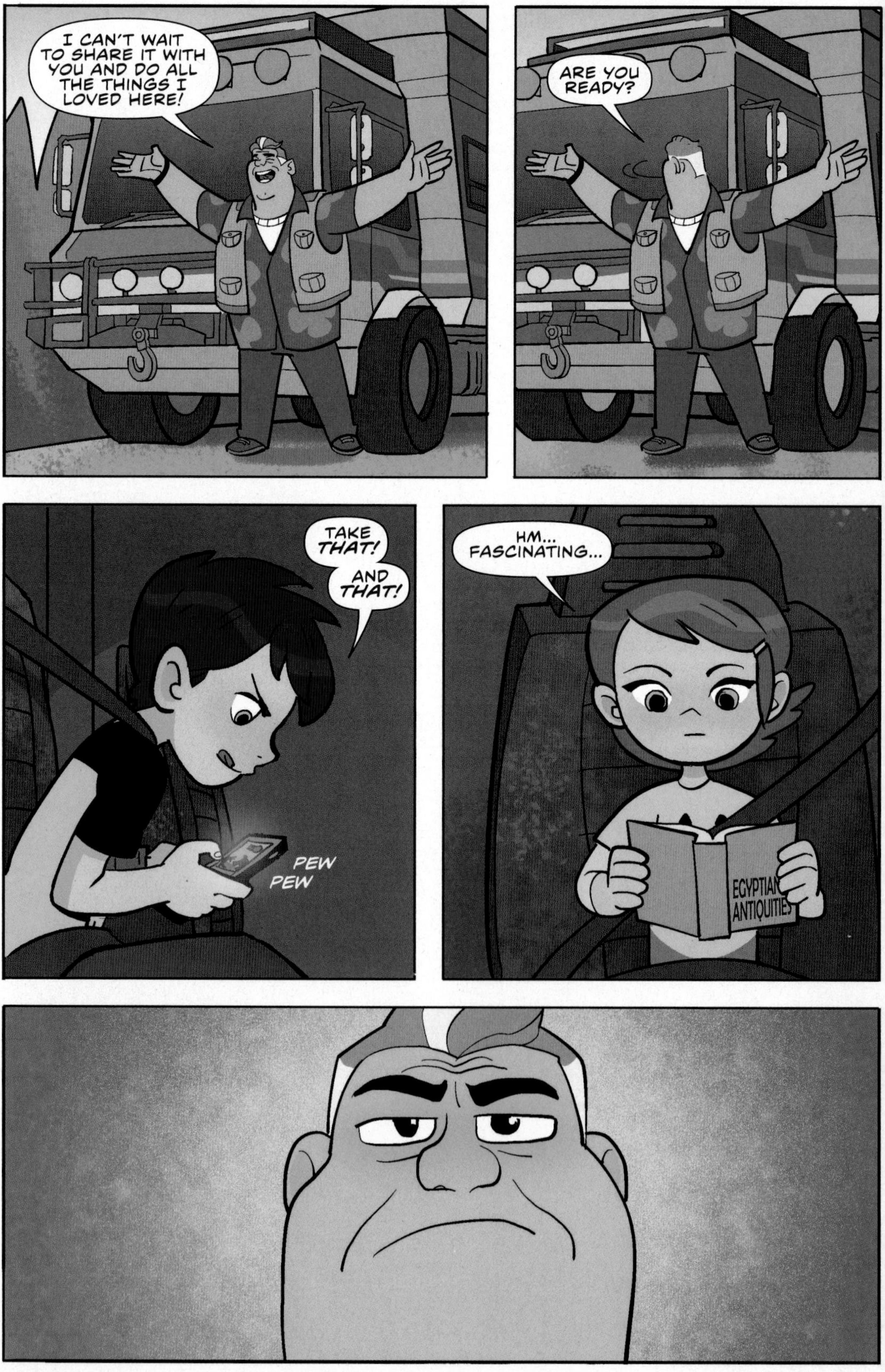
I CAN'T WAIT TO SHARE IT WITH YOU AND DO ALL THE THINGS I LOVED HERE!
ARE YOU READY?
TAKE THAT!
AND THAT!
PEW PEW
HM... FASCINATING...
EGYPTIAN ANTIQUITIES

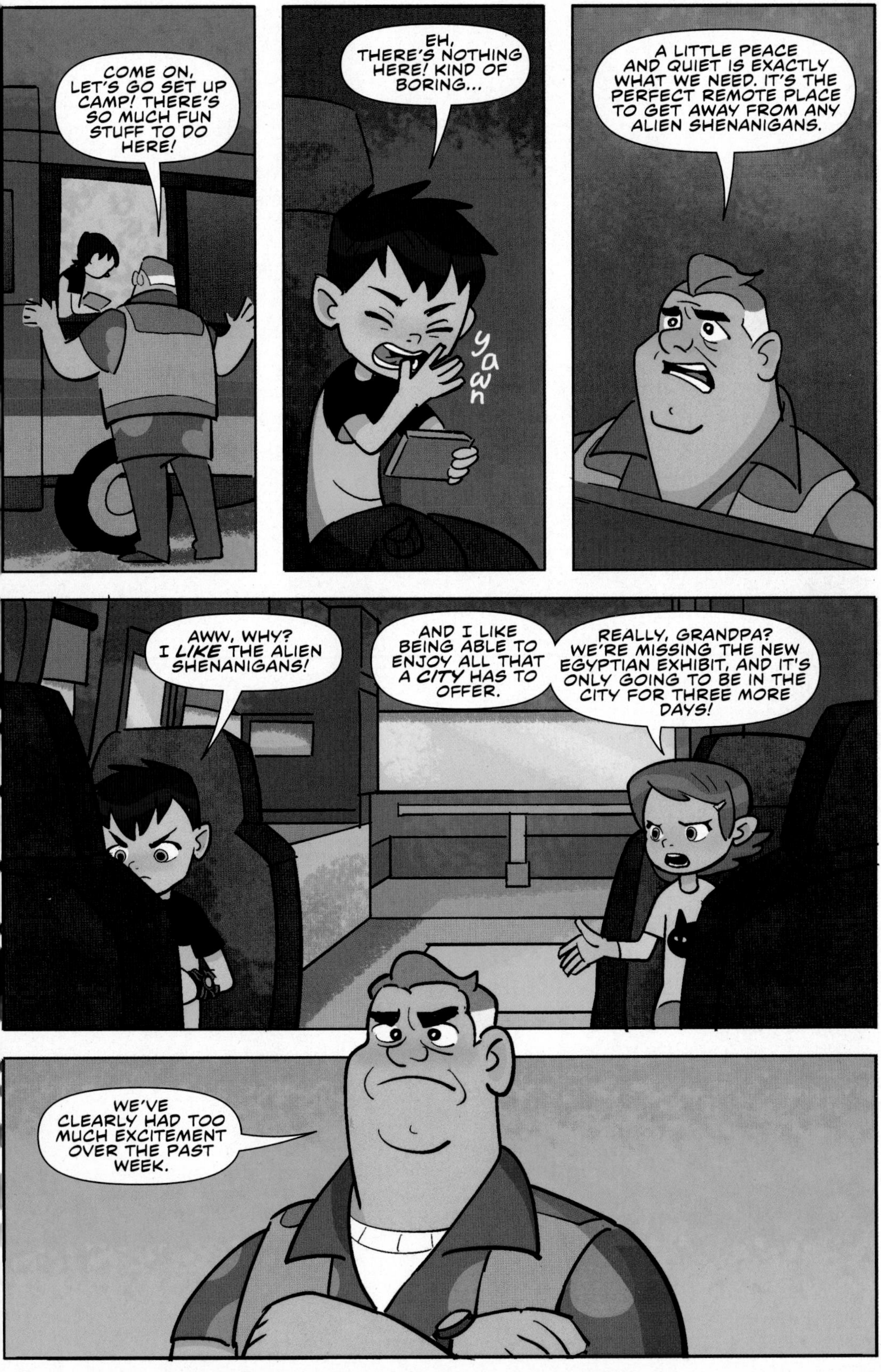
COME ON, LET'S GO SET UP CAMP! THERE'S SO MUCH FUN STUFF TO DO HERE!
EH, THERE'S NOTHING HERE! KIND OF BORING...
yawn
A LITTLE PEACE AND QUIET IS EXACTLY WHAT WE NEED. IT'S THE PERFECT REMOTE PLACE TO GET AWAY FROM ANY ALIEN SHENANIGANS.
AWW, WHY? I LIKE THE ALIEN SHENANIGANS!
AND I LIKE BEING ABLE TO ENJOY ALL THAT A CITY HAS TO OFFER.
REALLY, GRANDPA? WE'RE MISSING THE NEW EGYPTIAN EXHIBIT, AND IT'S ONLY GOING TO BE IN THE CITY FOR THREE MORE DAYS!
WE'VE CLEARLY HAD TOO MUCH EXCITEMENT OVER THE PAST WEEK.

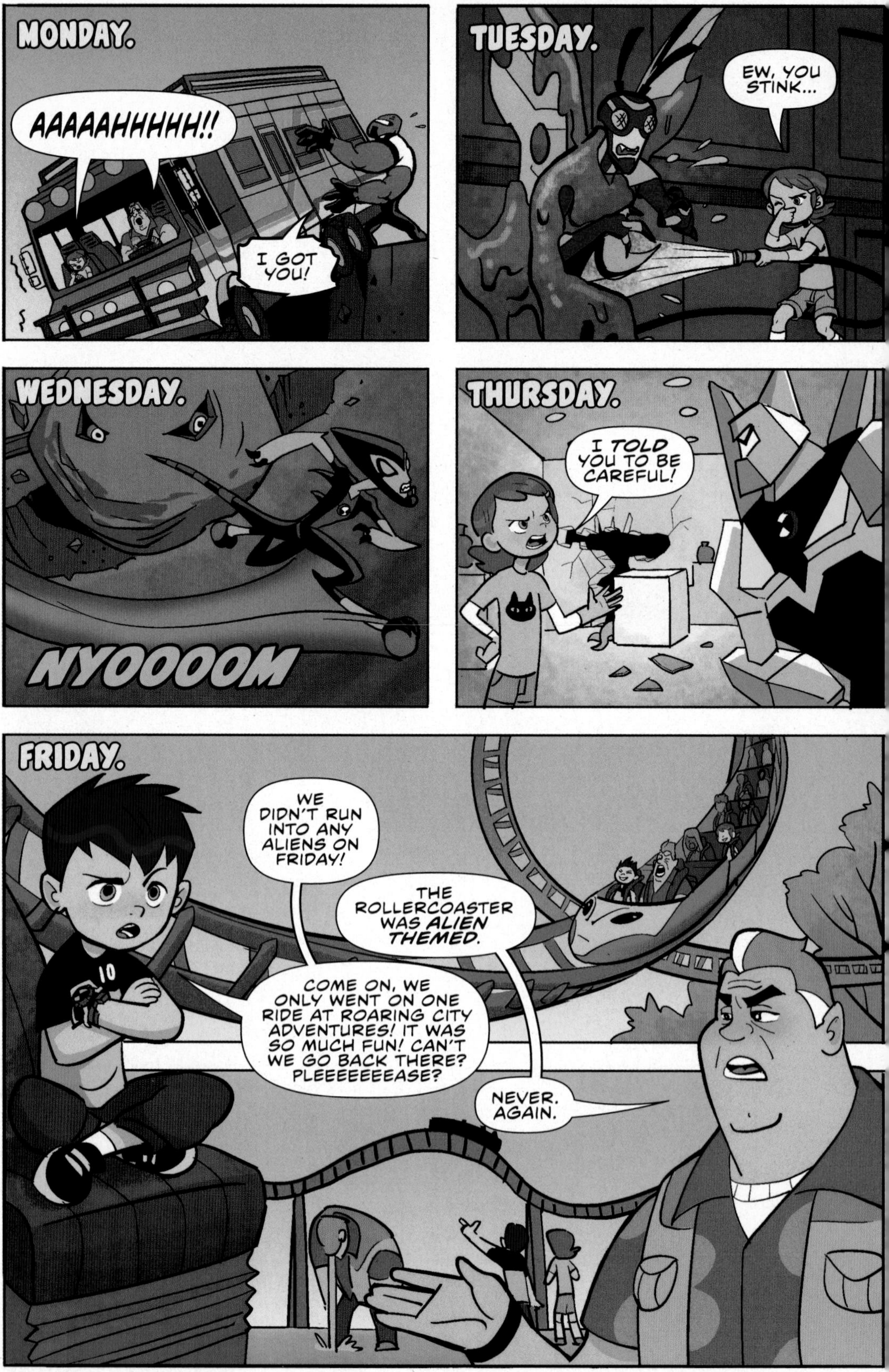
MONDAY.
AAAAAHHHHH!!
I GOT YOU!
TUESDAY.
EW, YOU STINK...
WEDNESDAY.
NYOOOOM
THURSDAY.
I TOLD YOU TO BE CAREFUL!
FRIDAY.
WE DIDN'T RUN INTO ANY ALIENS ON FRIDAY!
THE ROLLERCOASTER WAS ALIEN THEMED.
COME ON, WE ONLY WENT ON ONE RIDE AT ROARING CITY ADVENTURES! IT WAS SO MUCH FUN! CAN'T WE GO BACK THERE? PLEEEEEEEASE?
NEVER. AGAIN.

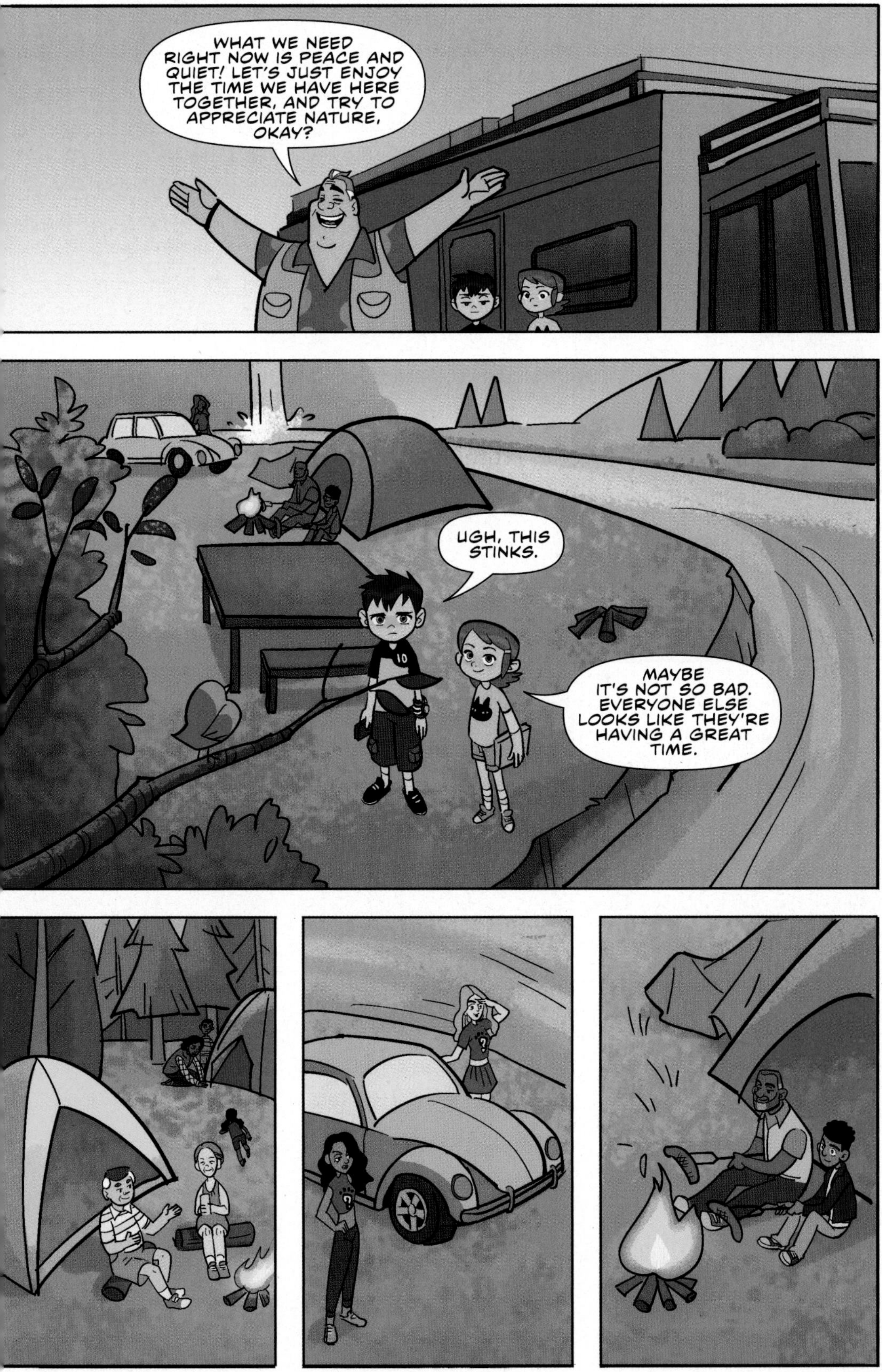
WHAT WE NEED RIGHT NOW IS PEACE AND QUIET! LET'S JUST ENJOY THE TIME WE HAVE HERE TOGETHER, AND TRY TO APPRECIATE NATURE, OKAY?
UGH, THIS STINKS.
MAYBE IT'S NOT SO BAD. EVERYONE ELSE LOOKS LIKE THEY'RE HAVING A GREAT TIME.

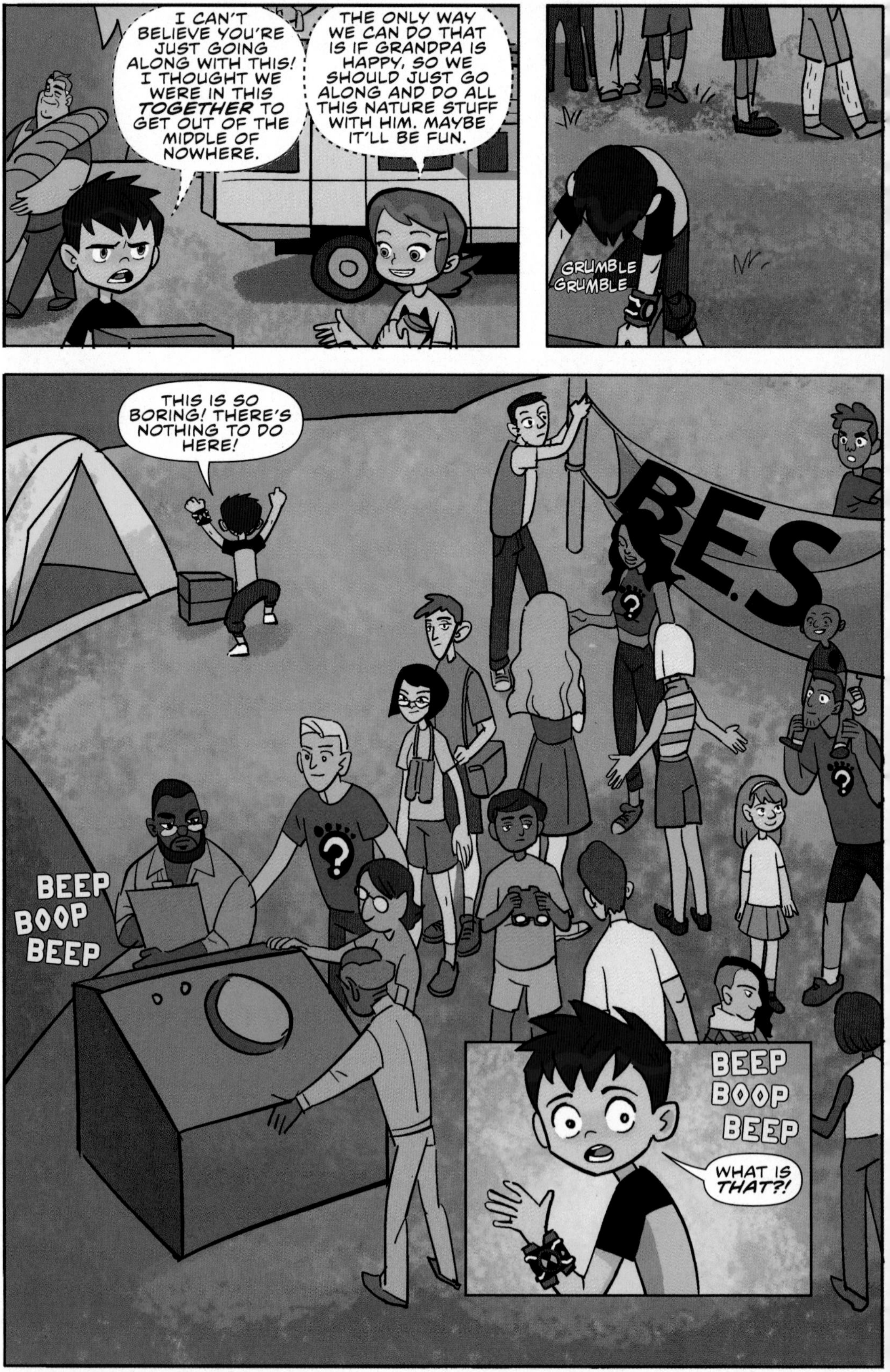
I CAN'T BELIEVE YOU'RE JUST GOING ALONG WITH THIS! I THOUGHT WE WERE IN THIS *TOGETHER* TO GET OUT OF THE MIDDLE OF NOWHERE.
THE ONLY WAY WE CAN DO THAT IS IF GRANDPA IS HAPPY, SO WE SHOULD JUST GO ALONG AND DO ALL THIS NATURE STUFF WITH HIM. MAYBE IT'LL BE FUN.
GRUMBLE GRUMBLE
THIS IS SO BORING! THERE'S NOTHING TO DO HERE!
B.E.S
BEEP BOOP BEEP
BEEP BOOP BEEP
WHAT IS *THAT?!*

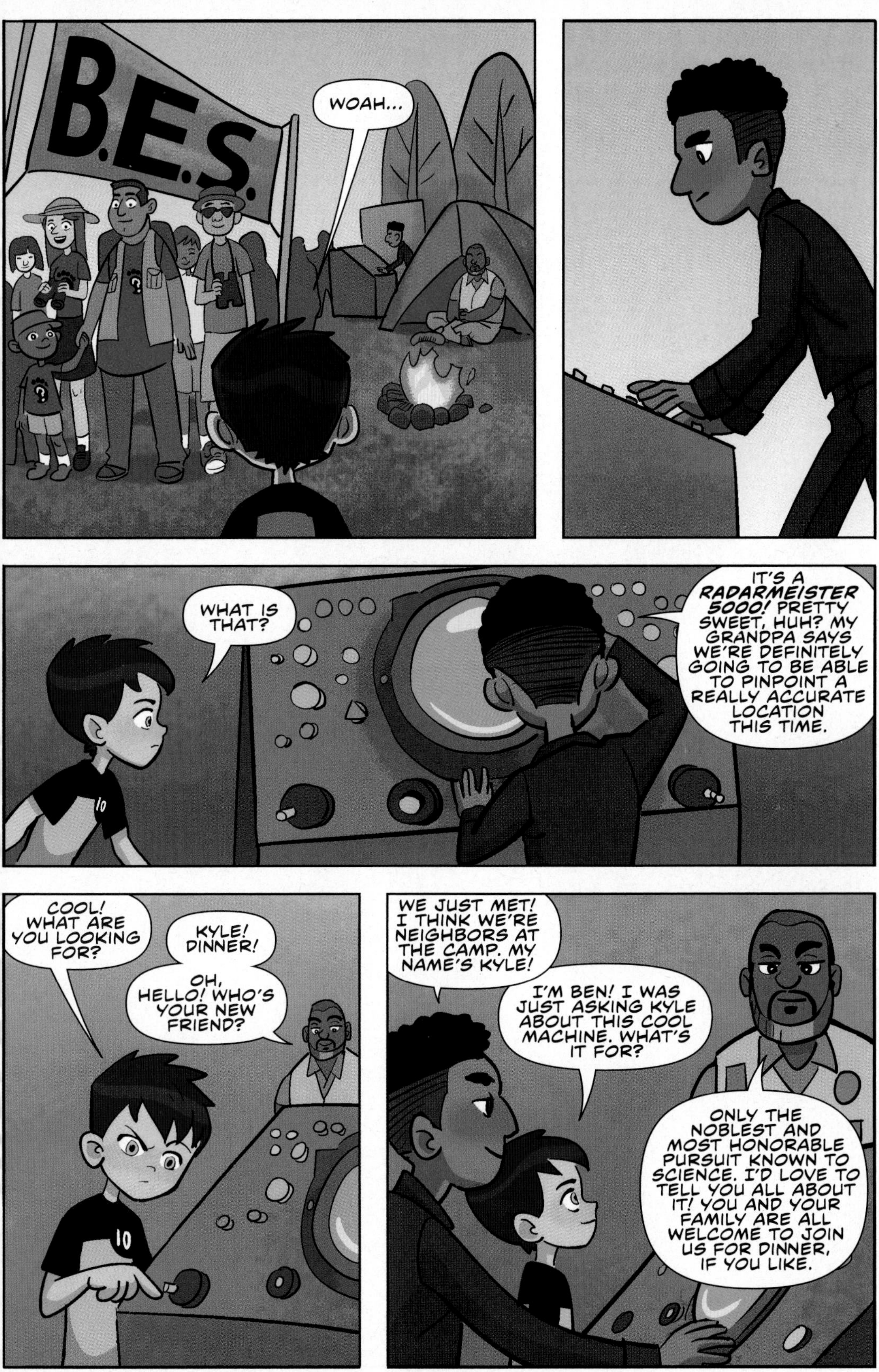
B.E.S.
WOAH...
WHAT IS THAT?
IT'S A *RADARMEISTER 5000!* PRETTY SWEET, HUH? MY GRANDPA SAYS WE'RE DEFINITELY GOING TO BE ABLE TO PINPOINT A REALLY ACCURATE LOCATION THIS TIME.
COOL! WHAT ARE YOU LOOKING FOR?
KYLE! DINNER!
OH, HELLO! WHO'S YOUR NEW FRIEND?
WE JUST MET! I THINK WE'RE NEIGHBORS AT THE CAMP. MY NAME'S KYLE!
I'M BEN! I WAS JUST ASKING KYLE ABOUT THIS COOL MACHINE. WHAT'S IT FOR?
ONLY THE NOBLEST AND MOST HONORABLE PURSUIT KNOWN TO SCIENCE. I'D LOVE TO TELL YOU ALL ABOUT IT! YOU AND YOUR FAMILY ARE ALL WELCOME TO JOIN US FOR DINNER, IF YOU LIKE.

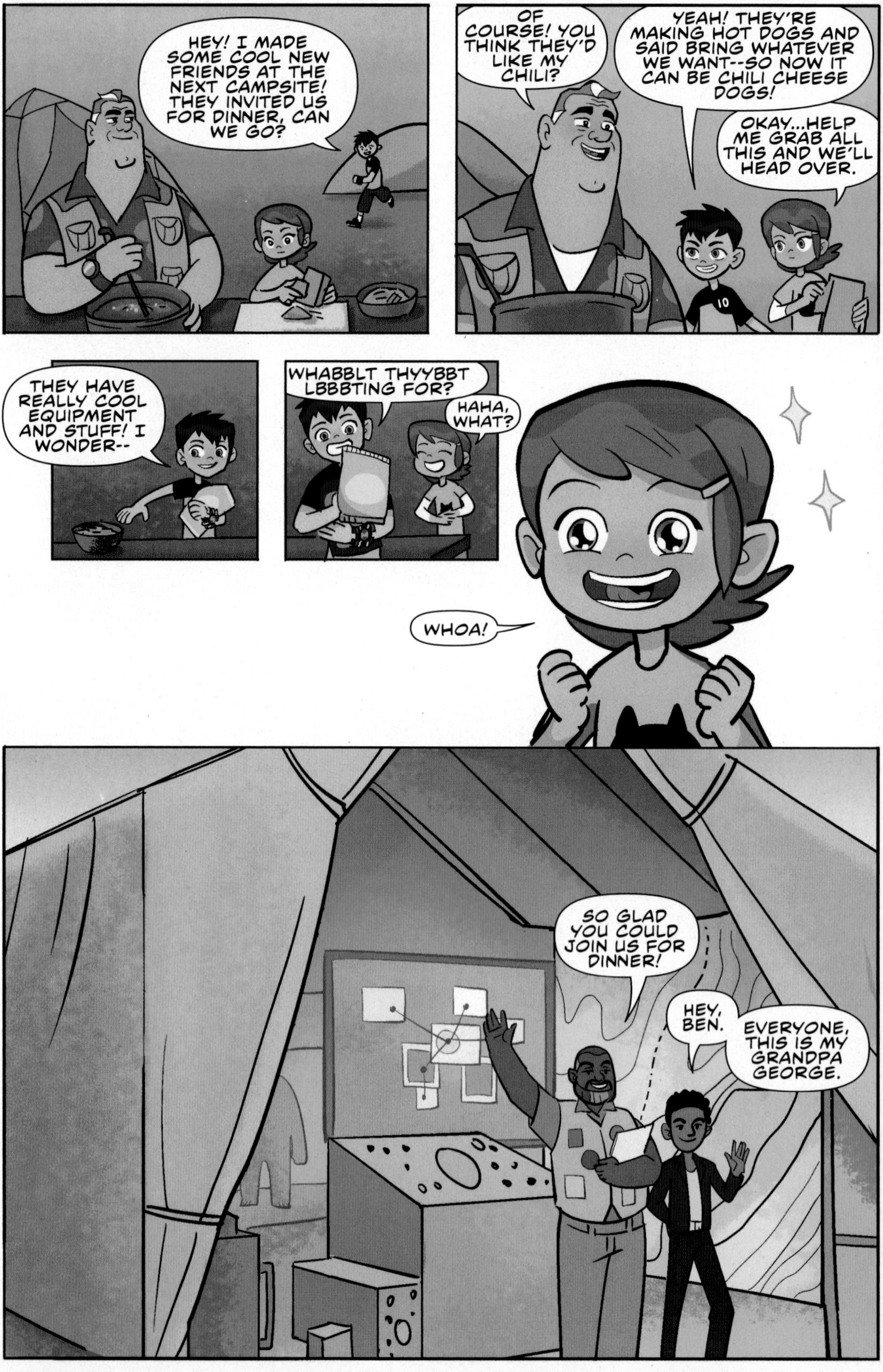
HEY! I MADE SOME COOL NEW FRIENDS AT THE NEXT CAMPSITE! THEY INVITED US FOR DINNER, CAN WE GO?
OF COURSE! YOU THINK THEY'D LIKE MY CHILI?
YEAH! THEY'RE MAKING HOT DOGS AND SAID BRING WHATEVER WE WANT--SO NOW IT CAN BE CHILI CHEESE DOGS!
OKAY...HELP ME GRAB ALL THIS AND WE'LL HEAD OVER.
THEY HAVE REALLY COOL EQUIPMENT AND STUFF! I WONDER--
WHABBLT THYYBBT LBBBTING FOR?
HAHA, WHAT?
WHOA!
SO GLAD YOU COULD JOIN US FOR DINNER!
HEY, BEN.
EVERYONE, THIS IS MY GRANDPA GEORGE.

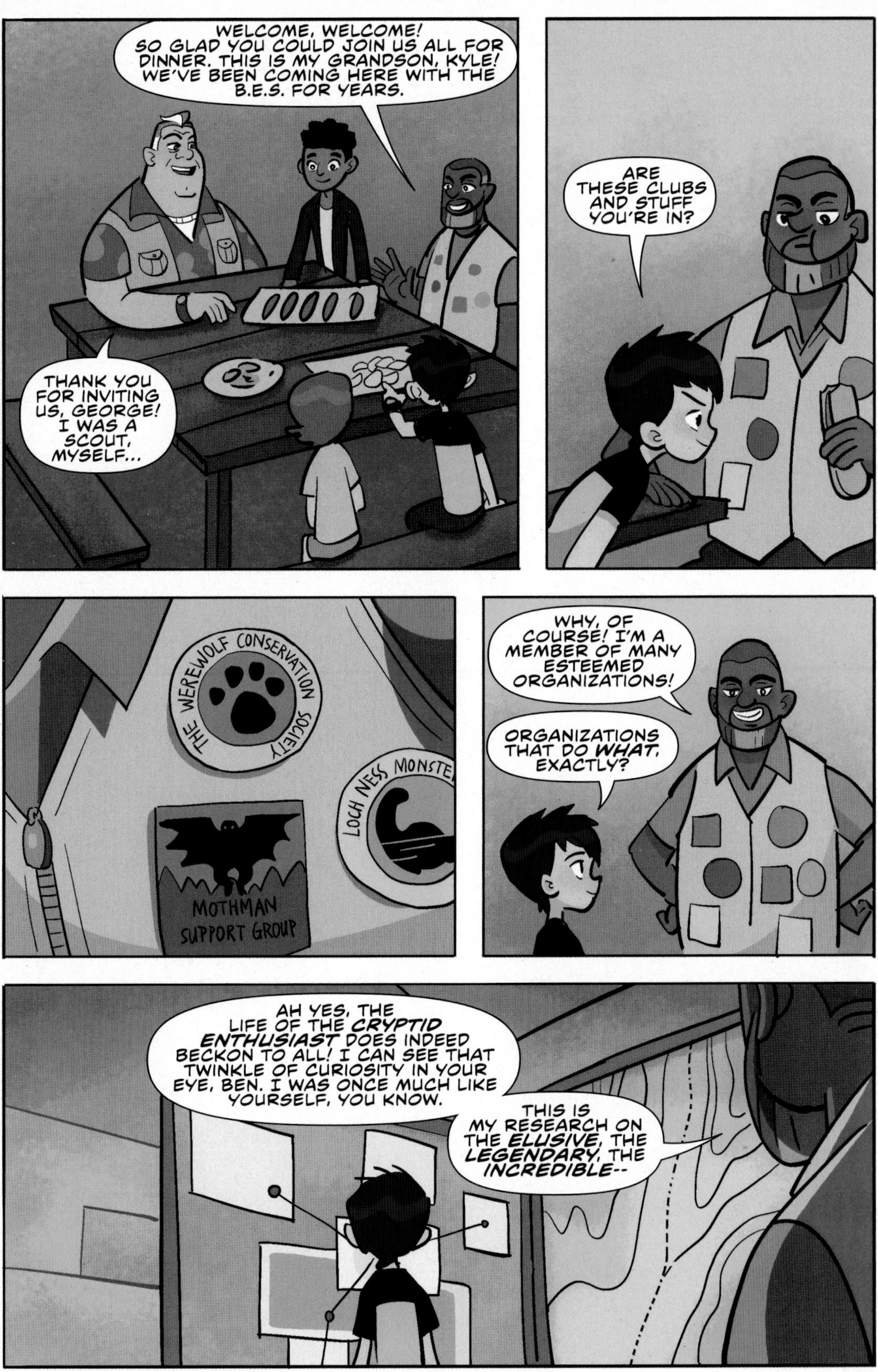

WELCOME, WELCOME! SO GLAD YOU COULD JOIN US ALL FOR DINNER. THIS IS MY GRANDSON, KYLE! WE'VE BEEN COMING HERE WITH THE B.E.S. FOR YEARS.
THANK YOU FOR INVITING US, GEORGE! I WAS A SCOUT, MYSELF...
ARE THESE CLUBS AND STUFF YOU'RE IN?
THE WEREWOLF CONSERVATION SOCIETY
LOCH NESS MONSTE
MOTHMAN SUPPORT GROUP
WHY, OF COURSE! I'M A MEMBER OF MANY ESTEEMED ORGANIZATIONS!
ORGANIZATIONS THAT DO *WHAT*, EXACTLY?
AH YES, THE LIFE OF THE *CRYPTID ENTHUSIAST* DOES INDEED BECKON TO ALL! I CAN SEE THAT TWINKLE OF CURIOSITY IN YOUR EYE, BEN. I WAS ONCE MUCH LIKE YOURSELF, YOU KNOW.
THIS IS MY RESEARCH ON THE *ELUSIVE*, THE *LEGENDARY*, THE *INCREDIBLE*--

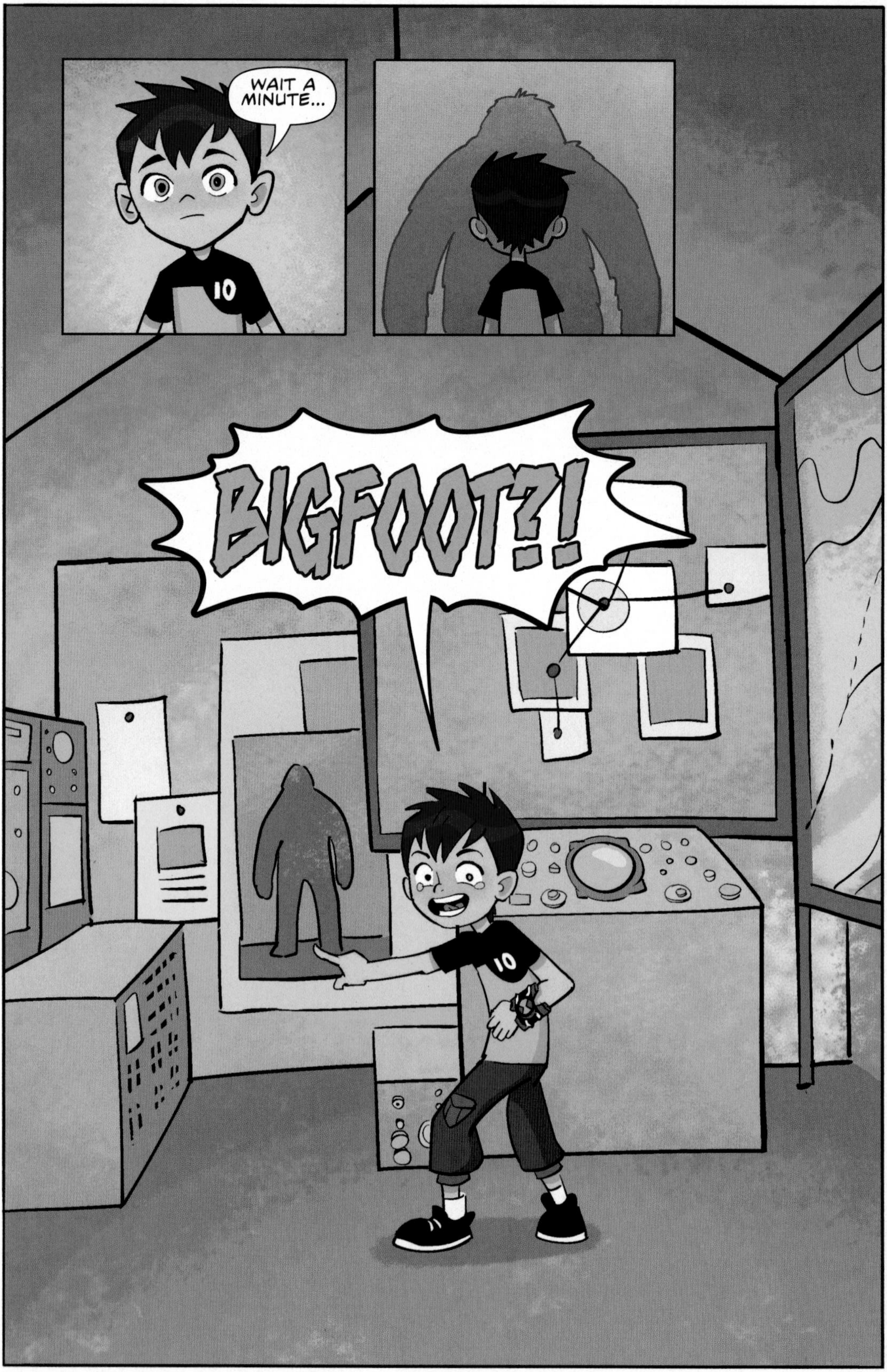
WAIT A MINUTE...
BIGFOOT?!

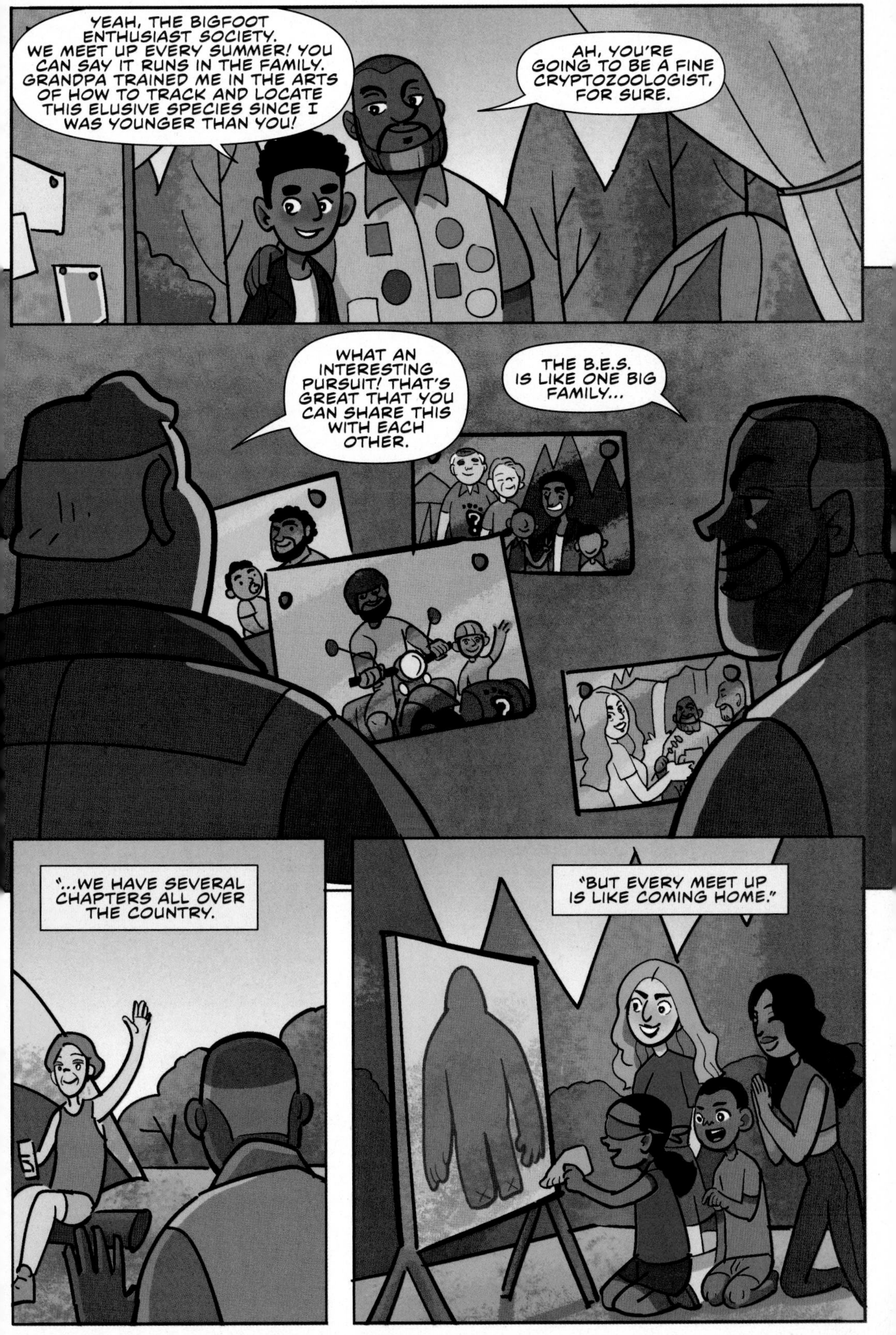
YEAH, THE BIGFOOT ENTHUSIAST SOCIETY. WE MEET UP EVERY SUMMER! YOU CAN SAY IT RUNS IN THE FAMILY. GRANDPA TRAINED ME IN THE ARTS OF HOW TO TRACK AND LOCATE THIS ELUSIVE SPECIES SINCE I WAS YOUNGER THAN YOU!
AH, YOU'RE GOING TO BE A FINE CRYPTOZOOLOGIST, FOR SURE.
WHAT AN INTERESTING PURSUIT! THAT'S GREAT THAT YOU CAN SHARE THIS WITH EACH OTHER.
THE B.E.S. IS LIKE ONE BIG FAMILY...
"...WE HAVE SEVERAL CHAPTERS ALL OVER THE COUNTRY.
"BUT EVERY MEET UP IS LIKE COMING HOME."

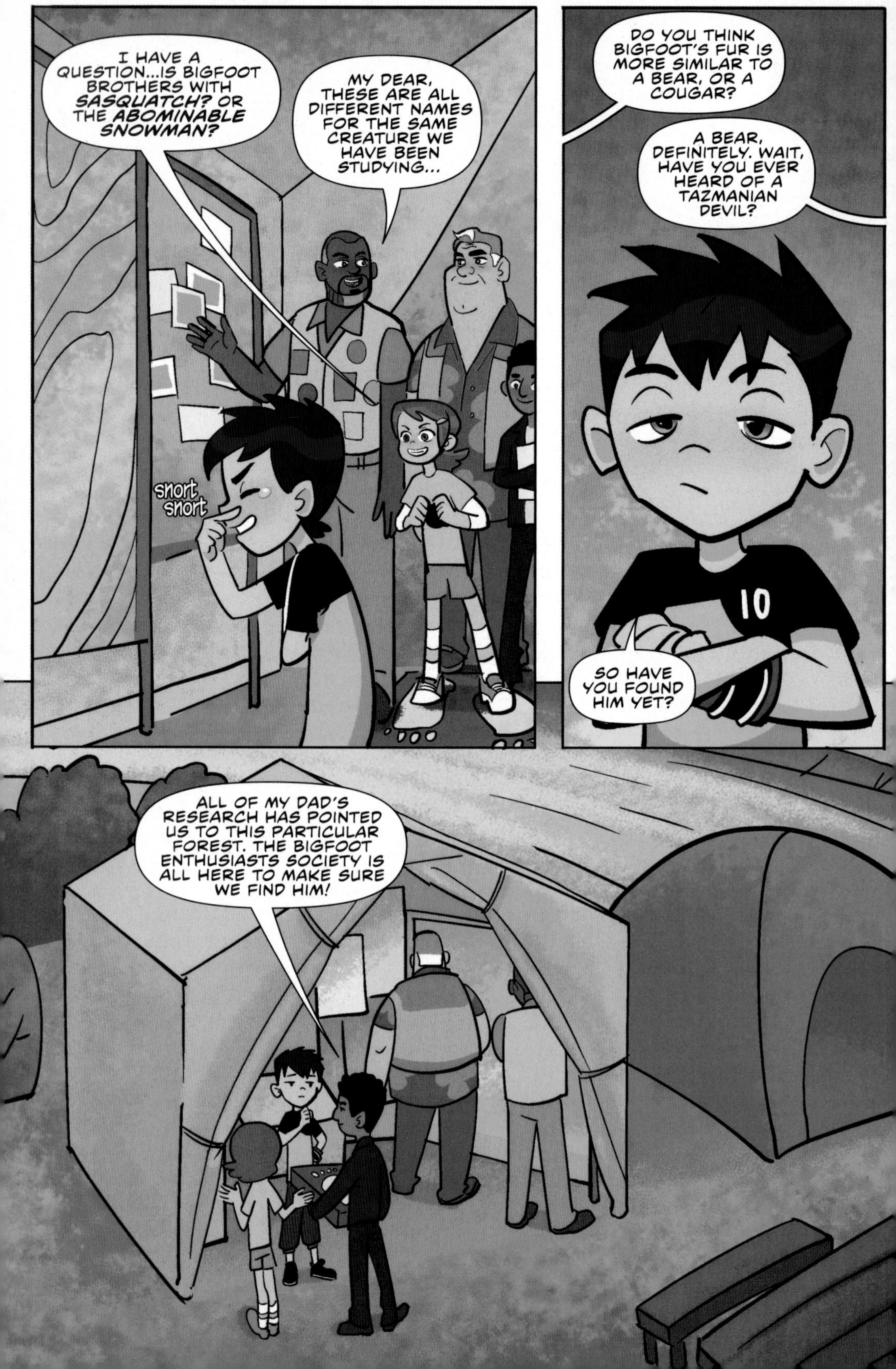

I HAVE A QUESTION...IS BIGFOOT BROTHERS WITH *SASQUATCH?* OR THE *ABOMINABLE SNOWMAN?*
MY DEAR, THESE ARE ALL DIFFERENT NAMES FOR THE SAME CREATURE WE HAVE BEEN STUDYING...
snort snort
DO YOU THINK BIGFOOT'S FUR IS MORE SIMILAR TO A BEAR, OR A COUGAR?
A BEAR, DEFINITELY. WAIT, HAVE YOU EVER HEARD OF A TAZMANIAN DEVIL?
10
SO HAVE YOU FOUND HIM YET?
ALL OF MY DAD'S RESEARCH HAS POINTED US TO THIS PARTICULAR FOREST. THE BIGFOOT ENTHUSIASTS SOCIETY IS ALL HERE TO MAKE SURE WE FIND HIM!

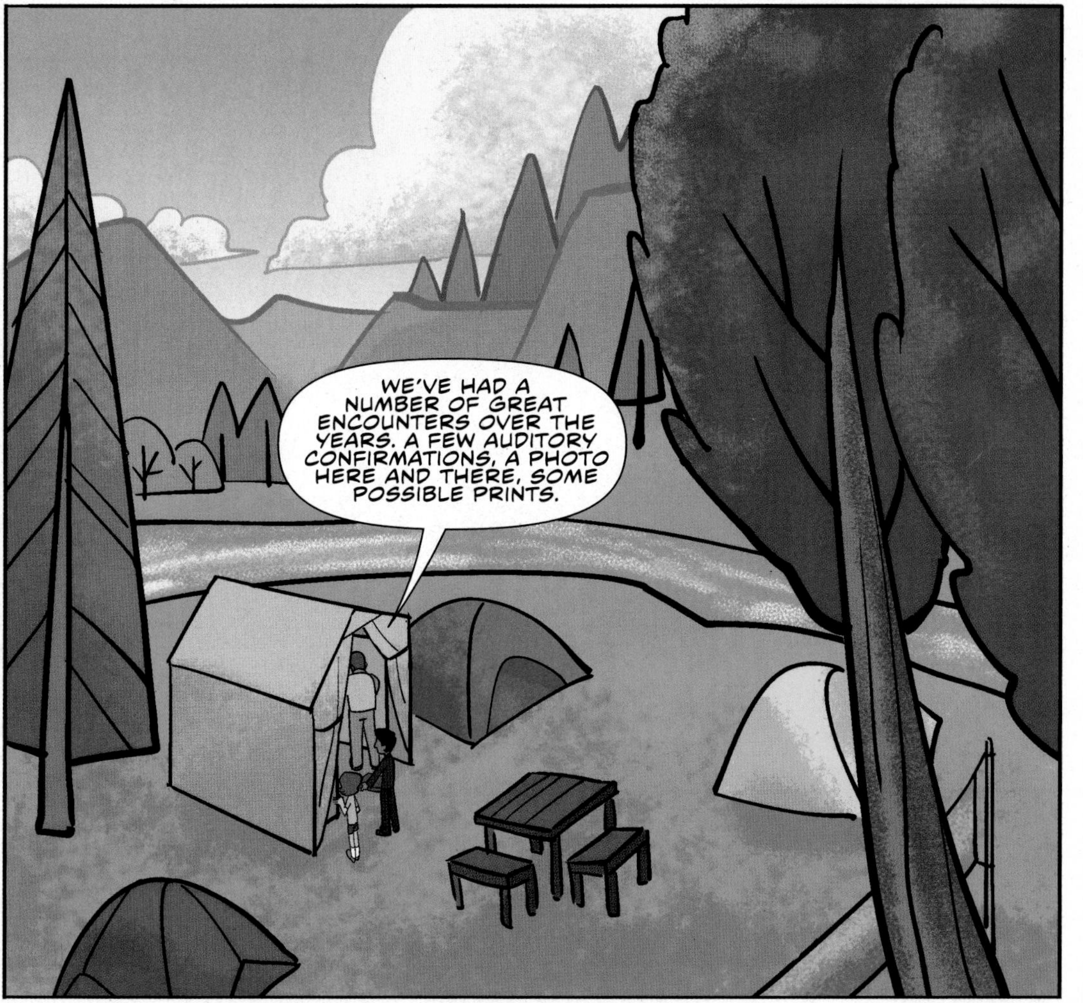
WE'VE HAD A NUMBER OF GREAT ENCOUNTERS OVER THE YEARS. A FEW AUDITORY CONFIRMATIONS, A PHOTO HERE AND THERE, SOME POSSIBLE PRINTS.

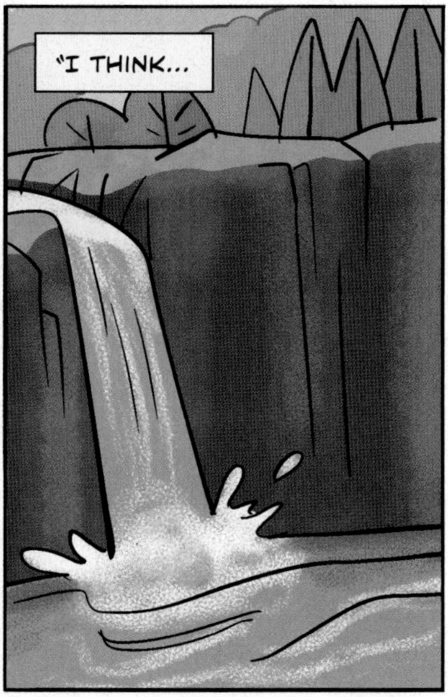
"I THINK...

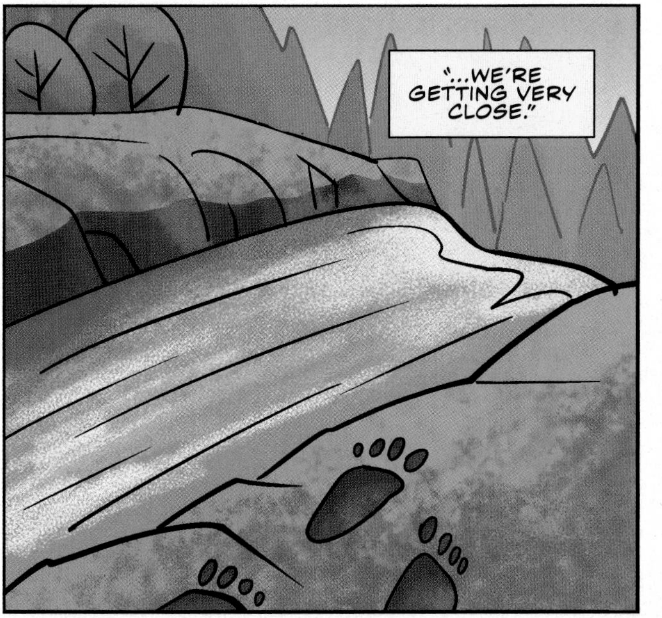
"...WE'RE GETTING VERY CLOSE."

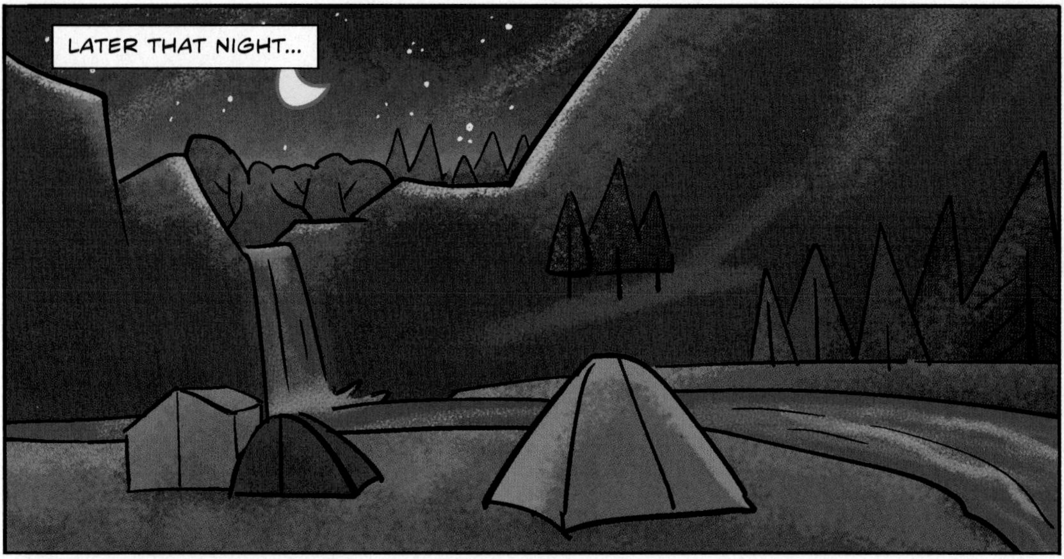
LATER THAT NIGHT...

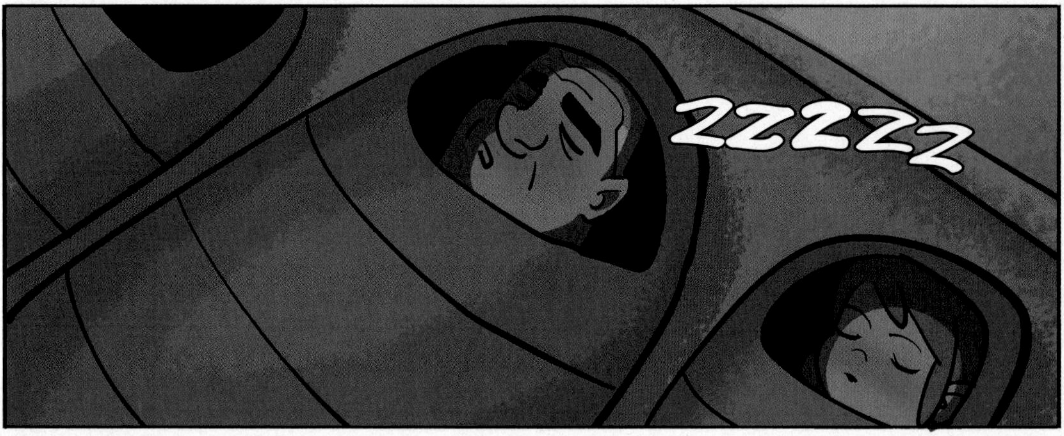
ZZZZZ

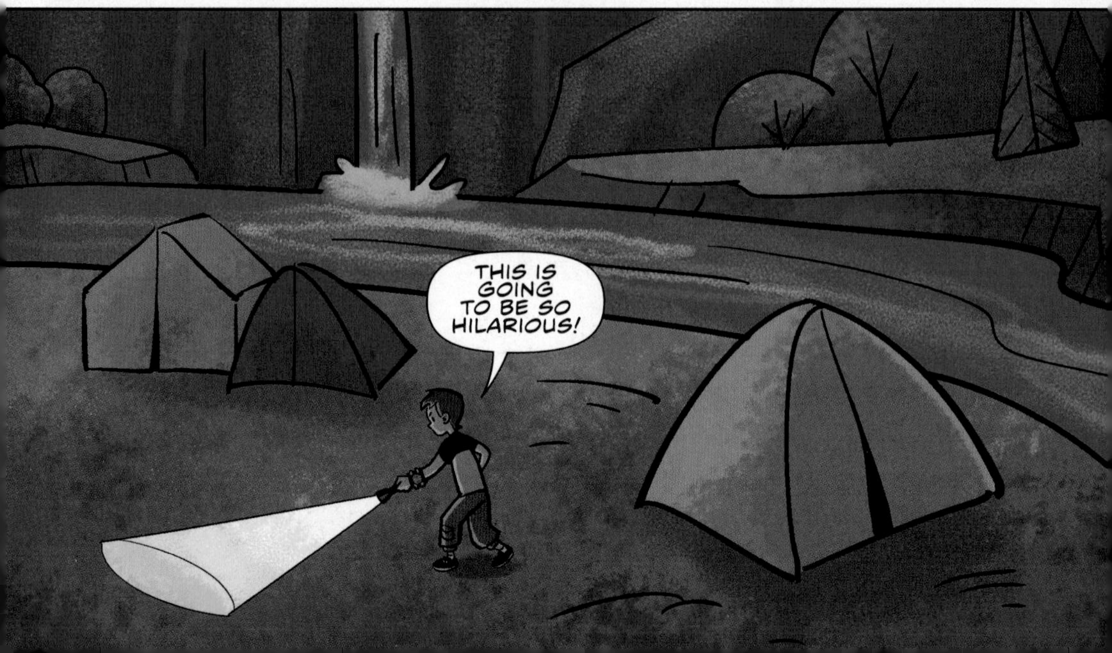
THIS IS GOING TO BE SO HILARIOUS!

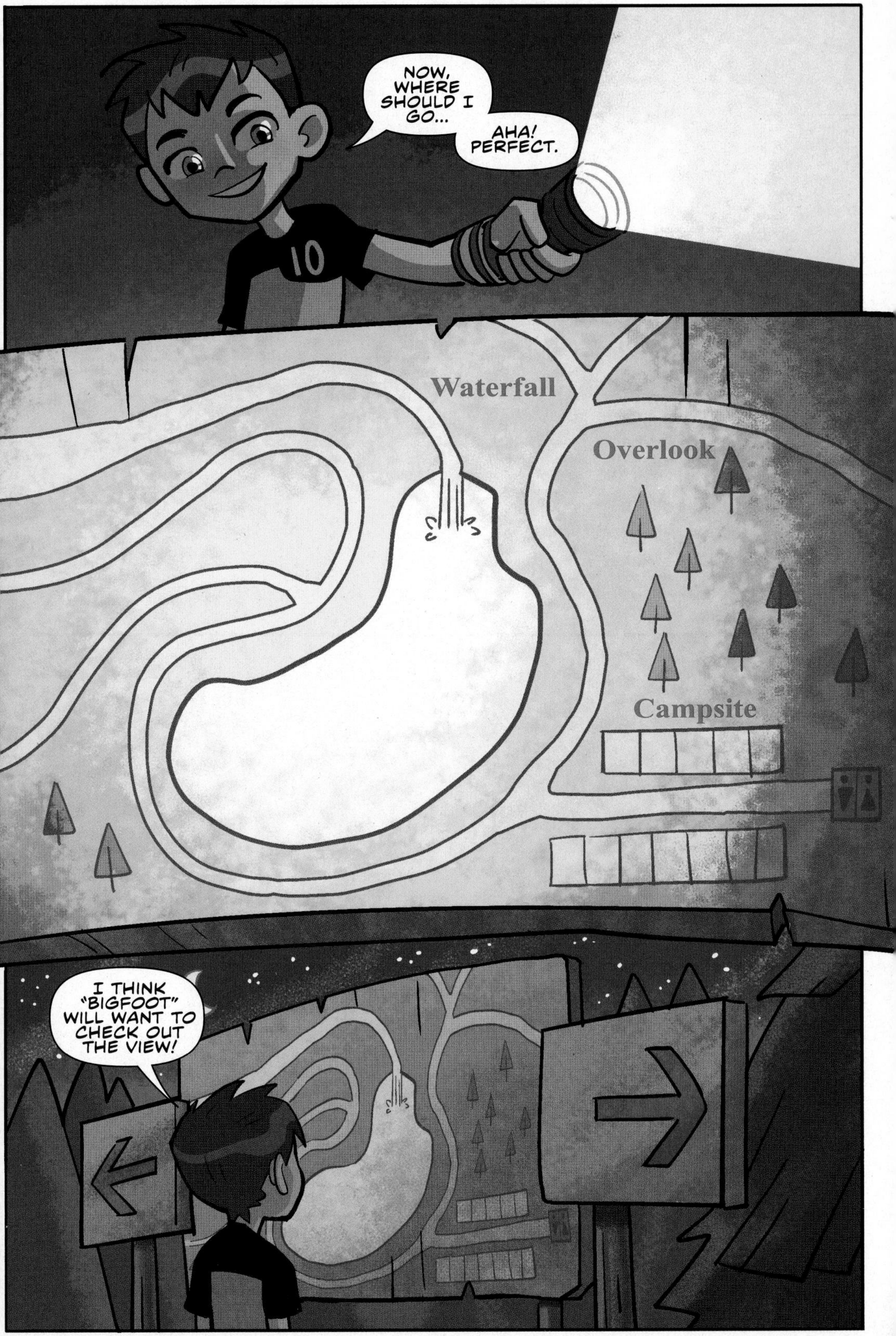
NOW, WHERE SHOULD I GO...
AHA! PERFECT.
10
Waterfall
Overlook
Campsite
I THINK "BIGFOOT" WILL WANT TO CHECK OUT THE VIEW!

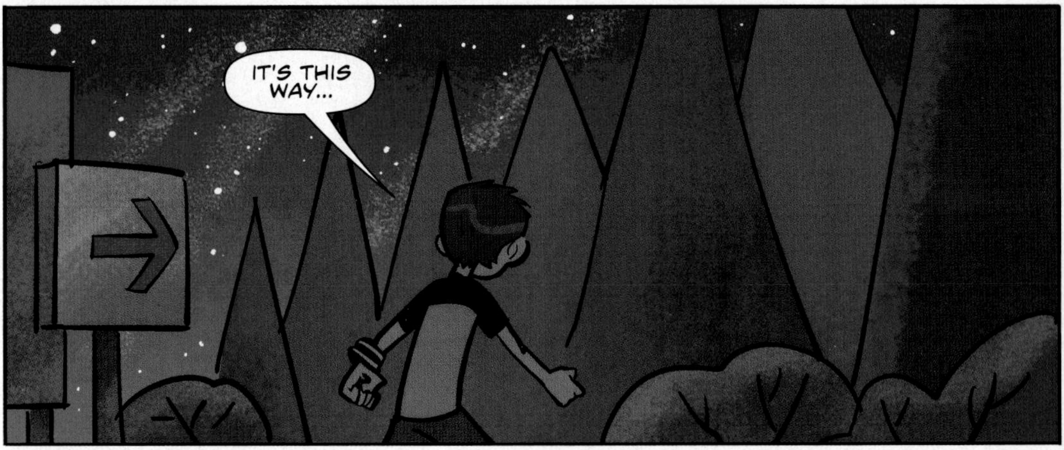
IT'S THIS WAY...

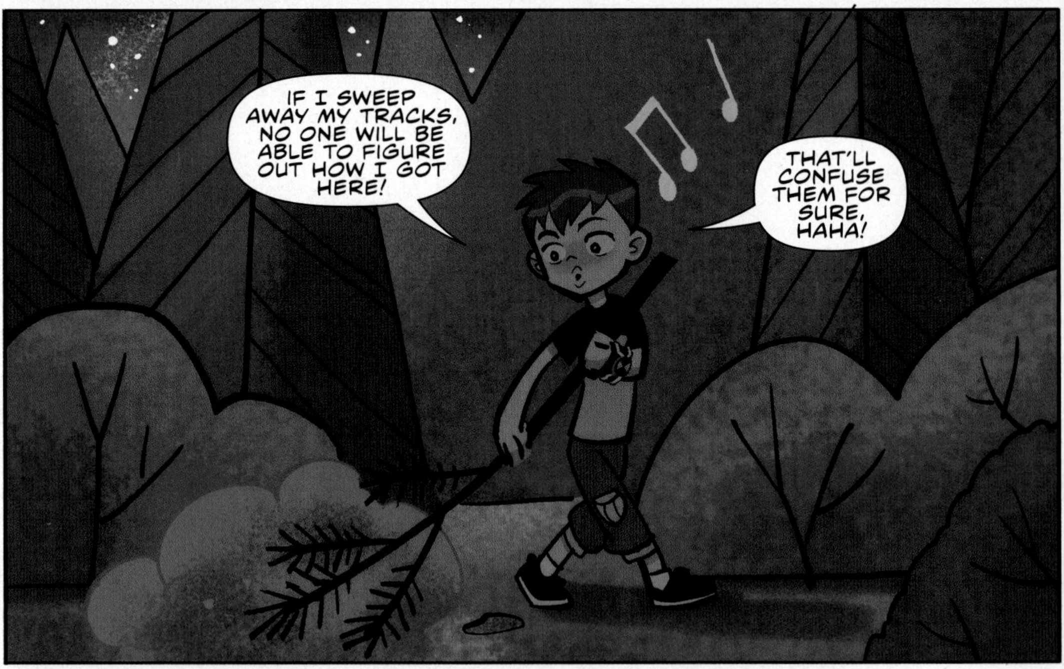
IF I SWEEP AWAY MY TRACKS, NO ONE WILL BE ABLE TO FIGURE OUT HOW I GOT HERE!
THAT'LL CONFUSE THEM FOR SURE, HAHA!

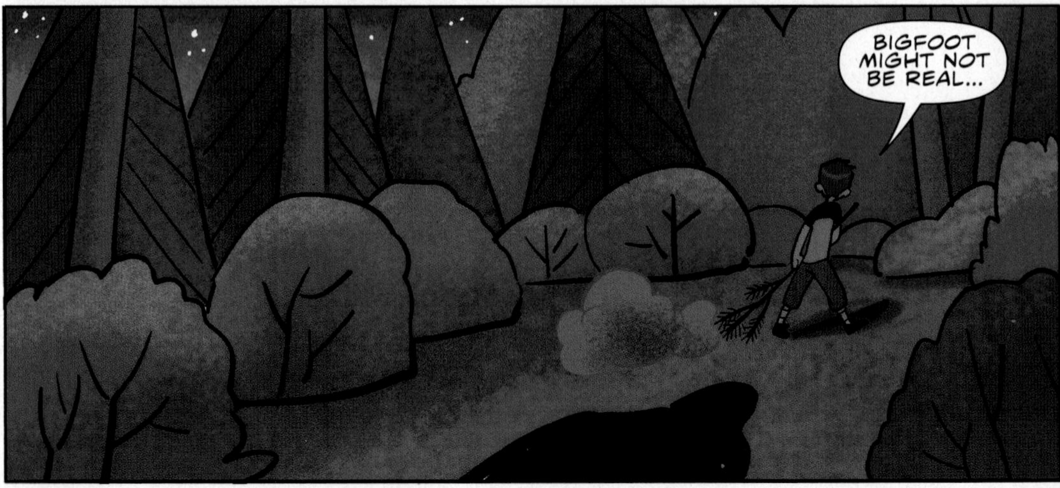
BIGFOOT MIGHT NOT BE REAL...

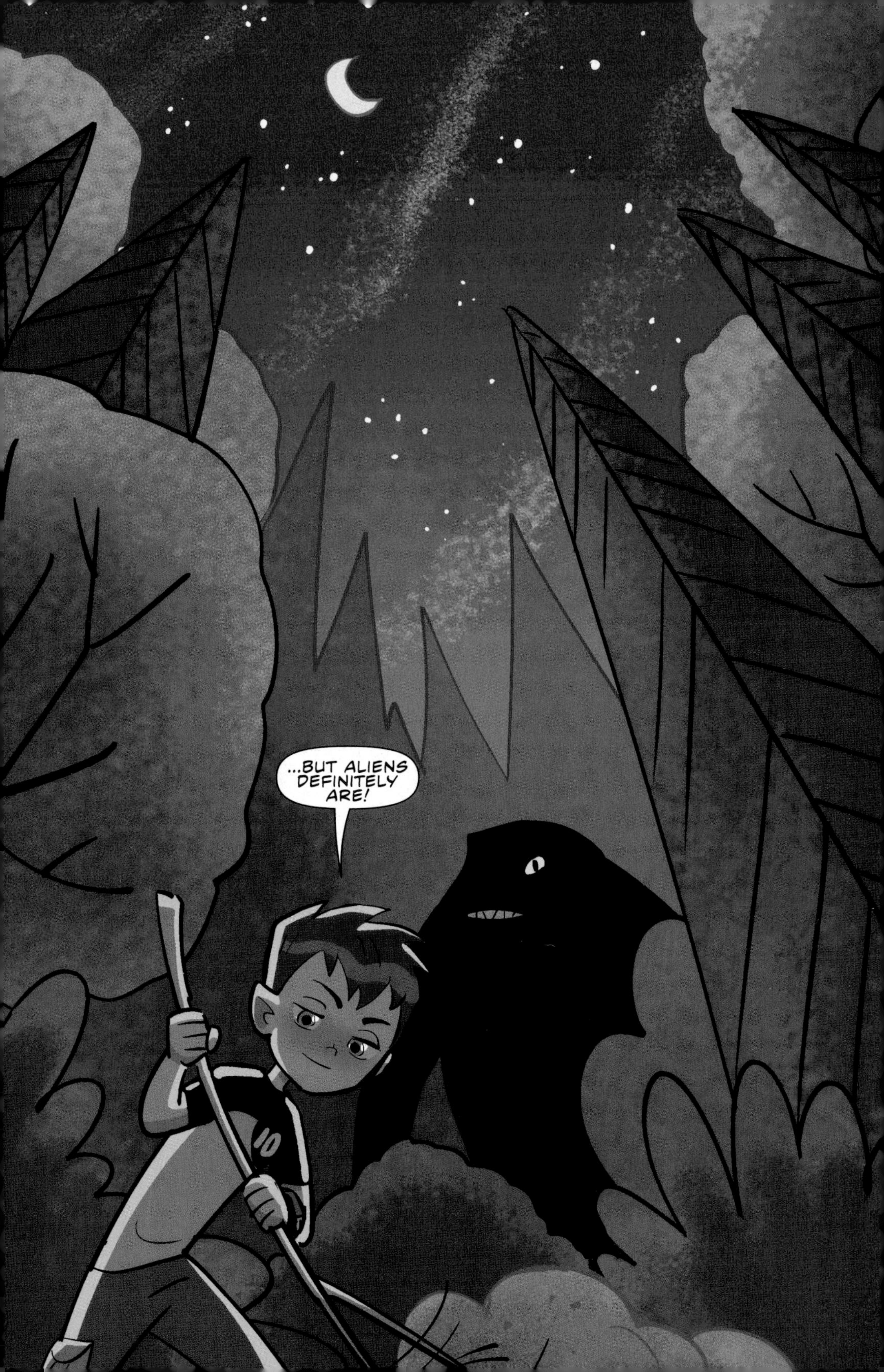
...BUT ALIENS DEFINITELY ARE!

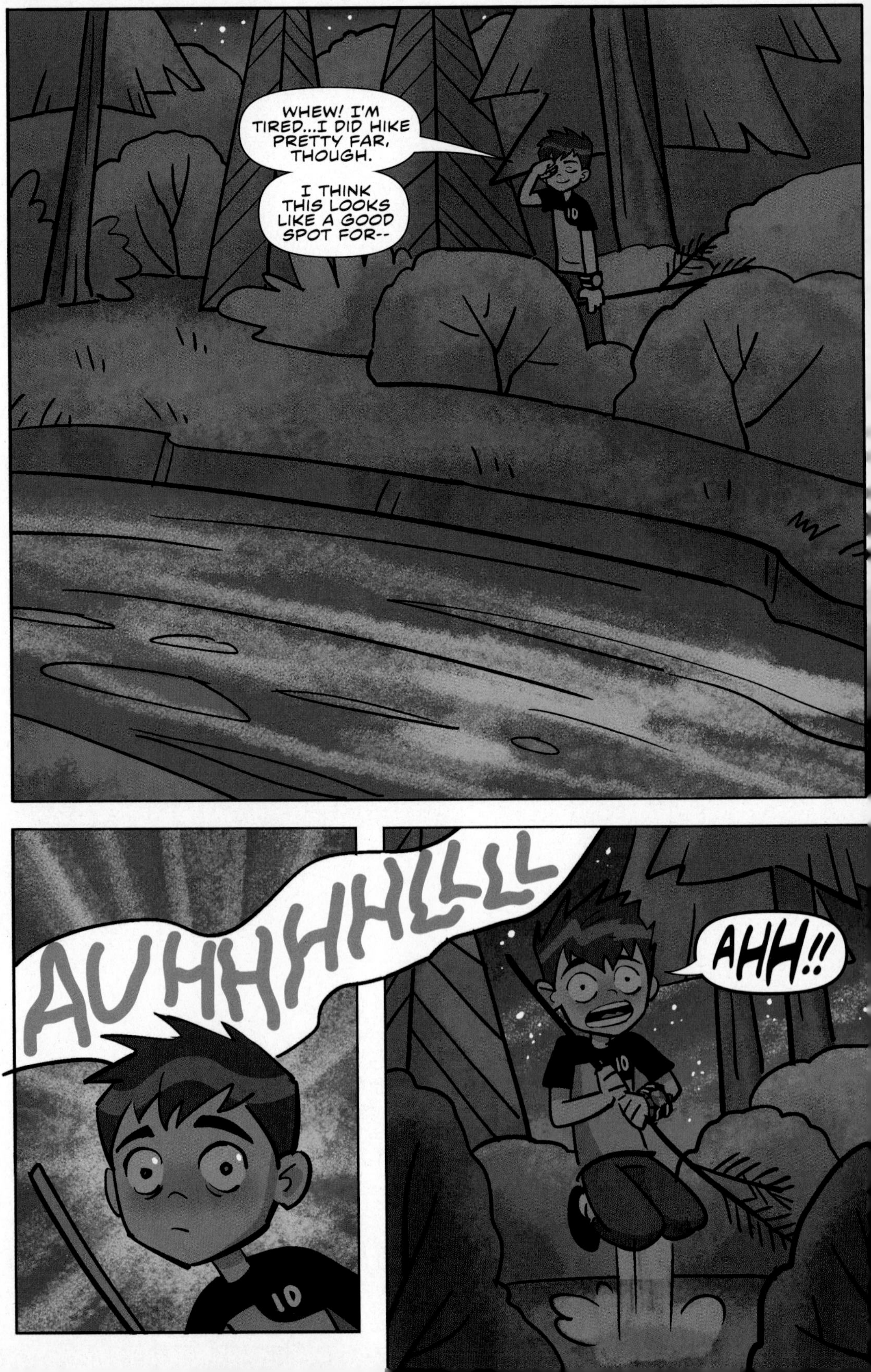
WHEW! I'M TIRED...I DID HIKE PRETTY FAR, THOUGH.
I THINK THIS LOOKS LIKE A GOOD SPOT FOR--
AUHHHLLL
AHH!!

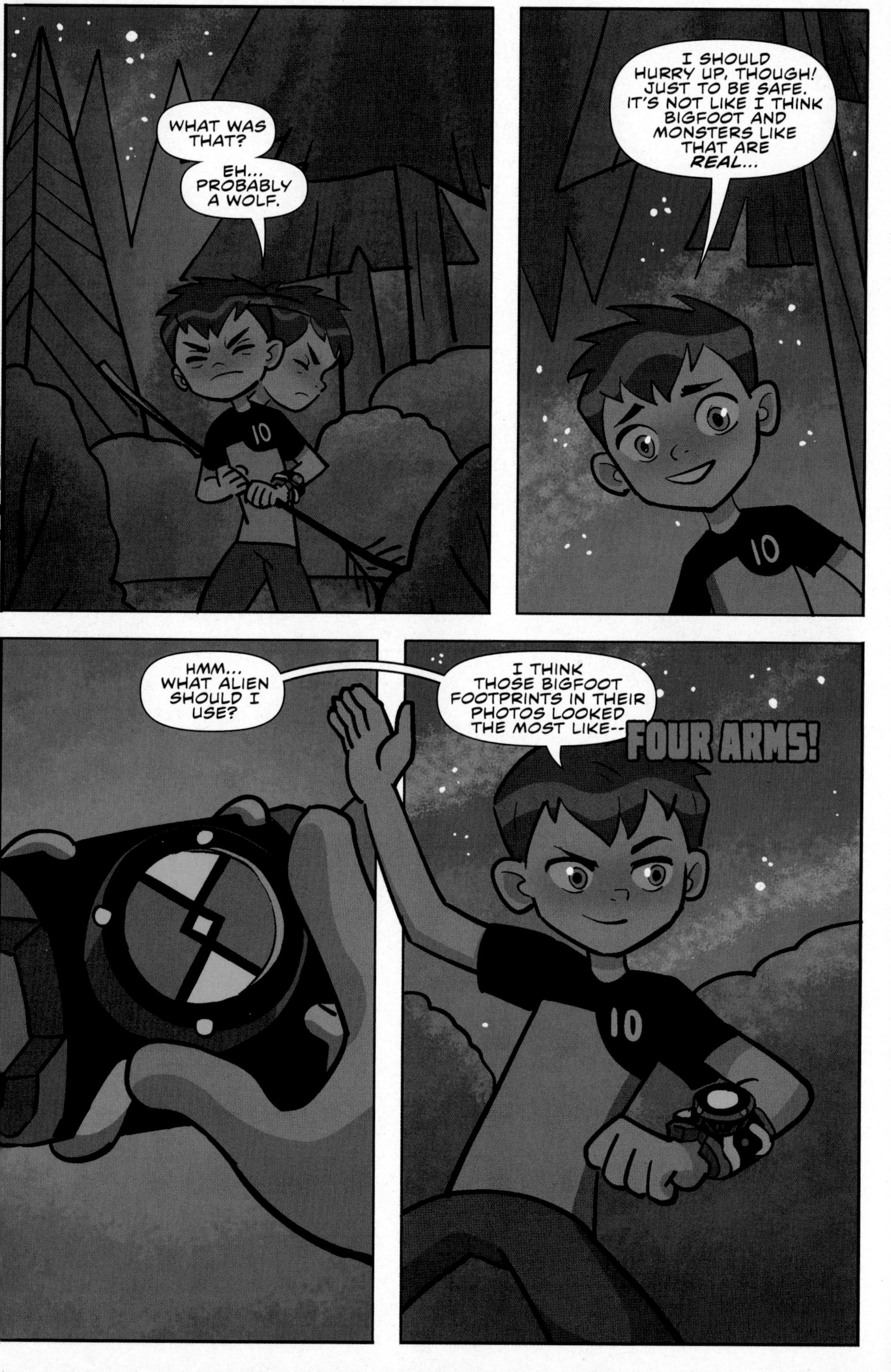
WHAT WAS THAT?
EH... PROBABLY A WOLF.
I SHOULD HURRY UP, THOUGH! JUST TO BE SAFE. IT'S NOT LIKE I THINK BIGFOOT AND MONSTERS LIKE THAT ARE REAL...
HMM... WHAT ALIEN SHOULD I USE?
I THINK THOSE BIGFOOT FOOTPRINTS IN THEIR PHOTOS LOOKED THE MOST LIKE--
FOUR ARMS!
10
10
10

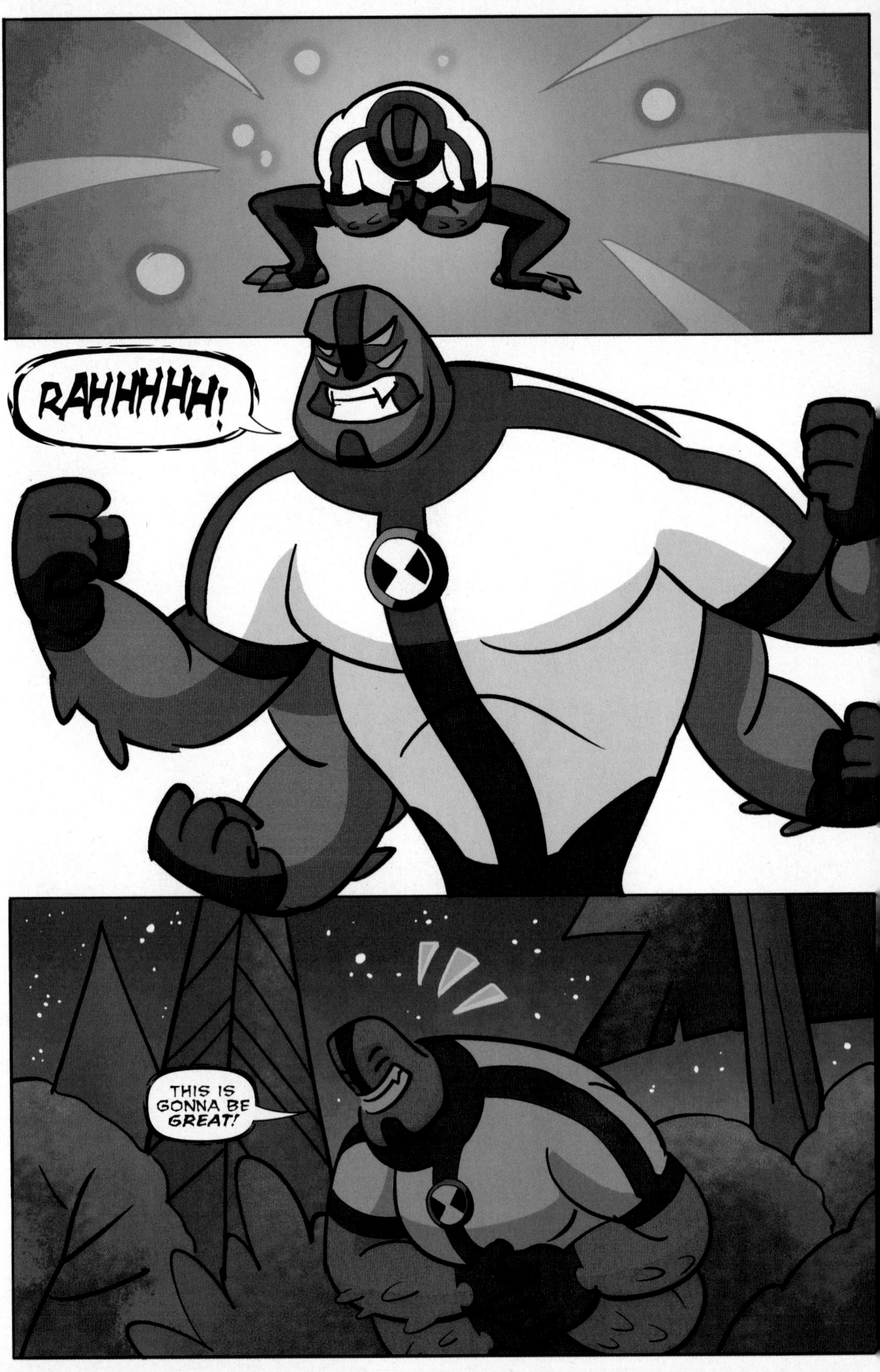
RAHHHHH!
THIS IS GONNA BE GREAT!

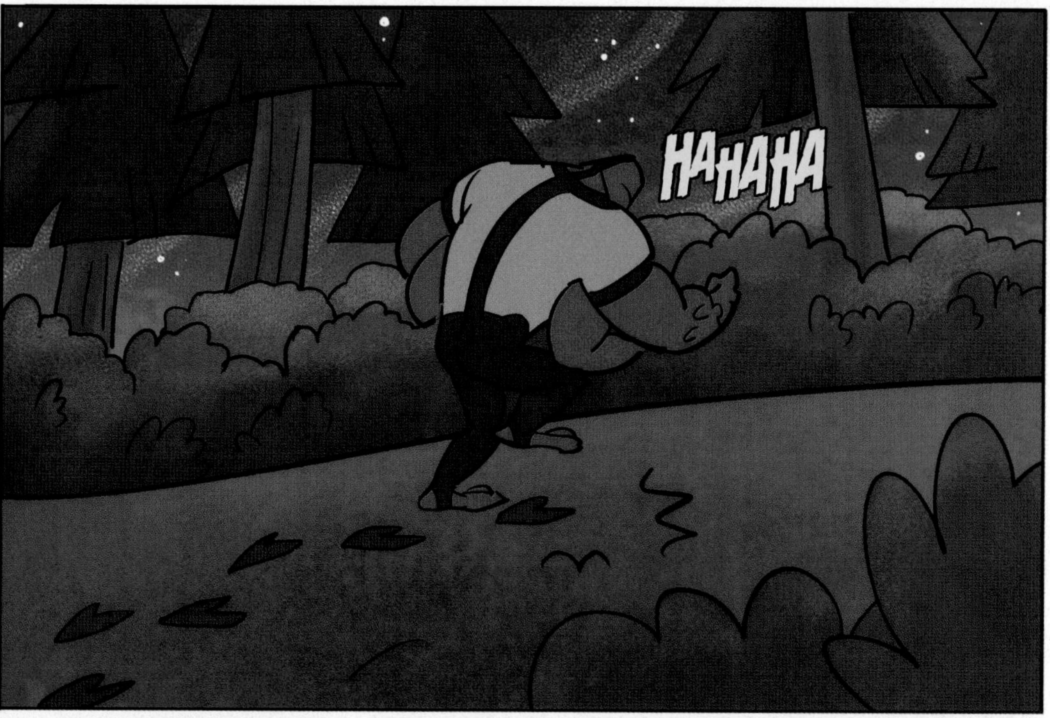
HAHAHA

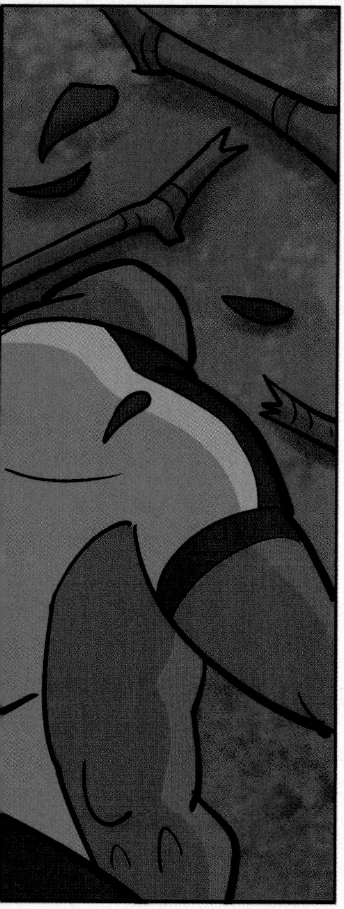

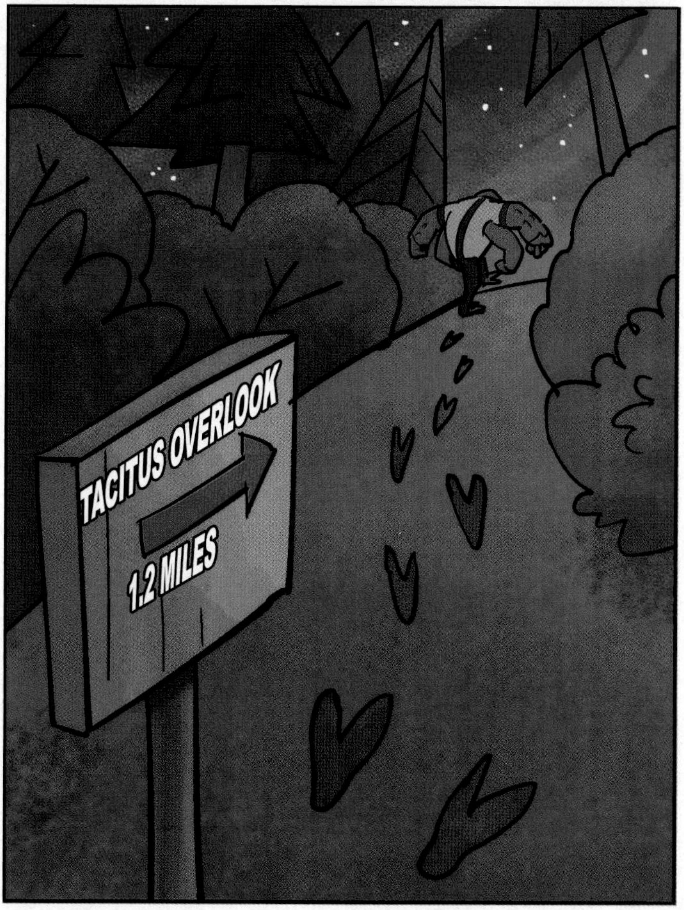
TACITUS OVERLOOK
1.2 MILES

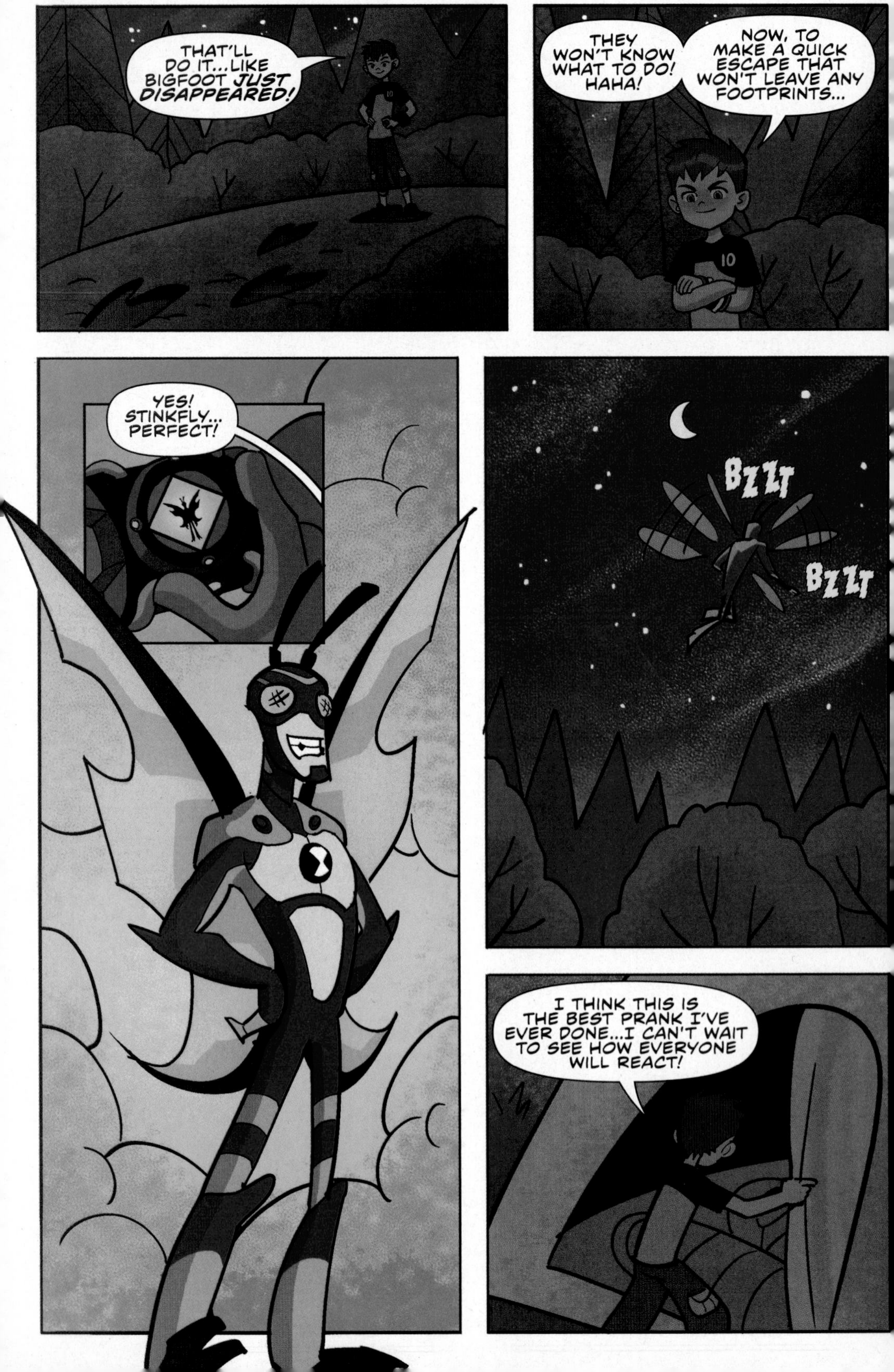
THAT'LL DO IT...LIKE BIGFOOT JUST DISAPPEARED!
THEY WON'T KNOW WHAT TO DO! HAHA!
NOW, TO MAKE A QUICK ESCAPE THAT WON'T LEAVE ANY FOOTPRINTS...
YES! STINKFLY... PERFECT!
BZZT
BZZT
I THINK THIS IS THE BEST PRANK I'VE EVER DONE...I CAN'T WAIT TO SEE HOW EVERYONE WILL REACT!

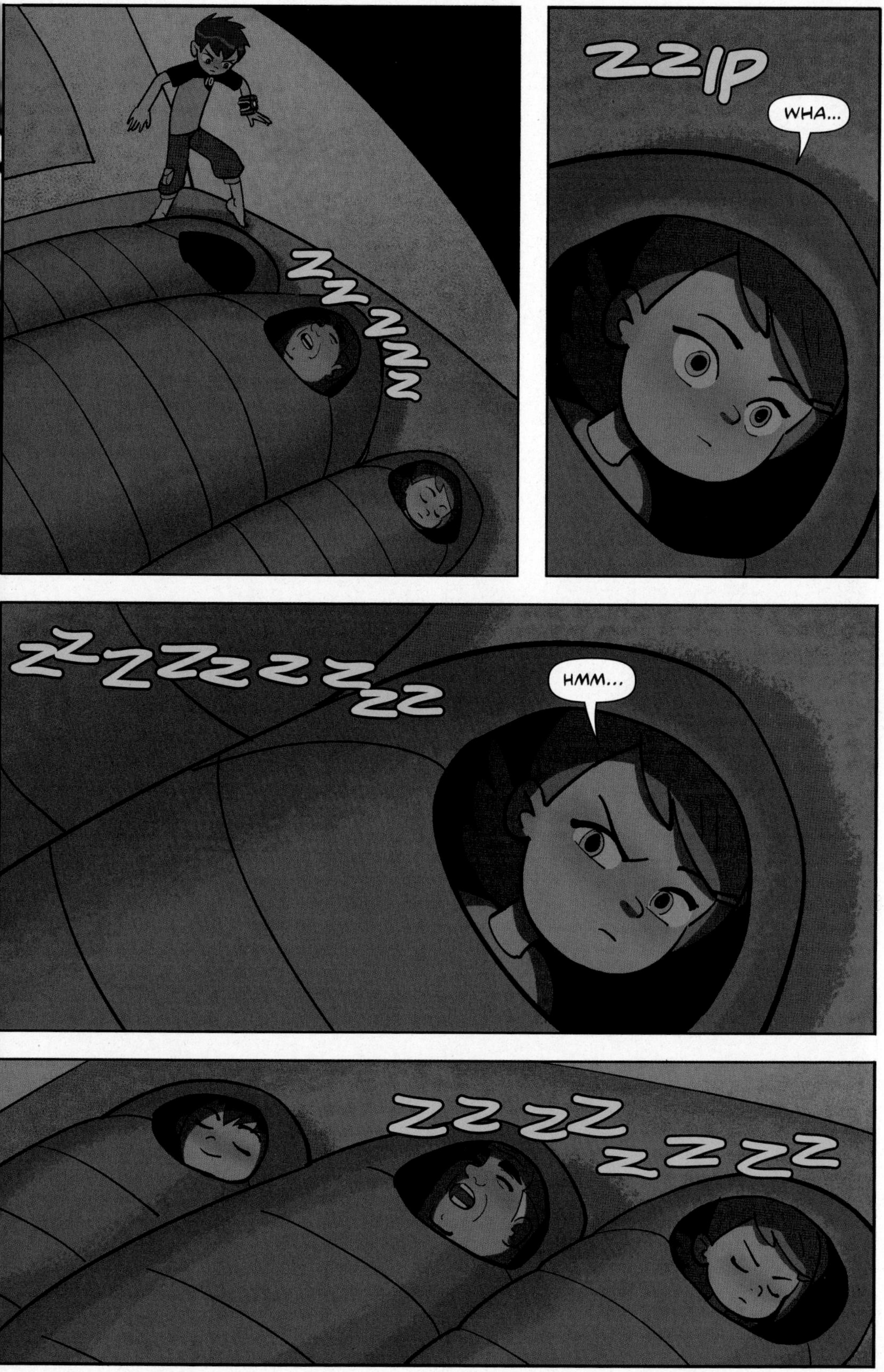
ZZZZZ
ZZIP
WHA...
ZZZZZZZZZ
HMM...
ZZZZZZZZ

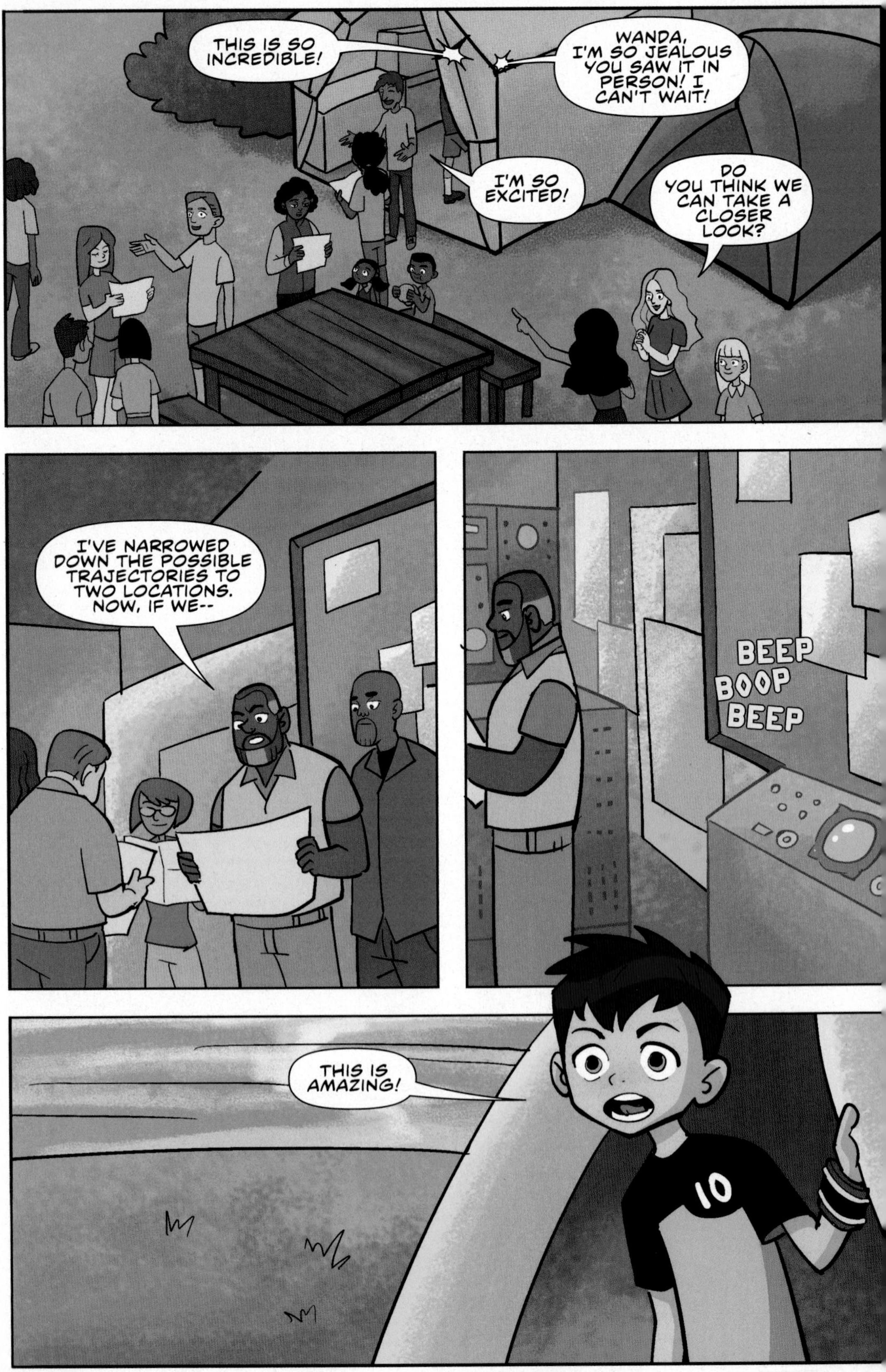
THIS IS SO INCREDIBLE!
WANDA, I'M SO JEALOUS YOU SAW IT IN PERSON! I CAN'T WAIT!
I'M SO EXCITED!
DO YOU THINK WE CAN TAKE A CLOSER LOOK?
I'VE NARROWED DOWN THE POSSIBLE TRAJECTORIES TO TWO LOCATIONS. NOW, IF WE--
BEEP
BOOP
BEEP
THIS IS AMAZING!
10

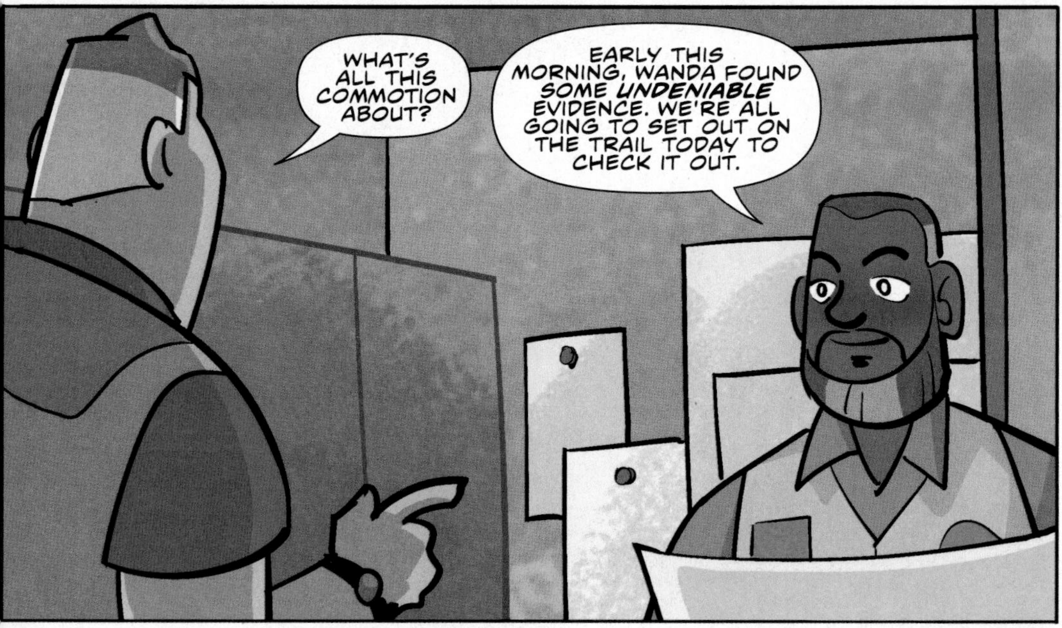
WHAT'S ALL THIS COMMOTION ABOUT?
EARLY THIS MORNING, WANDA FOUND *SOME UNDENIABLE* EVIDENCE. WE'RE ALL GOING TO SET OUT ON THE TRAIL TODAY TO CHECK IT OUT.

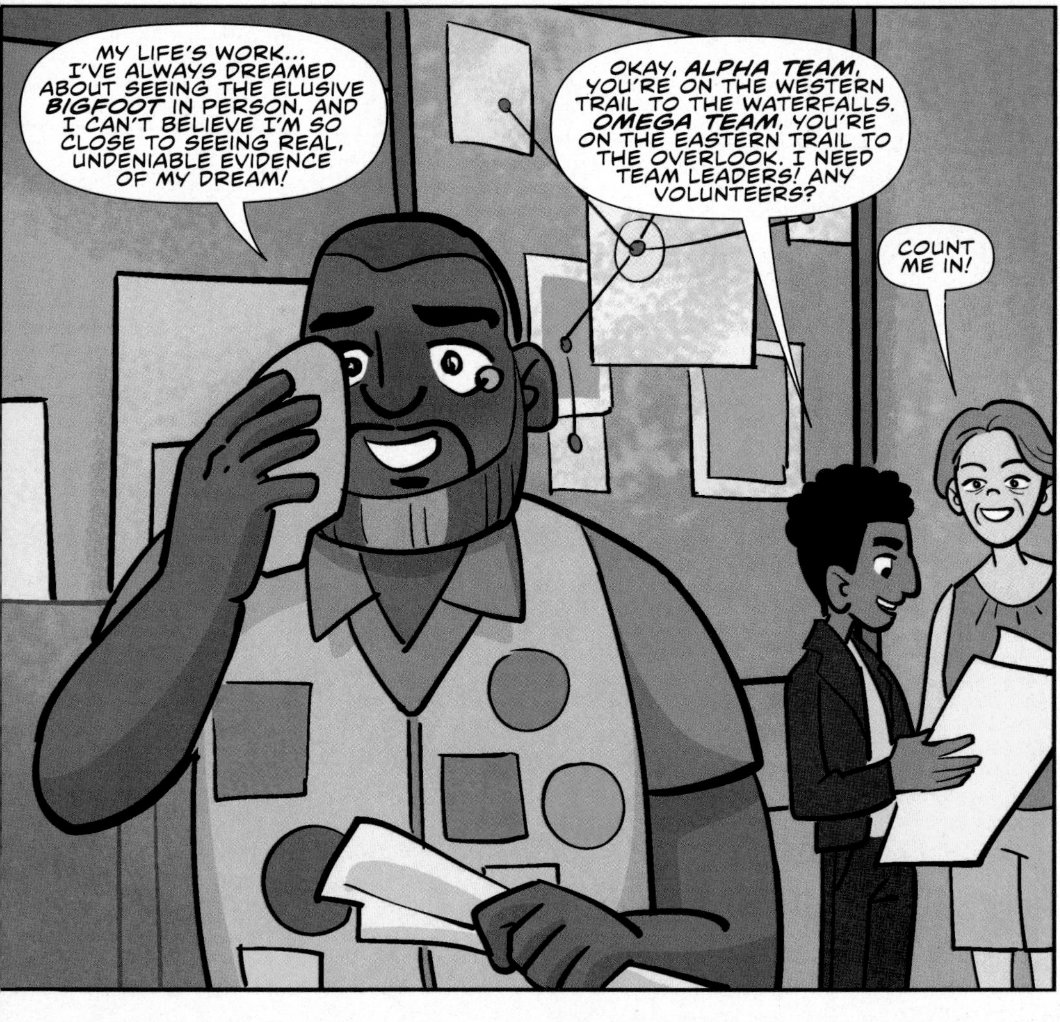
MY LIFE'S WORK... I'VE ALWAYS DREAMED ABOUT SEEING THE ELUSIVE *BIGFOOT* IN PERSON, AND I CAN'T BELIEVE I'M SO CLOSE TO SEEING REAL, UNDENIABLE EVIDENCE OF MY DREAM!
OKAY, *ALPHA TEAM*, YOU'RE ON THE WESTERN TRAIL TO THE WATERFALLS. *OMEGA TEAM*, YOU'RE ON THE EASTERN TRAIL TO THE OVERLOOK. I NEED TEAM LEADERS! ANY VOLUNTEERS?
COUNT ME IN!

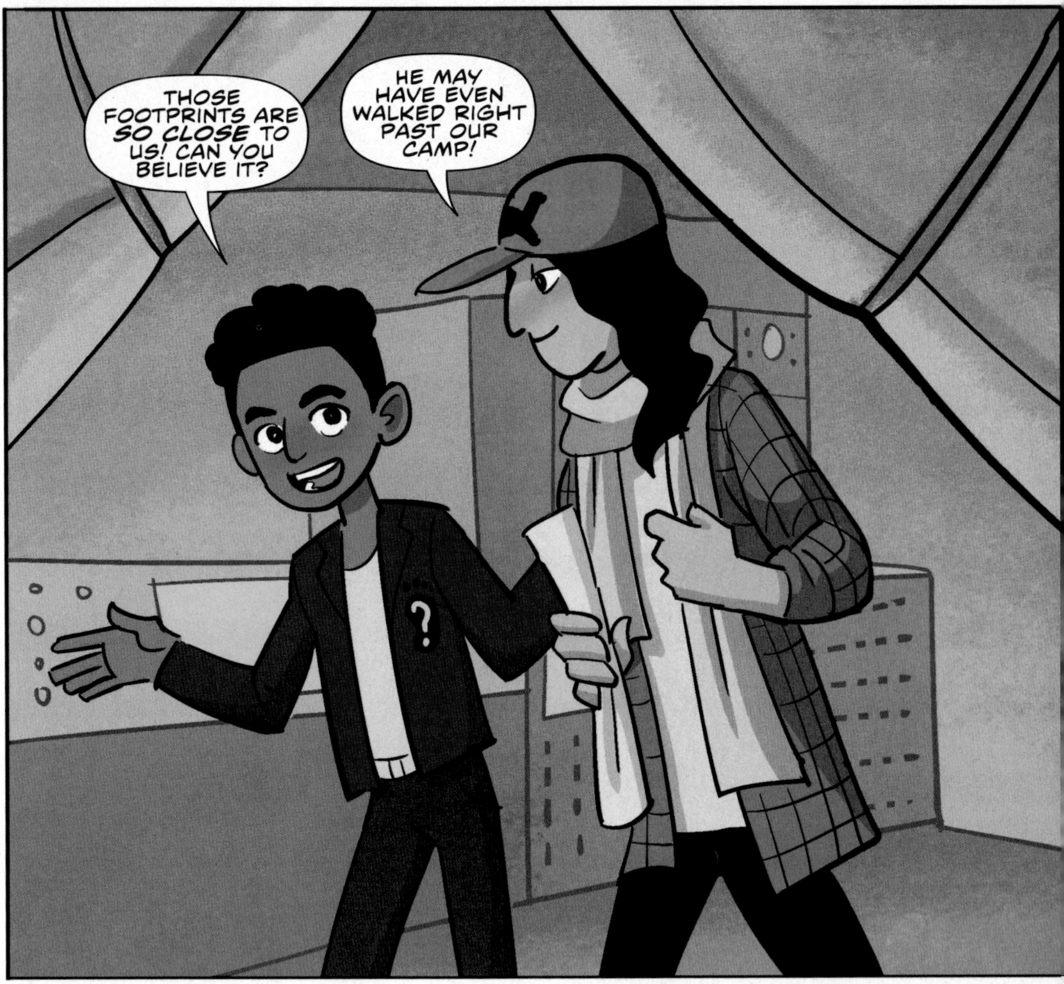
THOSE FOOTPRINTS ARE SO CLOSE TO US! CAN YOU BELIEVE IT?
HE MAY HAVE EVEN WALKED RIGHT PAST OUR CAMP!

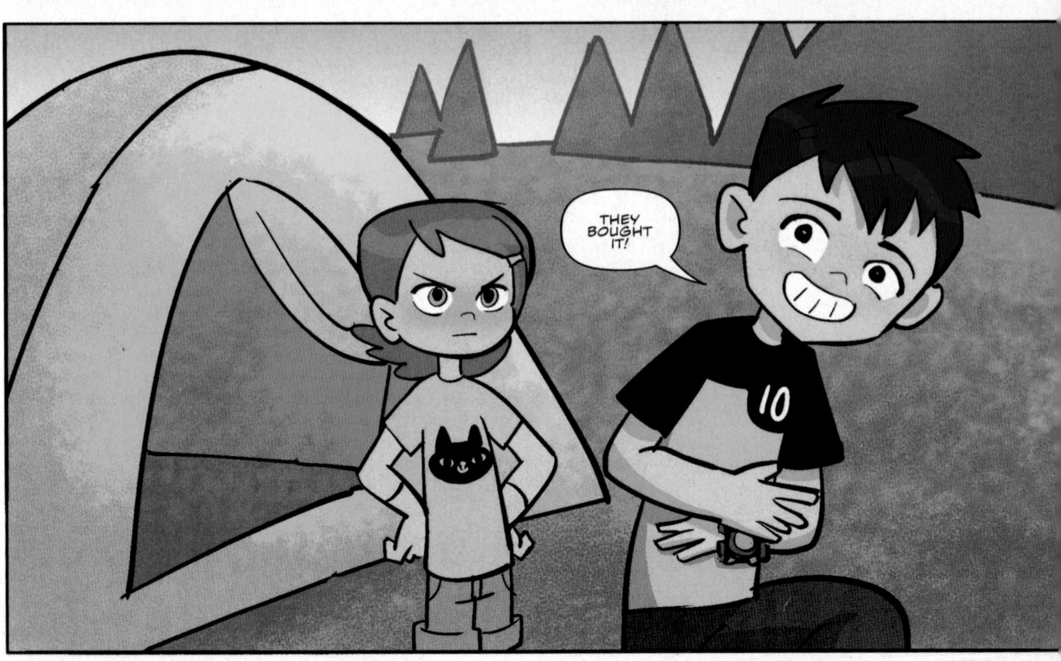
THEY BOUGHT IT!

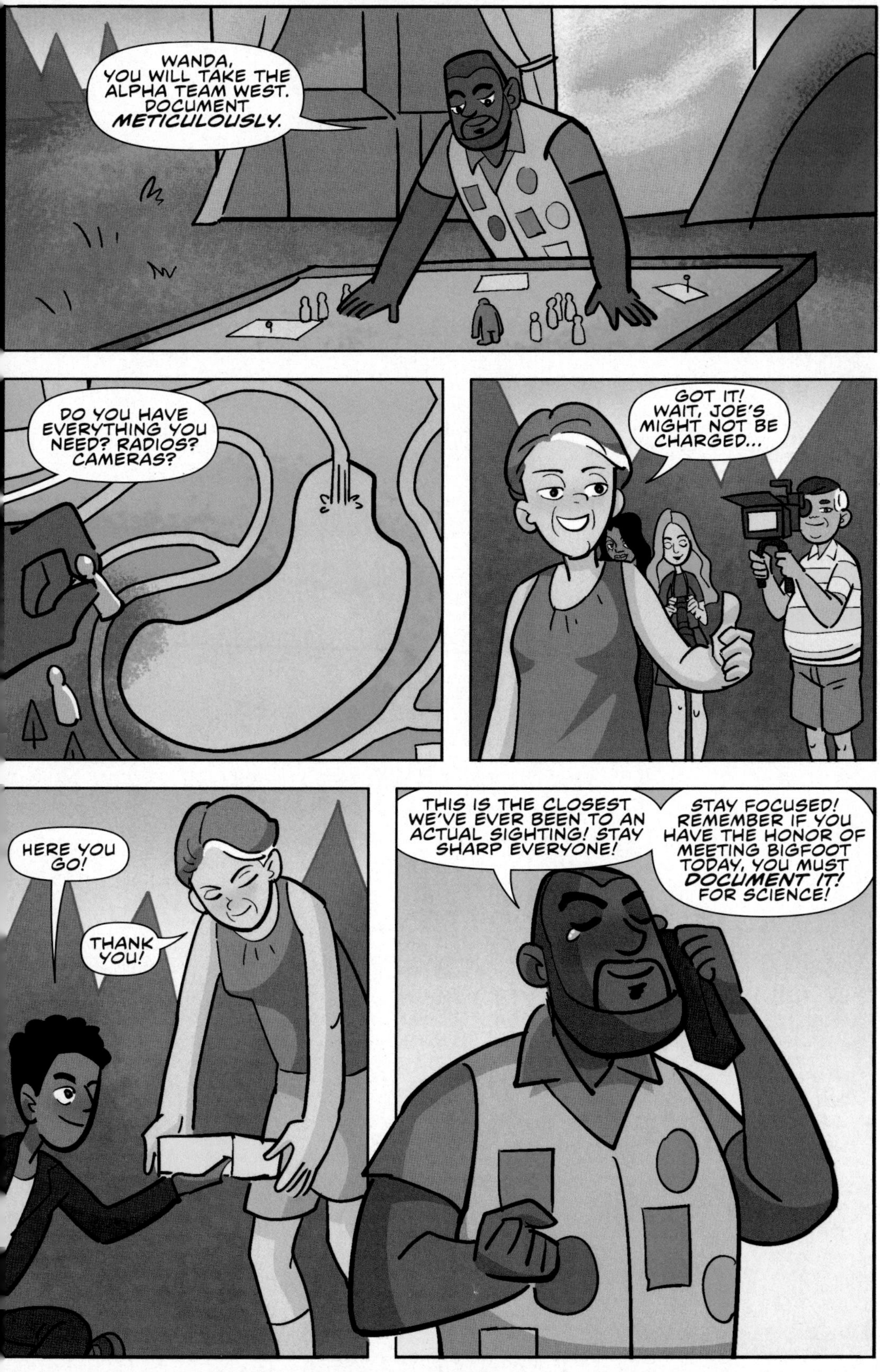
WANDA, YOU WILL TAKE THE ALPHA TEAM WEST. DOCUMENT METICULOUSLY.
DO YOU HAVE EVERYTHING YOU NEED? RADIOS? CAMERAS?
GOT IT! WAIT, JOE'S MIGHT NOT BE CHARGED...
HERE YOU GO!
THANK YOU!
THIS IS THE CLOSEST WE'VE EVER BEEN TO AN ACTUAL SIGHTING! STAY SHARP EVERYONE!
STAY FOCUSED! REMEMBER IF YOU HAVE THE HONOR OF MEETING BIGFOOT TODAY, YOU MUST DOCUMENT IT! FOR SCIENCE!

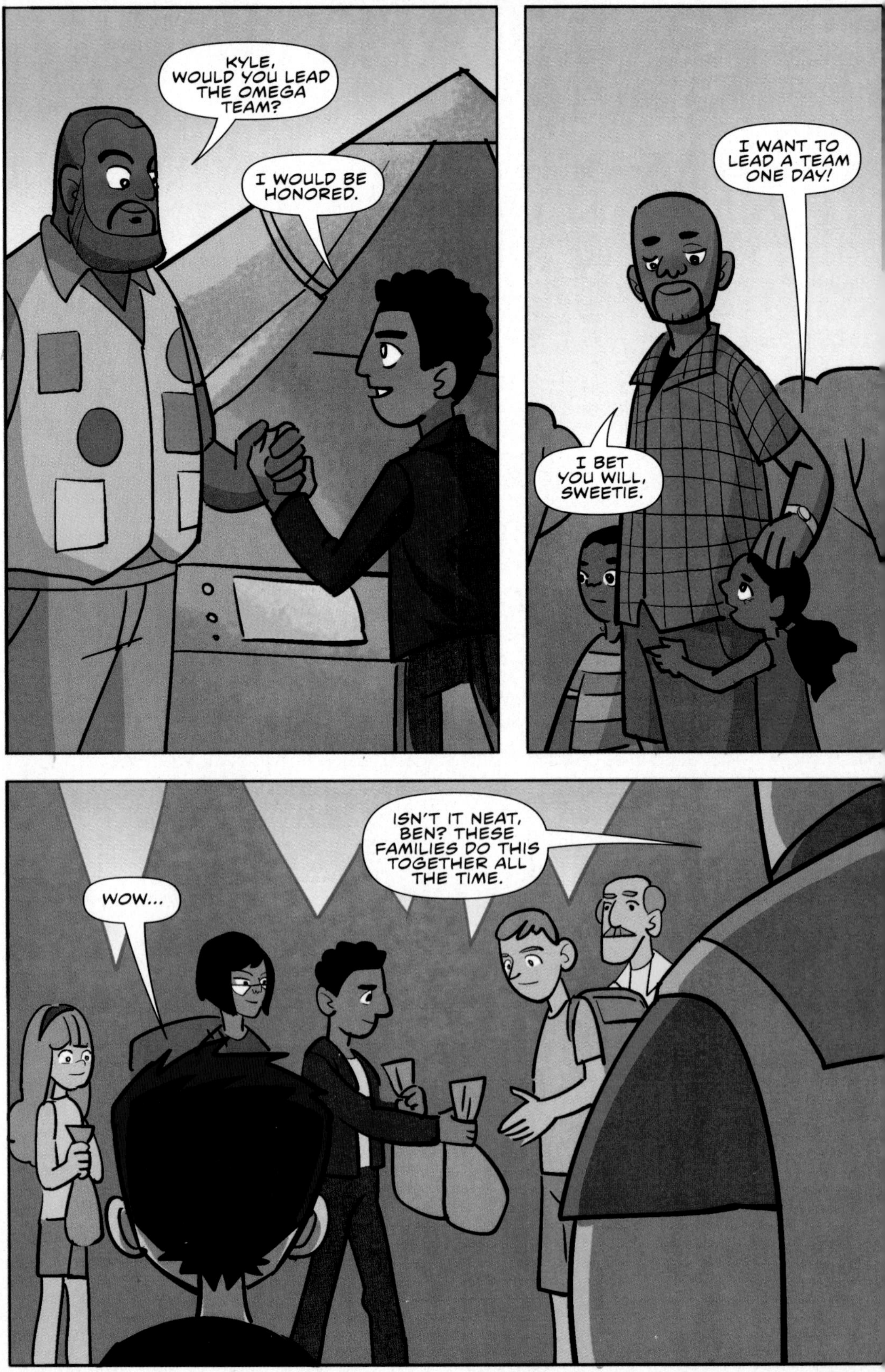
KYLE, WOULD YOU LEAD THE OMEGA TEAM?
I WOULD BE HONORED.
I WANT TO LEAD A TEAM ONE DAY!
I BET YOU WILL, SWEETIE.
ISN'T IT NEAT, BEN? THESE FAMILIES DO THIS TOGETHER ALL THE TIME.
WOW...

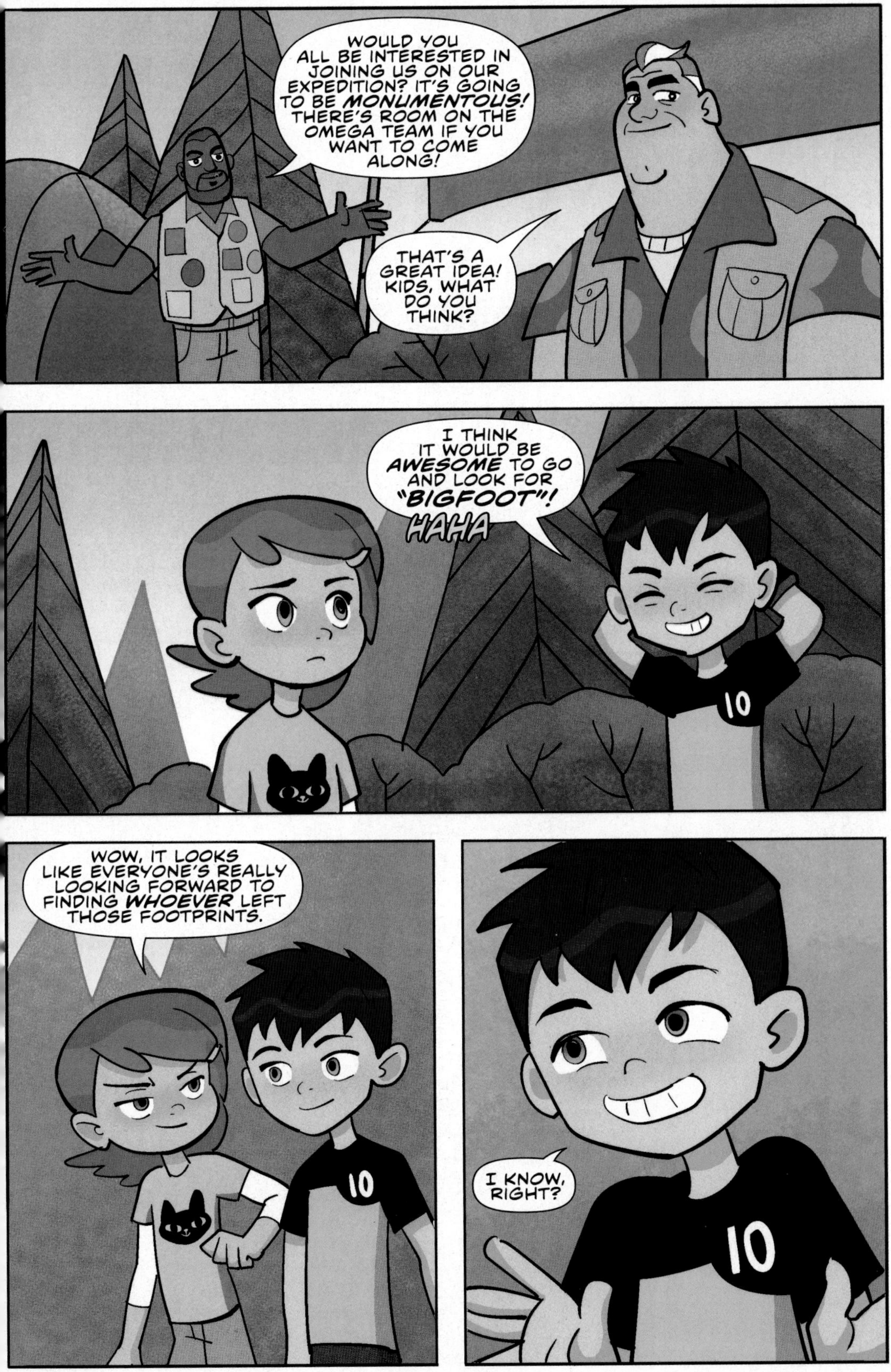
WOULD YOU ALL BE INTERESTED IN JOINING US ON OUR EXPEDITION? IT'S GOING TO BE MONUMENTOUS! THERE'S ROOM ON THE OMEGA TEAM IF YOU WANT TO COME ALONG!
THAT'S A GREAT IDEA! KIDS, WHAT DO YOU THINK?
I THINK IT WOULD BE AWESOME TO GO AND LOOK FOR "BIGFOOT"!
HAHA
WOW, IT LOOKS LIKE EVERYONE'S REALLY LOOKING FORWARD TO FINDING WHOEVER LEFT THOSE FOOTPRINTS.
I KNOW, RIGHT?

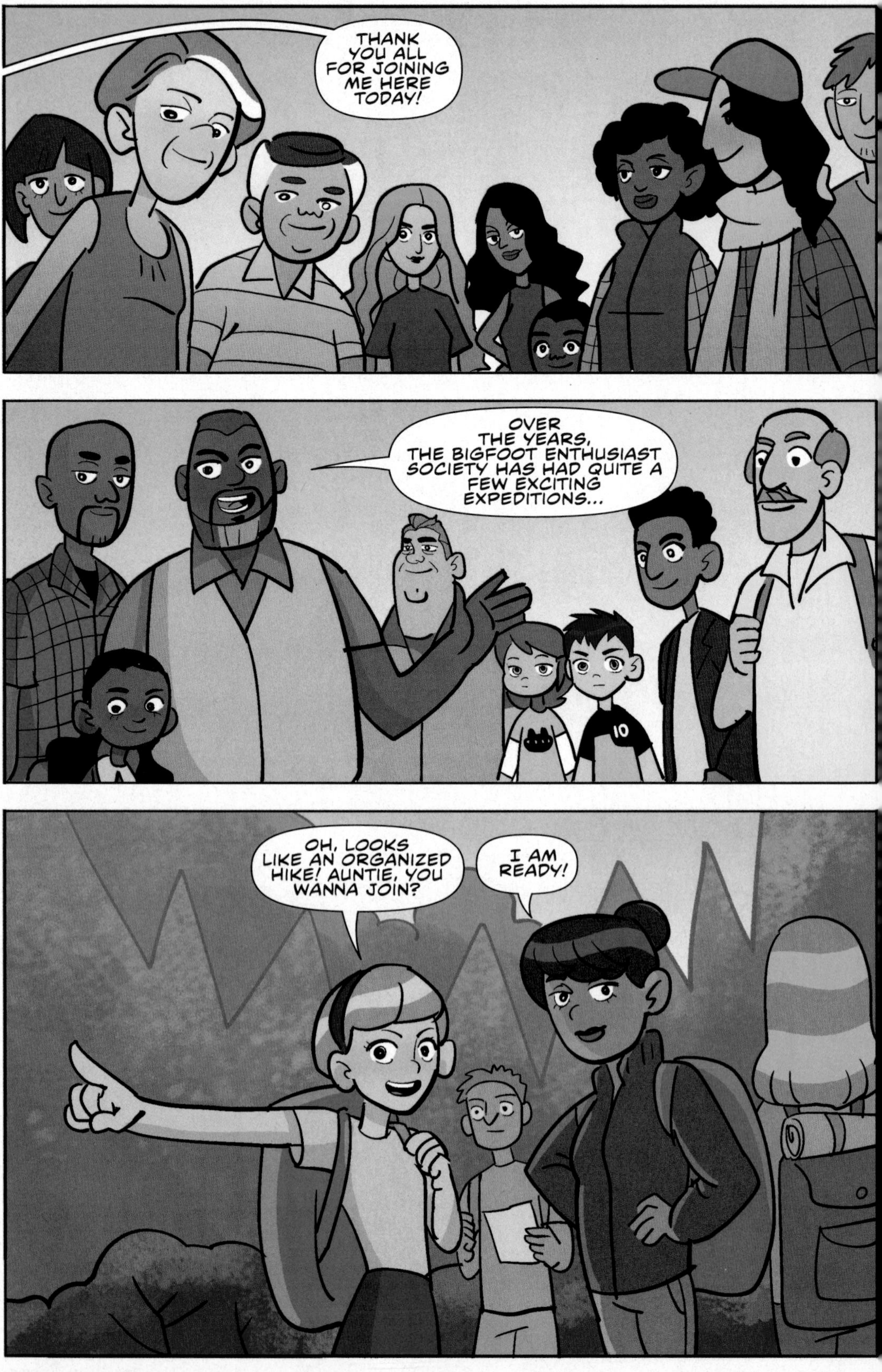
THANK YOU ALL FOR JOINING ME HERE TODAY!
OVER THE YEARS, THE BIGFOOT ENTHUSIAST SOCIETY HAS HAD QUITE A FEW EXCITING EXPEDITIONS...
OH, LOOKS LIKE AN ORGANIZED HIKE! AUNTIE, YOU WANNA JOIN?
I AM READY!

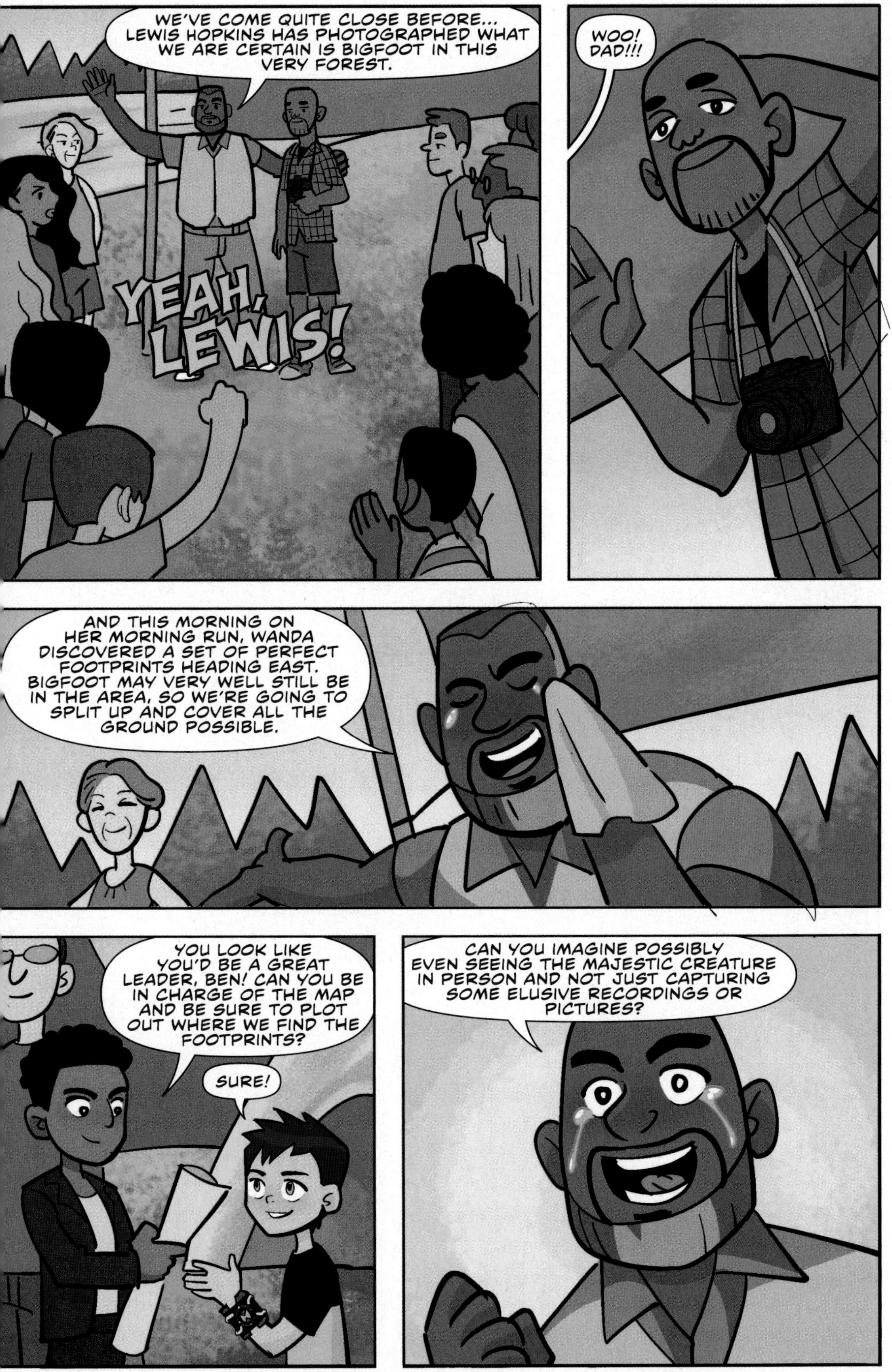
WE'VE COME QUITE CLOSE BEFORE... LEWIS HOPKINS HAS PHOTOGRAPHED WHAT WE ARE CERTAIN IS BIGFOOT IN THIS VERY FOREST.
YEAH, LEWIS!
WOO! DAD!!!
AND THIS MORNING ON HER MORNING RUN, WANDA DISCOVERED A SET OF PERFECT FOOTPRINTS HEADING EAST. BIGFOOT MAY VERY WELL STILL BE IN THE AREA, SO WE'RE GOING TO SPLIT UP AND COVER ALL THE GROUND POSSIBLE.
YOU LOOK LIKE YOU'D BE A GREAT LEADER, BEN! CAN YOU BE IN CHARGE OF THE MAP AND BE SURE TO PLOT OUT WHERE WE FIND THE FOOTPRINTS?
SURE!
CAN YOU IMAGINE POSSIBLY EVEN SEEING THE MAJESTIC CREATURE IN PERSON AND NOT JUST CAPTURING SOME ELUSIVE RECORDINGS OR PICTURES?

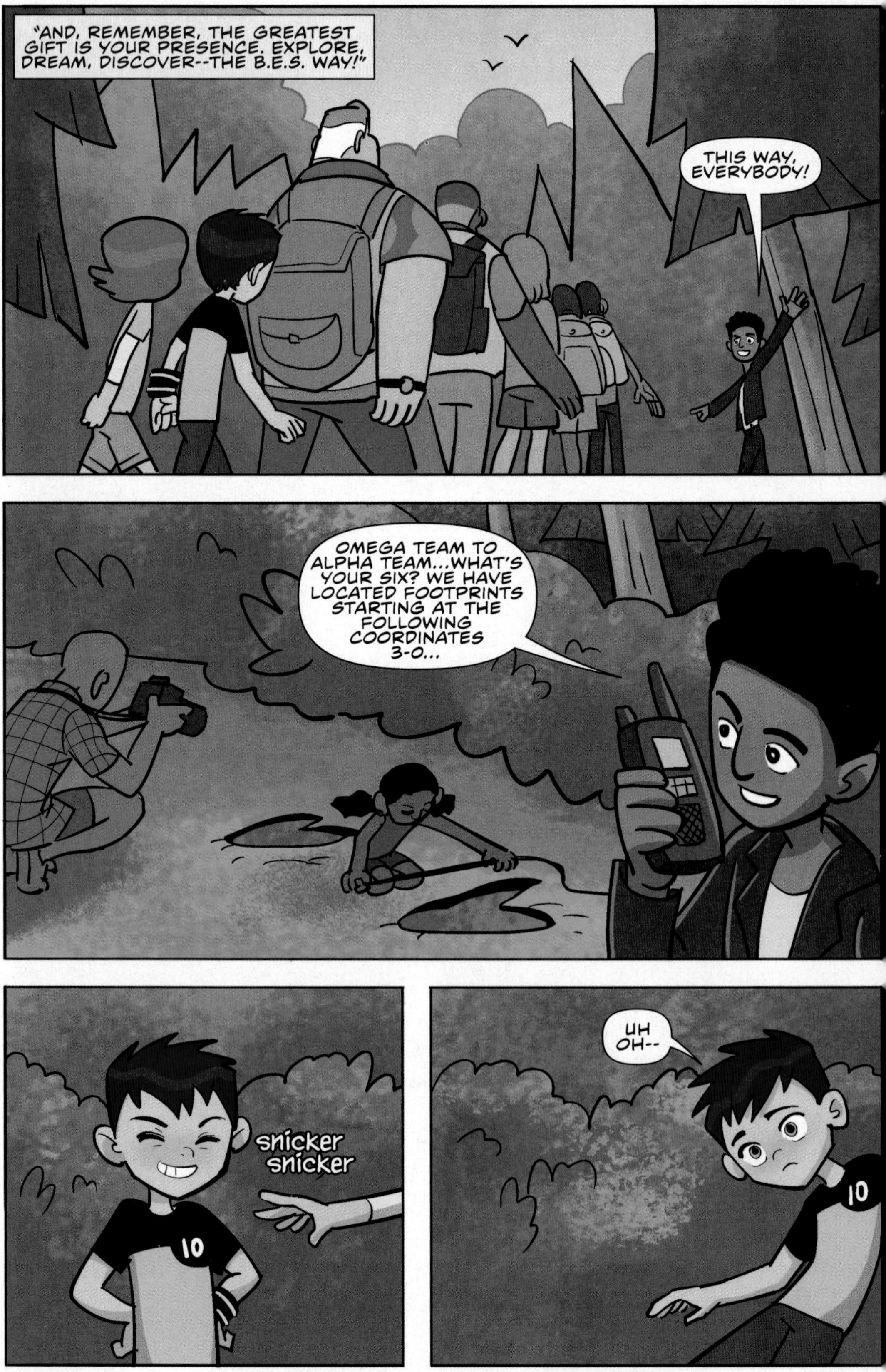
"AND, REMEMBER, THE GREATEST GIFT IS YOUR PRESENCE. EXPLORE, DREAM, DISCOVER--THE B.E.S. WAY!"
THIS WAY, EVERYBODY!
OMEGA TEAM TO ALPHA TEAM...WHAT'S YOUR SIX? WE HAVE LOCATED FOOTPRINTS STARTING AT THE FOLLOWING COORDINATES 3-0...
snicker snicker
10
UH OH--
10

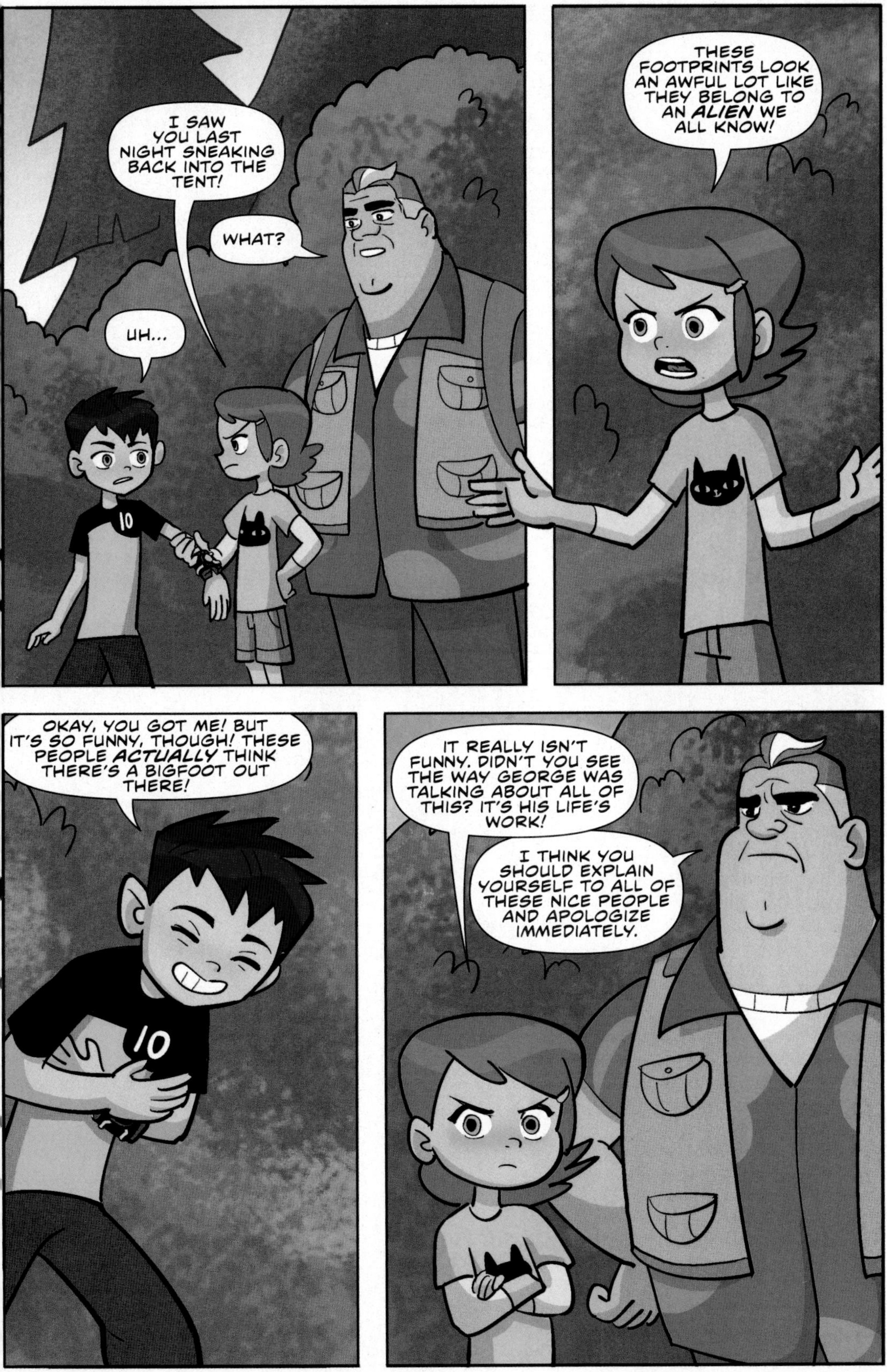
I SAW YOU LAST NIGHT SNEAKING BACK INTO THE TENT!
WHAT?
UH...
THESE FOOTPRINTS LOOK AN AWFUL LOT LIKE THEY BELONG TO AN *ALIEN* WE ALL KNOW!
OKAY, YOU GOT ME! BUT IT'S SO FUNNY, THOUGH! THESE PEOPLE *ACTUALLY* THINK THERE'S A BIGFOOT OUT THERE!
IT REALLY ISN'T FUNNY. DIDN'T YOU SEE THE WAY GEORGE WAS TALKING ABOUT ALL OF THIS? IT'S HIS LIFE'S WORK!
I THINK YOU SHOULD EXPLAIN YOURSELF TO ALL OF THESE NICE PEOPLE AND APOLOGIZE IMMEDIATELY.

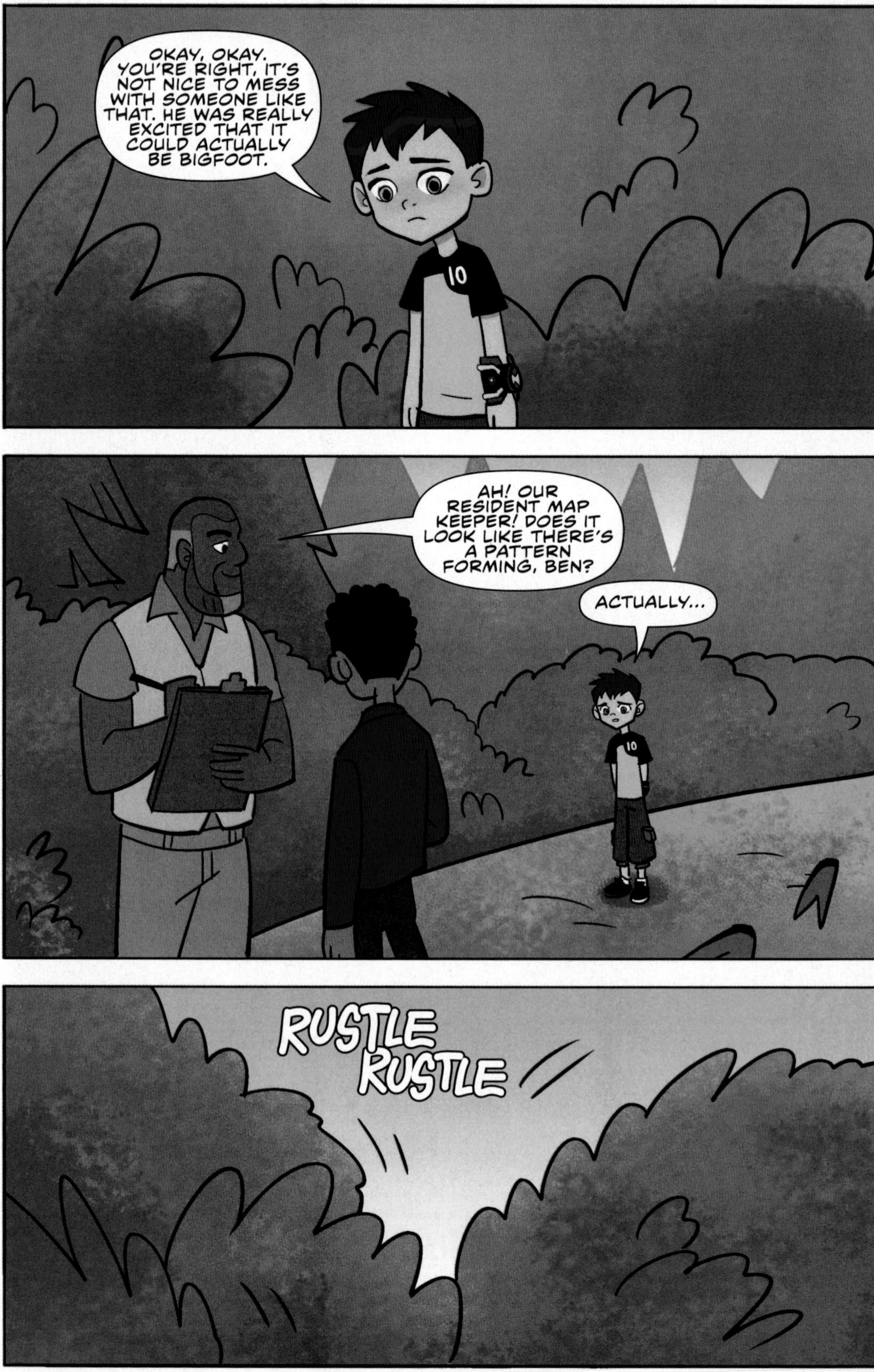
OKAY, OKAY. YOU'RE RIGHT, IT'S NOT NICE TO MESS WITH SOMEONE LIKE THAT. HE WAS REALLY EXCITED THAT IT COULD ACTUALLY BE BIGFOOT.
AH! OUR RESIDENT MAP KEEPER! DOES IT LOOK LIKE THERE'S A PATTERN FORMING, BEN?
ACTUALLY...
RUSTLE RUSTLE

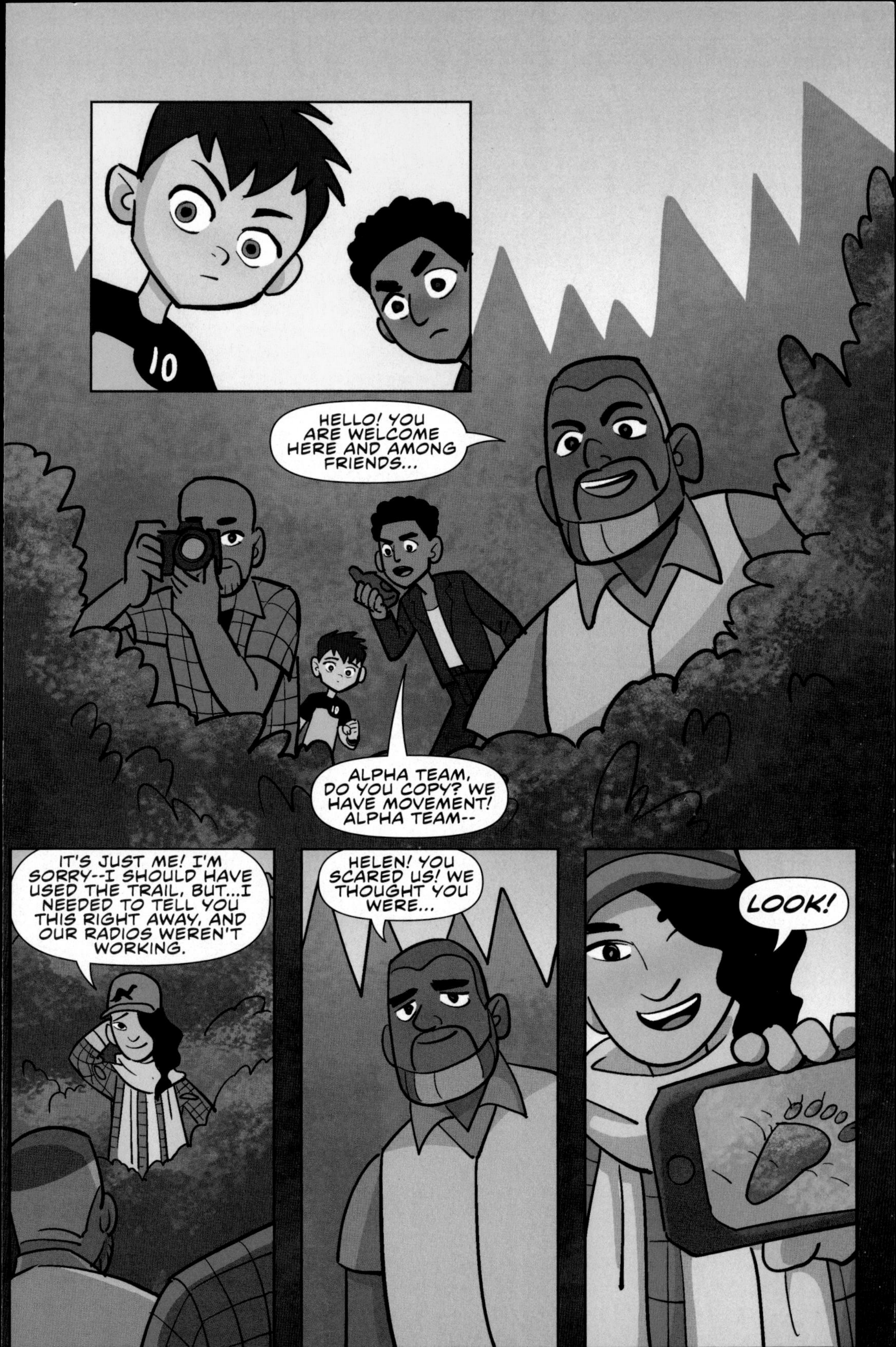
HELLO! YOU ARE WELCOME HERE AND AMONG FRIENDS...
ALPHA TEAM, DO YOU COPY? WE HAVE MOVEMENT! ALPHA TEAM--
IT'S JUST ME! I'M SORRY--I SHOULD HAVE USED THE TRAIL, BUT...I NEEDED TO TELL YOU THIS RIGHT AWAY, AND OUR RADIOS WEREN'T WORKING.
HELEN! YOU SCARED US! WE THOUGHT YOU WERE...
LOOK!

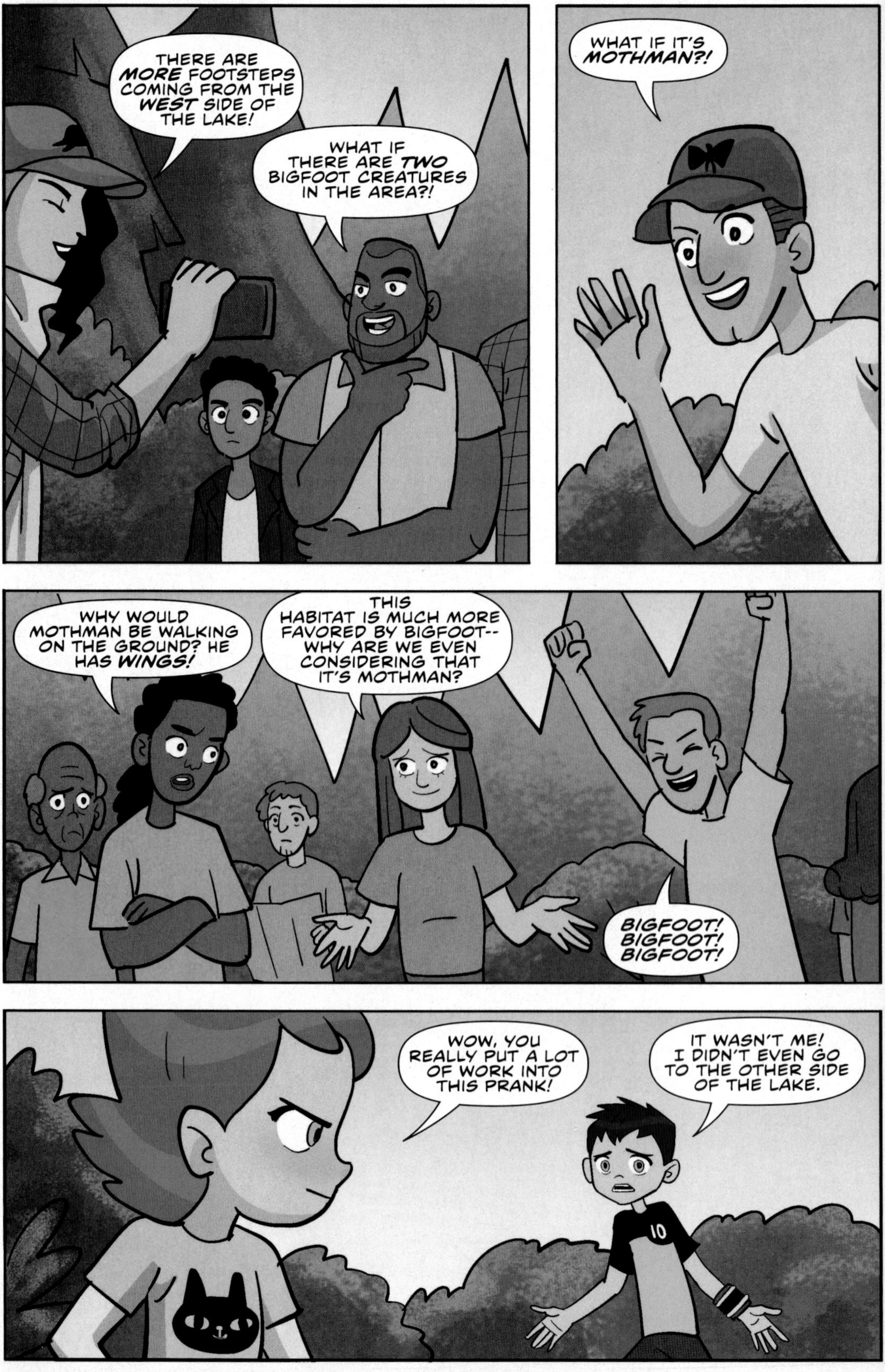
THERE ARE MORE FOOTSTEPS COMING FROM THE WEST SIDE OF THE LAKE!
WHAT IF THERE ARE TWO BIGFOOT CREATURES IN THE AREA?!
WHAT IF IT'S MOTHMAN?!
WHY WOULD MOTHMAN BE WALKING ON THE GROUND? HE HAS WINGS!
THIS HABITAT IS MUCH MORE FAVORED BY BIGFOOT-- WHY ARE WE EVEN CONSIDERING THAT IT'S MOTHMAN?
BIGFOOT! BIGFOOT! BIGFOOT!
WOW, YOU REALLY PUT A LOT OF WORK INTO THIS PRANK!
IT WASN'T ME! I DIDN'T EVEN GO TO THE OTHER SIDE OF THE LAKE.
10

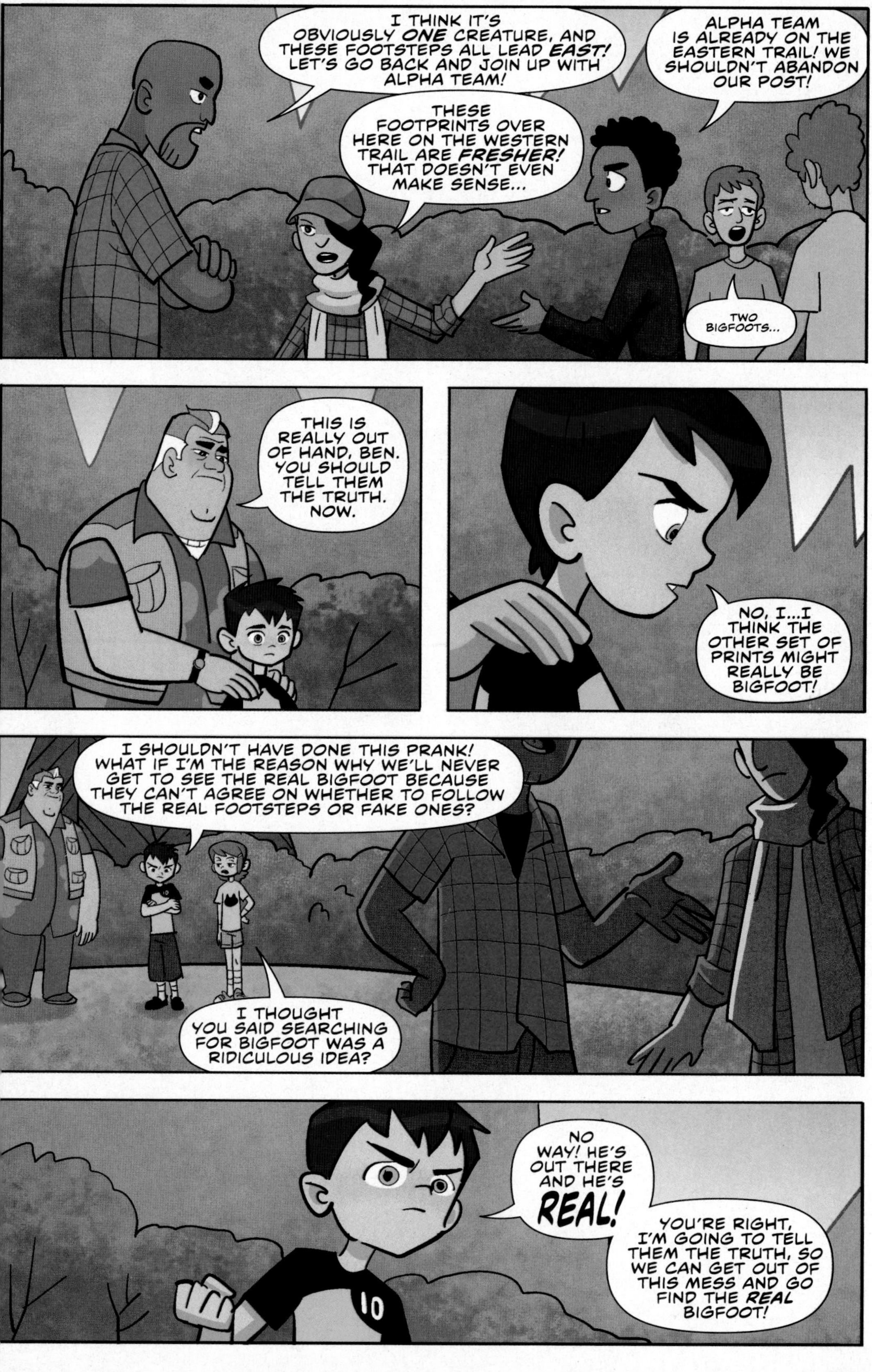
I THINK IT'S OBVIOUSLY ONE CREATURE, AND THESE FOOTSTEPS ALL LEAD EAST! LET'S GO BACK AND JOIN UP WITH ALPHA TEAM!
THESE FOOTPRINTS OVER HERE ON THE WESTERN TRAIL ARE FRESHER! THAT DOESN'T EVEN MAKE SENSE...
ALPHA TEAM IS ALREADY ON THE EASTERN TRAIL! WE SHOULDN'T ABANDON OUR POST!
TWO BIGFOOTS...
THIS IS REALLY OUT OF HAND, BEN. YOU SHOULD TELL THEM THE TRUTH. NOW.
NO, I...I THINK THE OTHER SET OF PRINTS MIGHT REALLY BE BIGFOOT!
I SHOULDN'T HAVE DONE THIS PRANK! WHAT IF I'M THE REASON WHY WE'LL NEVER GET TO SEE THE REAL BIGFOOT BECAUSE THEY CAN'T AGREE ON WHETHER TO FOLLOW THE REAL FOOTSTEPS OR FAKE ONES?
I THOUGHT YOU SAID SEARCHING FOR BIGFOOT WAS A RIDICULOUS IDEA?
NO WAY! HE'S OUT THERE AND HE'S REAL!
YOU'RE RIGHT, I'M GOING TO TELL THEM THE TRUTH, SO WE CAN GET OUT OF THIS MESS AND GO FIND THE REAL BIGFOOT!

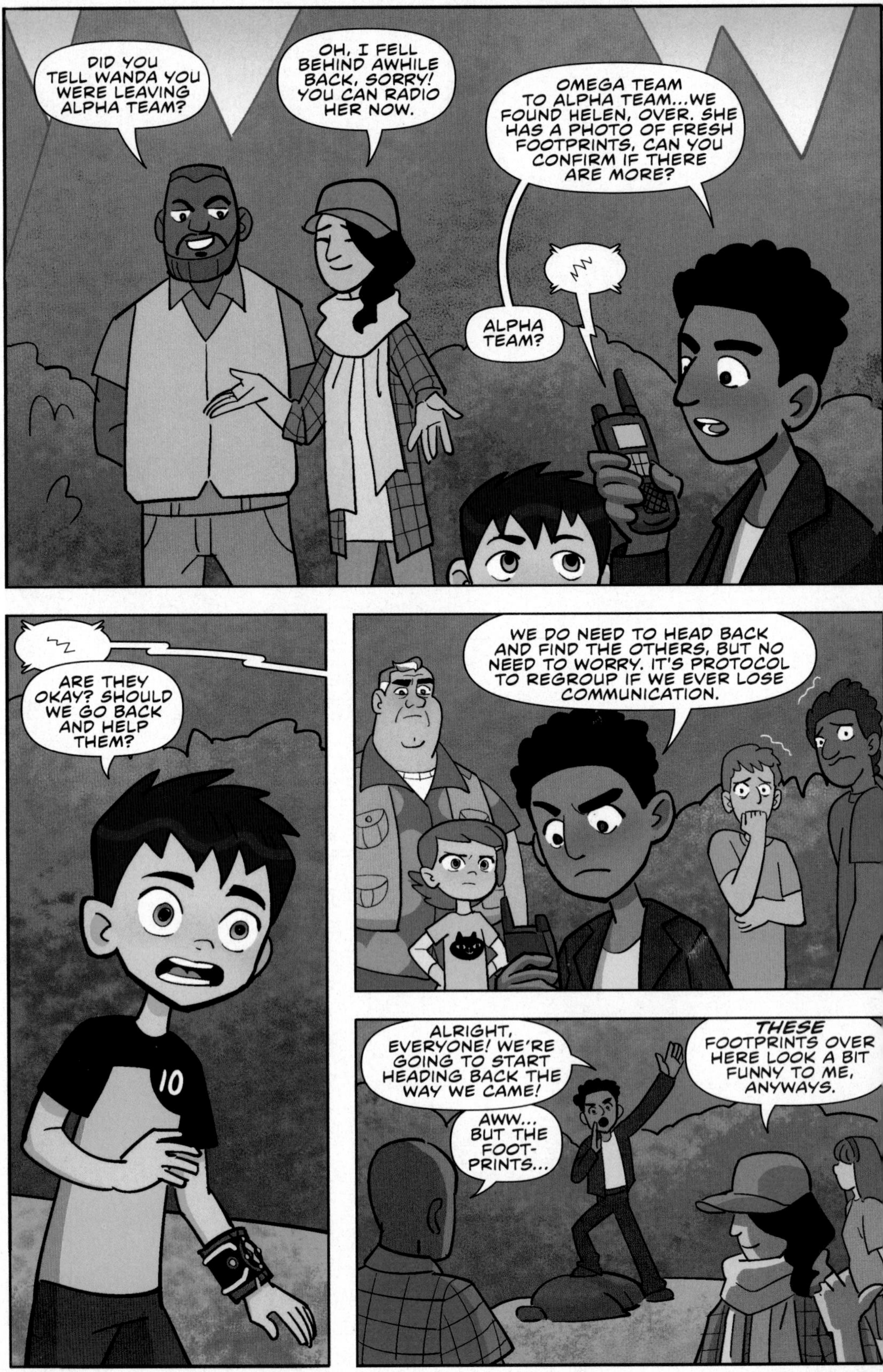
DID YOU TELL WANDA YOU WERE LEAVING ALPHA TEAM?
OH, I FELL BEHIND AWHILE BACK, SORRY! YOU CAN RADIO HER NOW.
OMEGA TEAM TO ALPHA TEAM...WE FOUND HELEN, OVER. SHE HAS A PHOTO OF FRESH FOOTPRINTS, CAN YOU CONFIRM IF THERE ARE MORE?
ALPHA TEAM?
ARE THEY OKAY? SHOULD WE GO BACK AND HELP THEM?
10
WE DO NEED TO HEAD BACK AND FIND THE OTHERS, BUT NO NEED TO WORRY. IT'S PROTOCOL TO REGROUP IF WE EVER LOSE COMMUNICATION.
ALRIGHT, EVERYONE! WE'RE GOING TO START HEADING BACK THE WAY WE CAME!
AWW... BUT THE FOOT-PRINTS...
THESE FOOTPRINTS OVER HERE LOOK A BIT FUNNY TO ME, ANYWAYS.

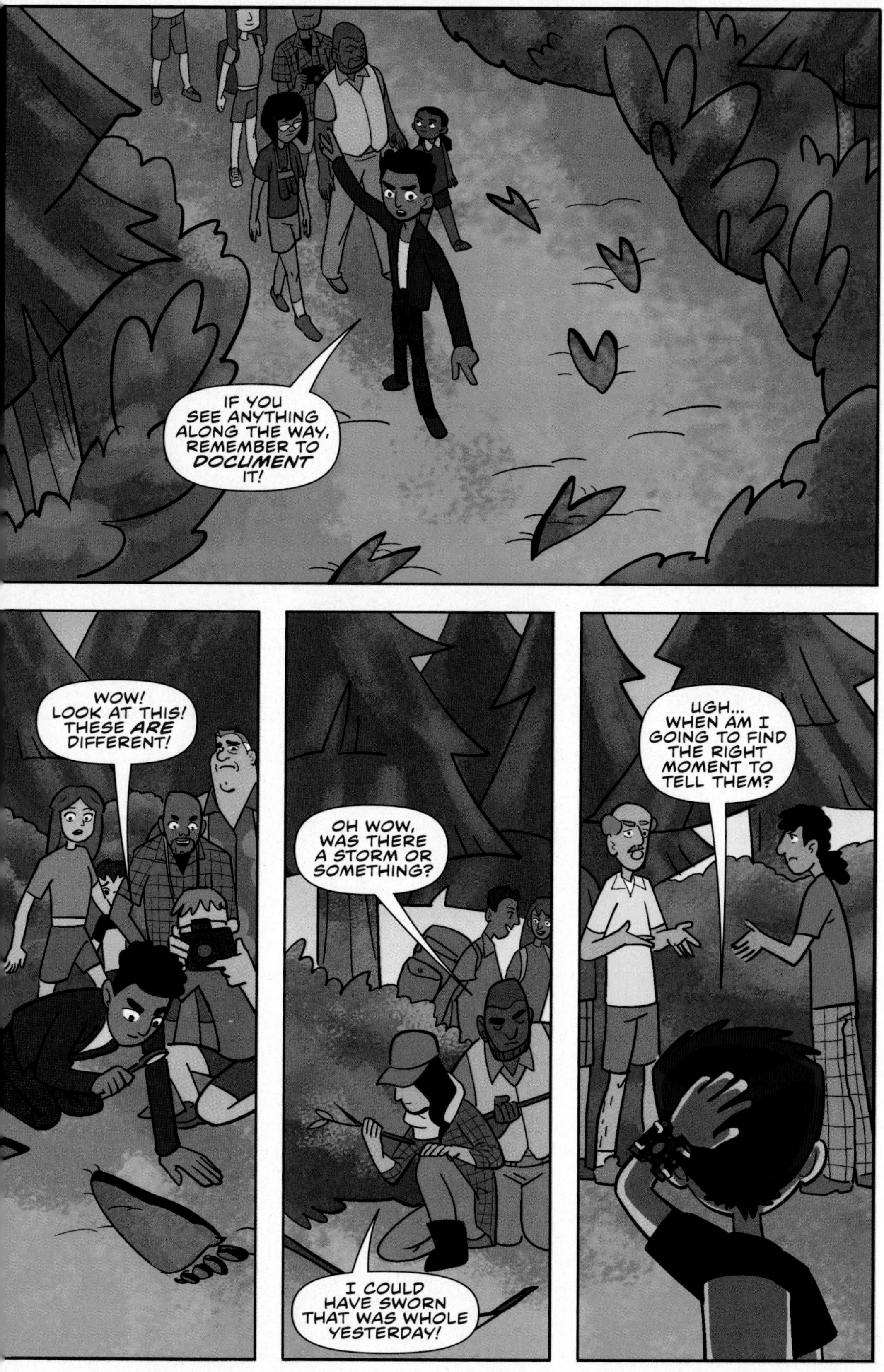
IF YOU SEE ANYTHING ALONG THE WAY, REMEMBER TO *DOCUMENT* IT!
WOW! LOOK AT THIS! THESE *ARE* DIFFERENT!
OH WOW, WAS THERE A STORM OR SOMETHING?
I COULD HAVE SWORN THAT WAS WHOLE YESTERDAY!
UGH... WHEN AM I GOING TO FIND THE RIGHT MOMENT TO TELL THEM?

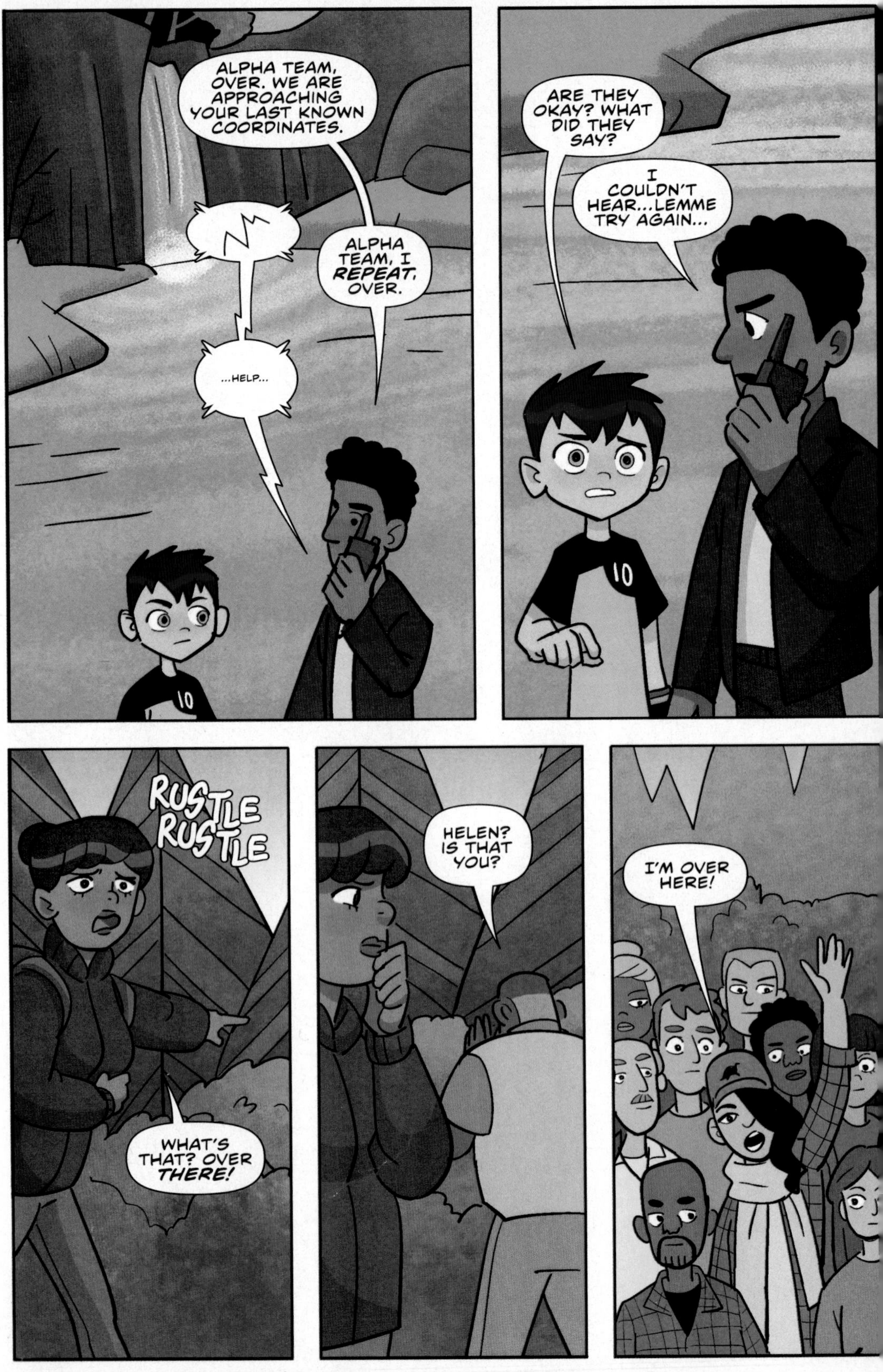
ALPHA TEAM, OVER. WE ARE APPROACHING YOUR LAST KNOWN COORDINATES.
...HELP...
ALPHA TEAM, I *REPEAT*, OVER.
ARE THEY OKAY? WHAT DID THEY SAY?
I COULDN'T HEAR...LEMME TRY AGAIN...
RUSTLE RUSTLE
WHAT'S THAT? OVER *THERE!*
HELEN? IS THAT YOU?
I'M OVER HERE!

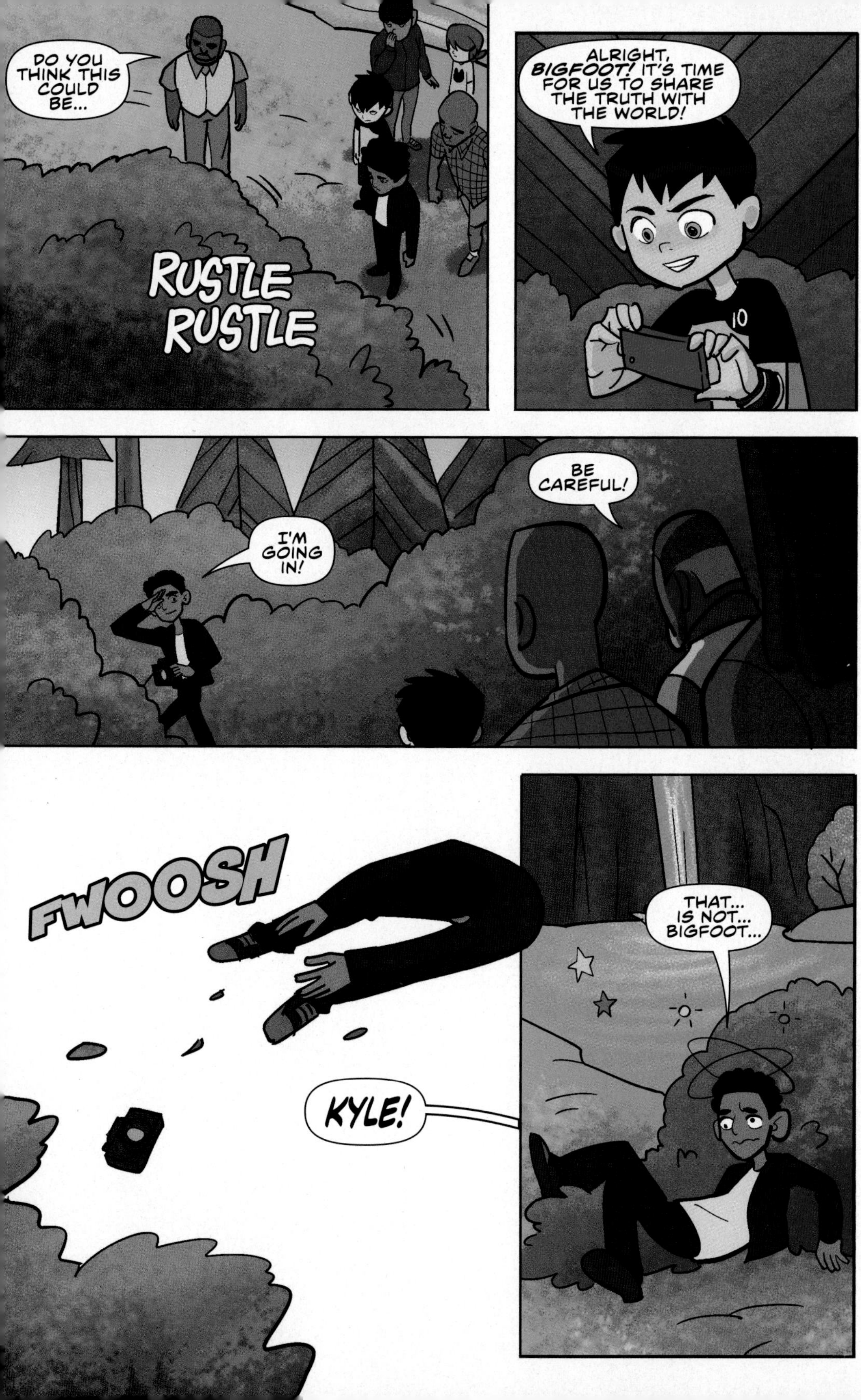
DO YOU THINK THIS COULD BE...
RUSTLE RUSTLE
ALRIGHT, BIGFOOT! IT'S TIME FOR US TO SHARE THE TRUTH WITH THE WORLD!
I'M GOING IN!
BE CAREFUL!
FWOOSH
KYLE!
THAT... IS NOT... BIGFOOT...

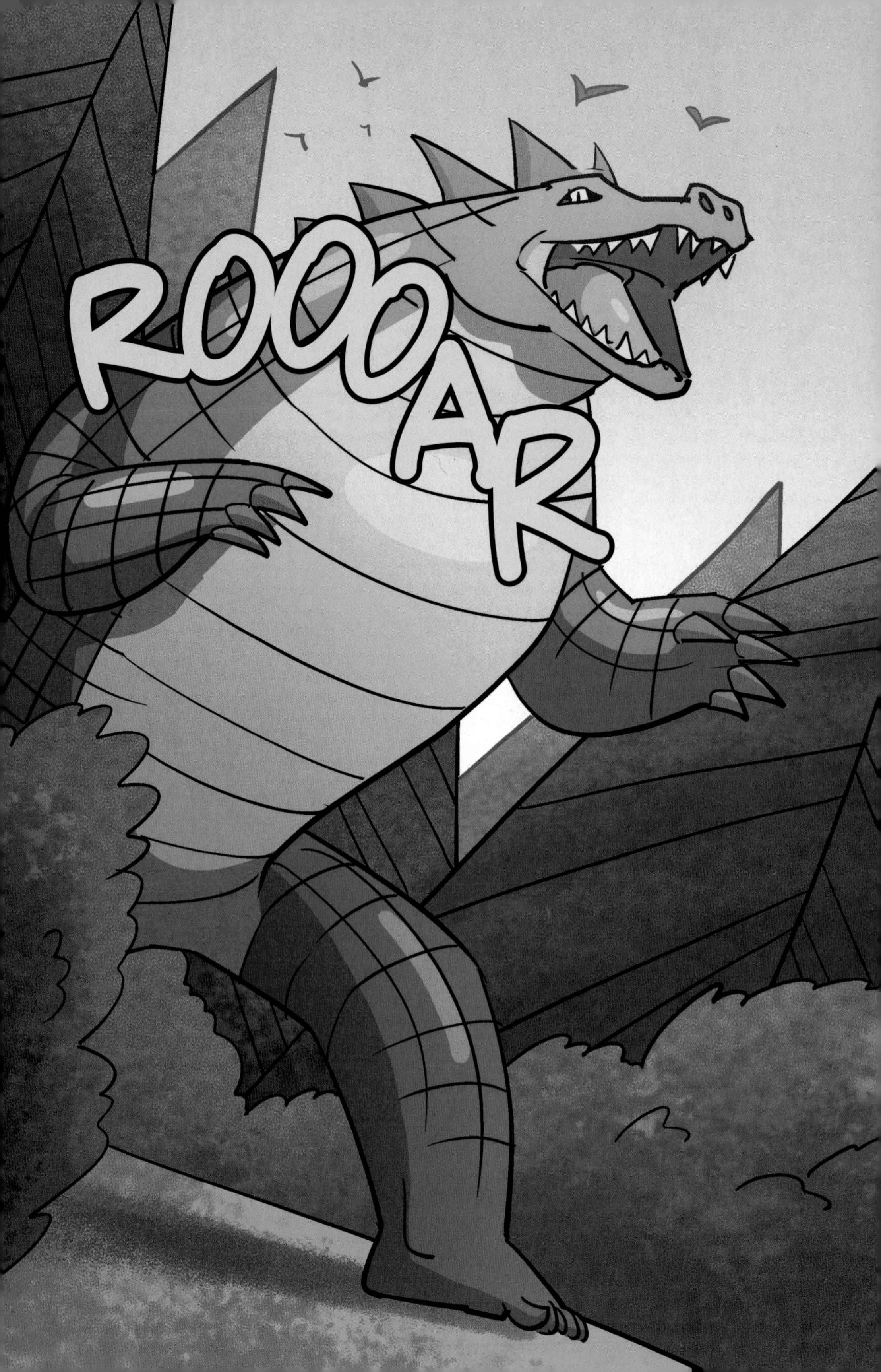
ROOOAR

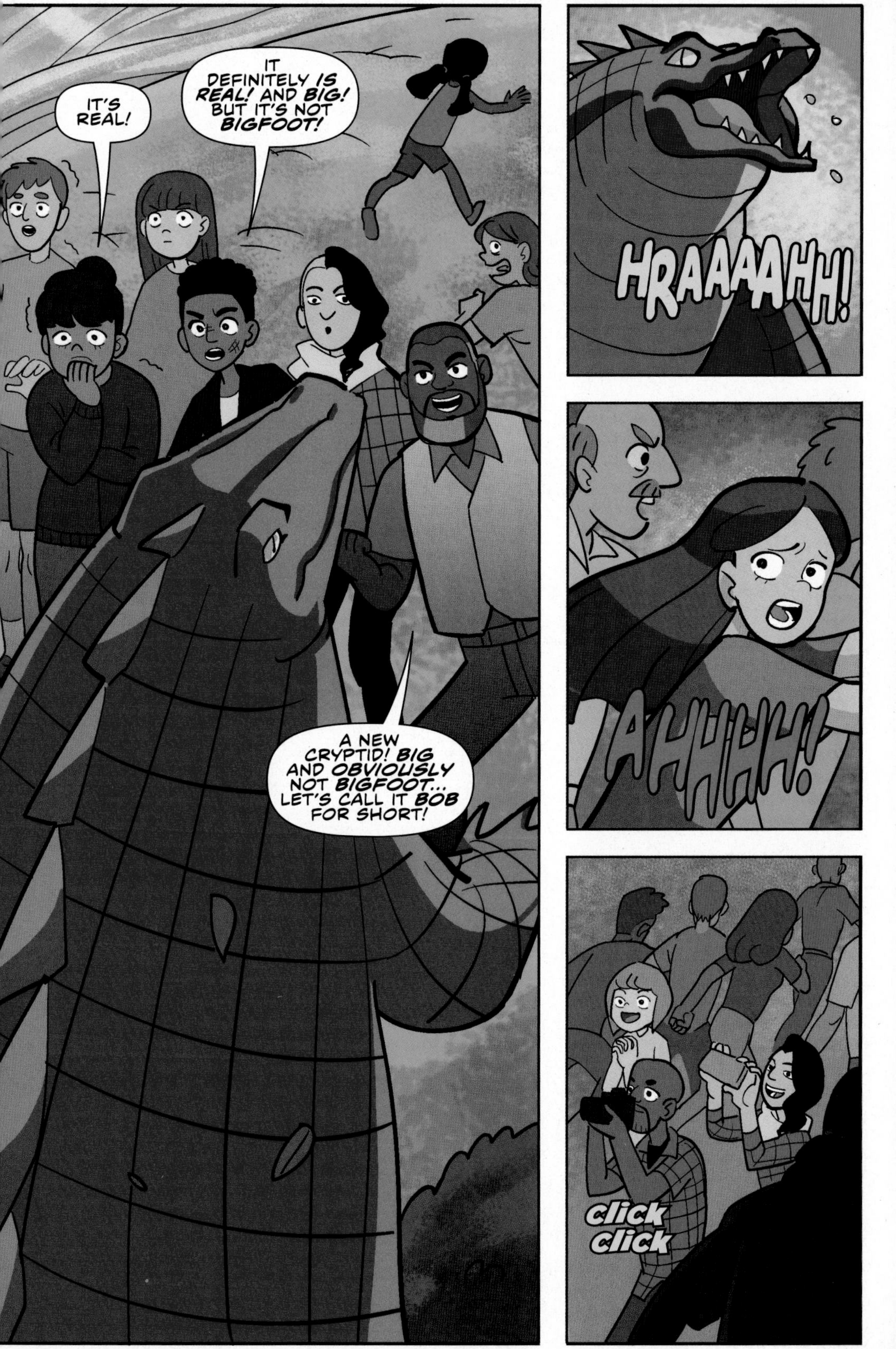
IT'S REAL!
IT DEFINITELY IS REAL! AND BIG! BUT IT'S NOT BIGFOOT!
A NEW CRYPTID! BIG AND OBVIOUSLY NOT BIGFOOT... LET'S CALL IT BOB FOR SHORT!
HRAAAAAHH!
AHHHH!
click click

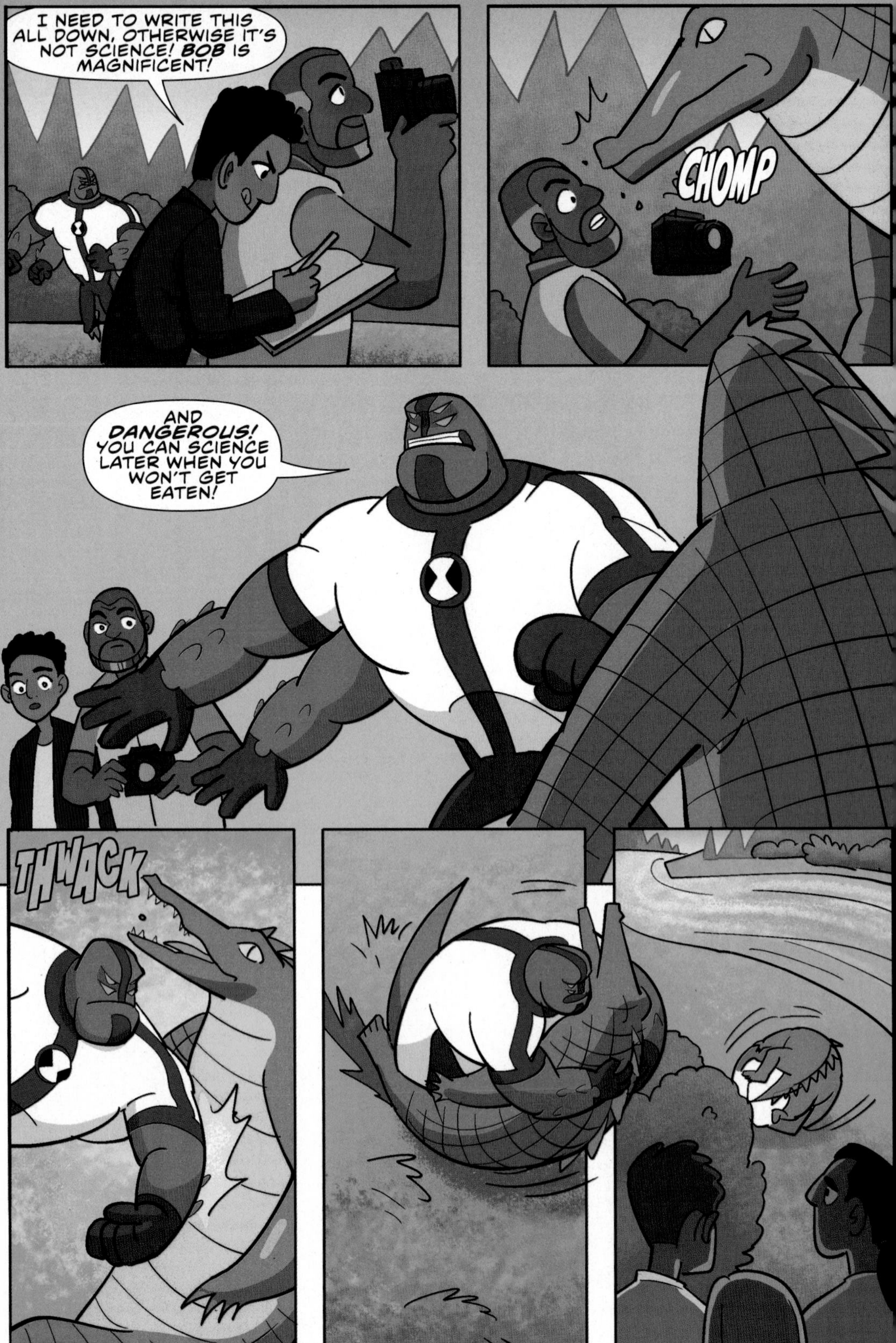
I NEED TO WRITE THIS ALL DOWN, OTHERWISE IT'S NOT SCIENCE! BOB IS MAGNIFICENT!
CHOMP
AND DANGEROUS! YOU CAN SCIENCE LATER WHEN YOU WON'T GET EATEN!
THWACK

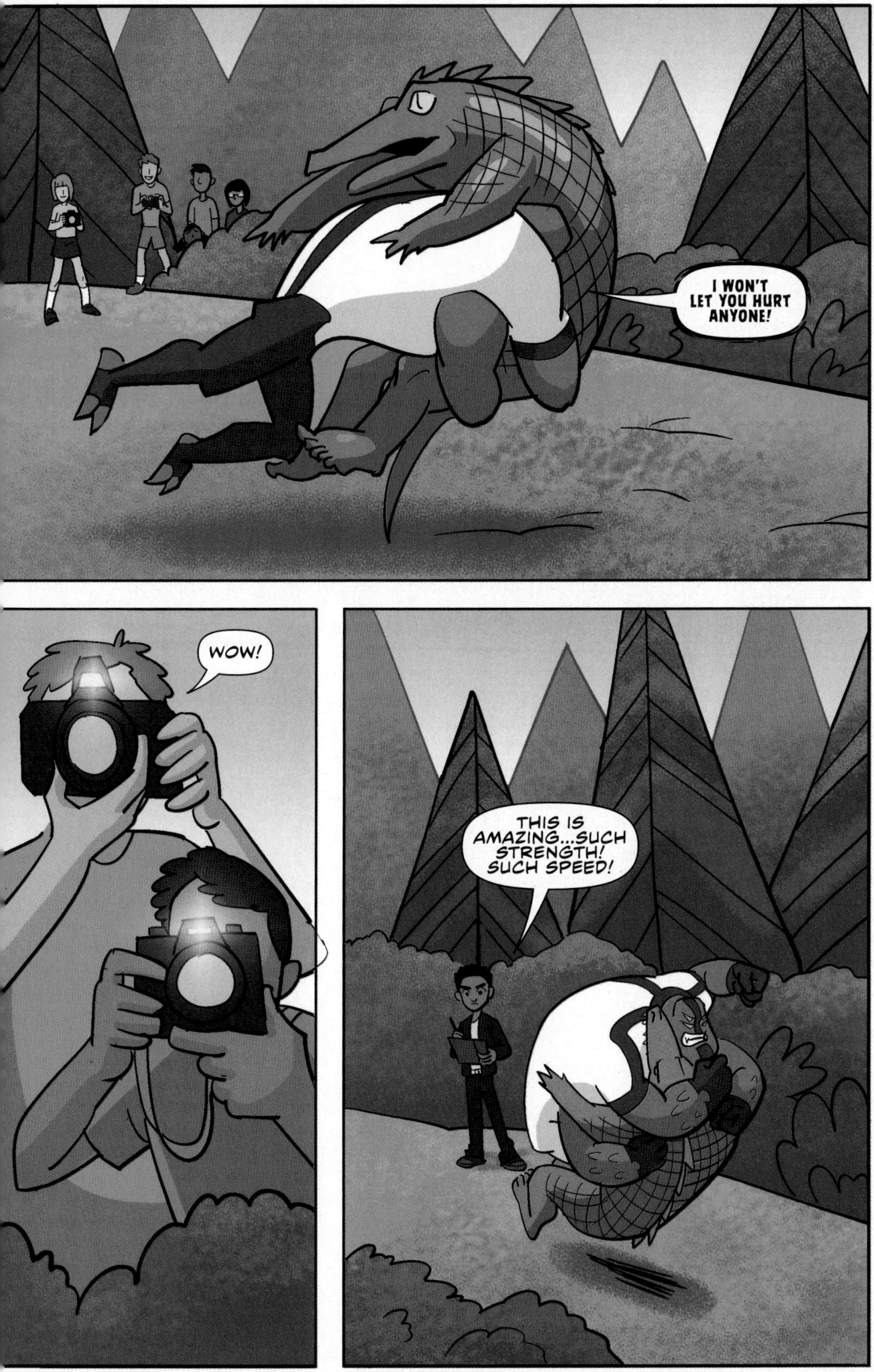
I WON'T LET YOU HURT ANYONE!
WOW!
THIS IS AMAZING...SUCH STRENGTH! SUCH SPEED!

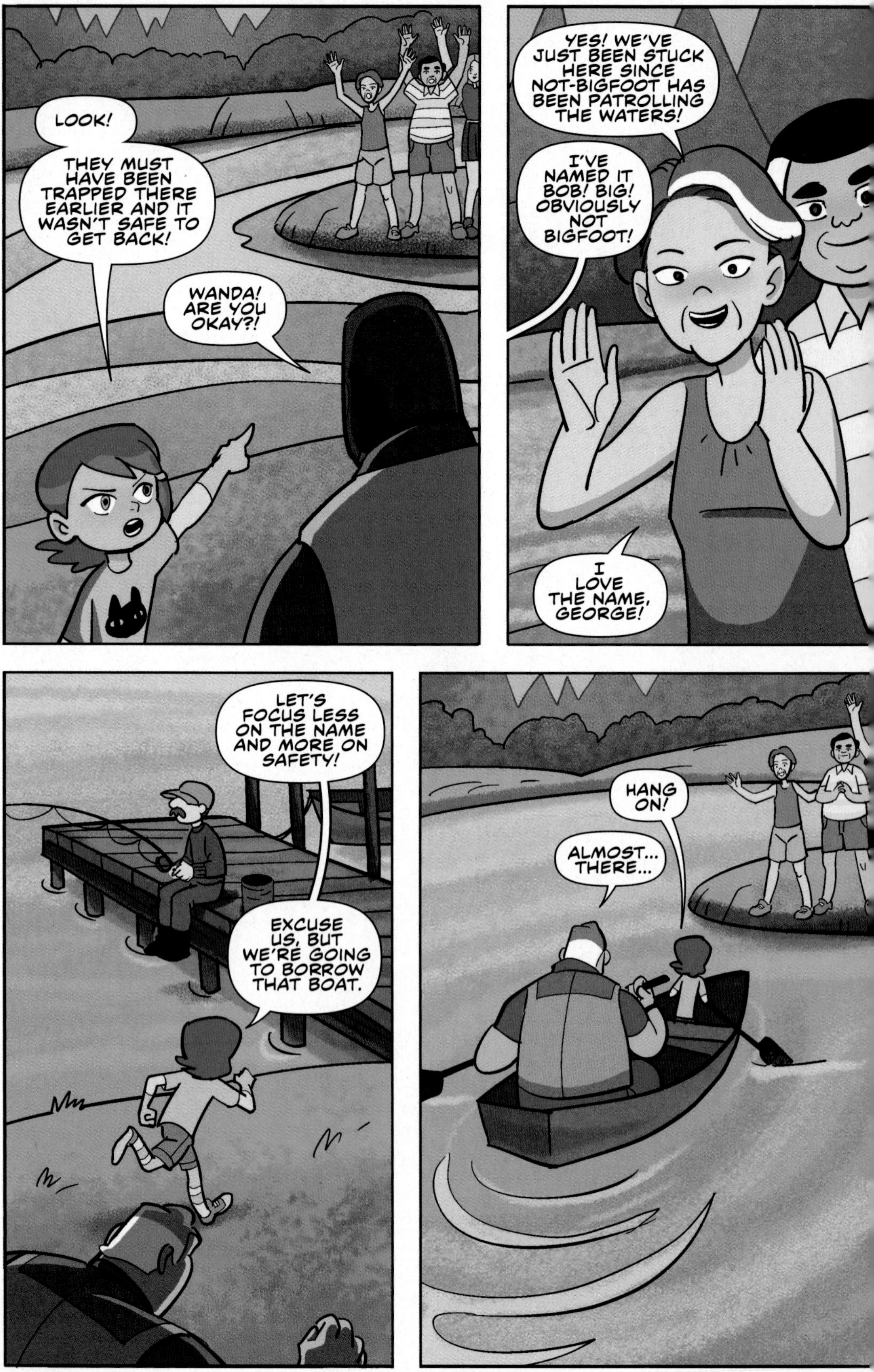
LOOK!
THEY MUST HAVE BEEN TRAPPED THERE EARLIER AND IT WASN'T SAFE TO GET BACK!
WANDA! ARE YOU OKAY?!
YES! WE'VE JUST BEEN STUCK HERE SINCE NOT-BIGFOOT HAS BEEN PATROLLING THE WATERS!
I'VE NAMED IT BOB! BIG! OBVIOUSLY NOT BIGFOOT!
I LOVE THE NAME, GEORGE!
LET'S FOCUS LESS ON THE NAME AND MORE ON SAFETY!
EXCUSE US, BUT WE'RE GOING TO BORROW THAT BOAT.
HANG ON!
ALMOST... THERE...

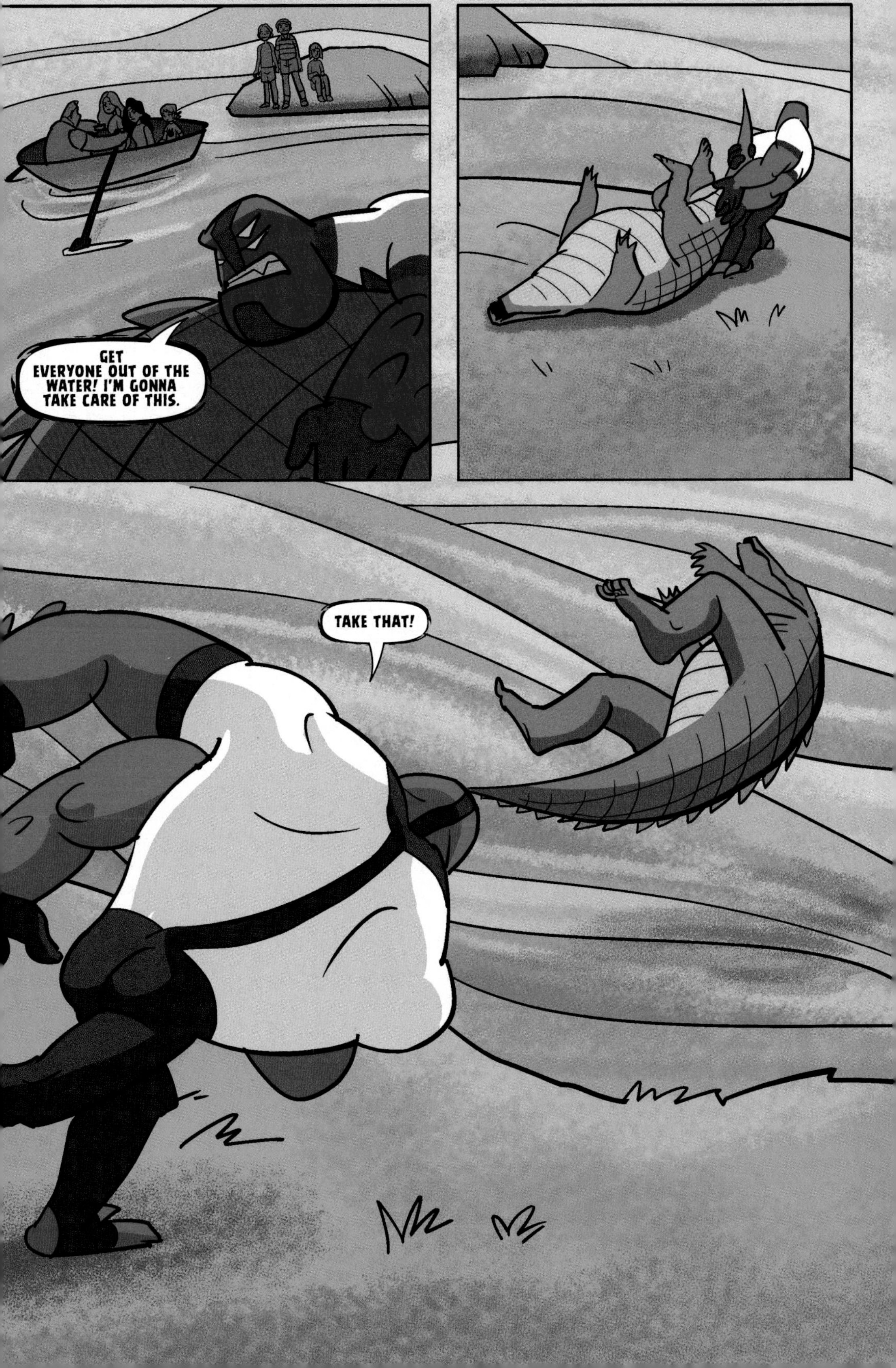
GET EVERYONE OUT OF THE WATER! I'M GONNA TAKE CARE OF THIS.
TAKE THAT!

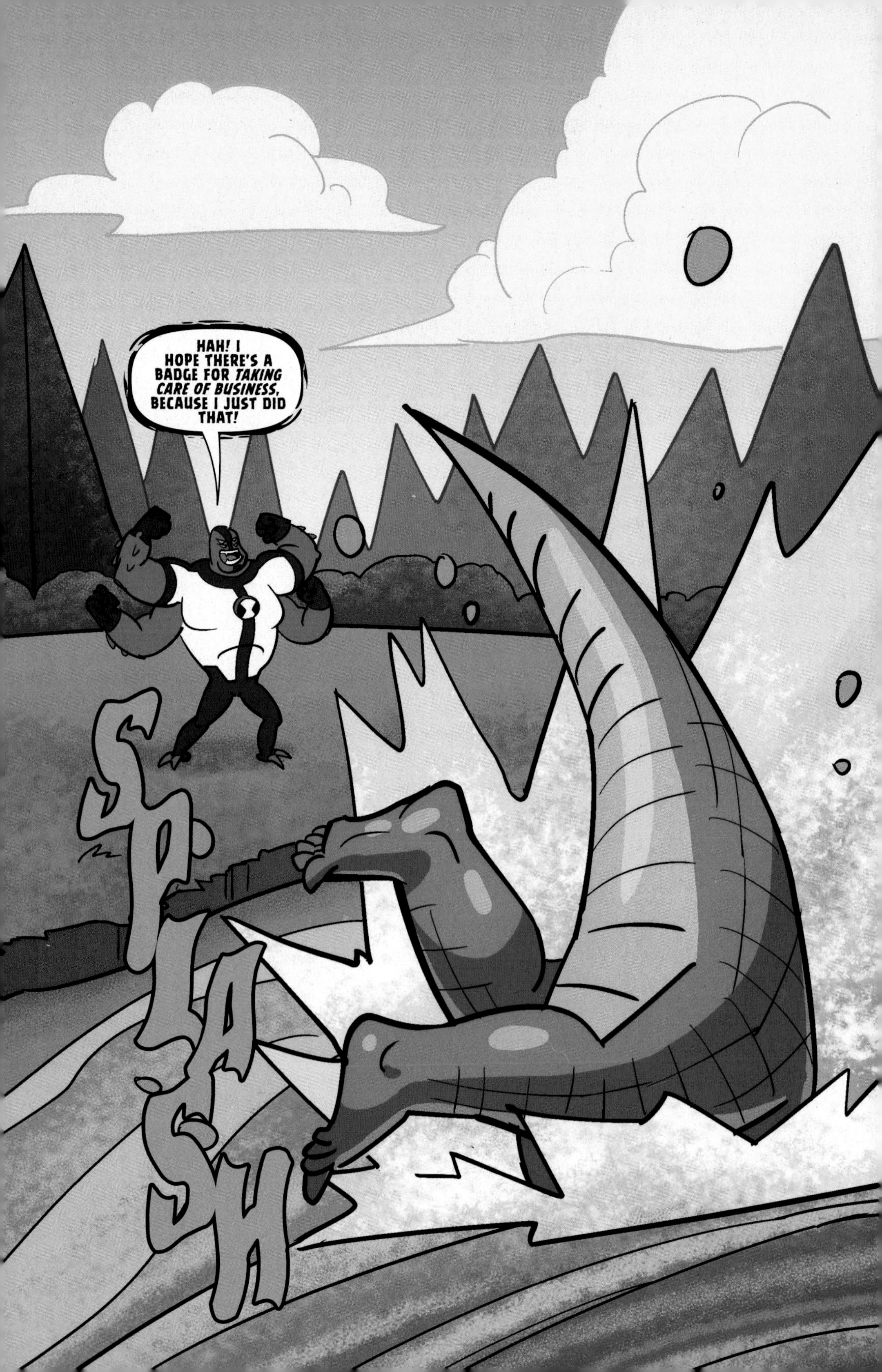
HAH! I HOPE THERE'S A BADGE FOR *TAKING CARE OF BUSINESS*, BECAUSE I JUST DID THAT!
SPLASH

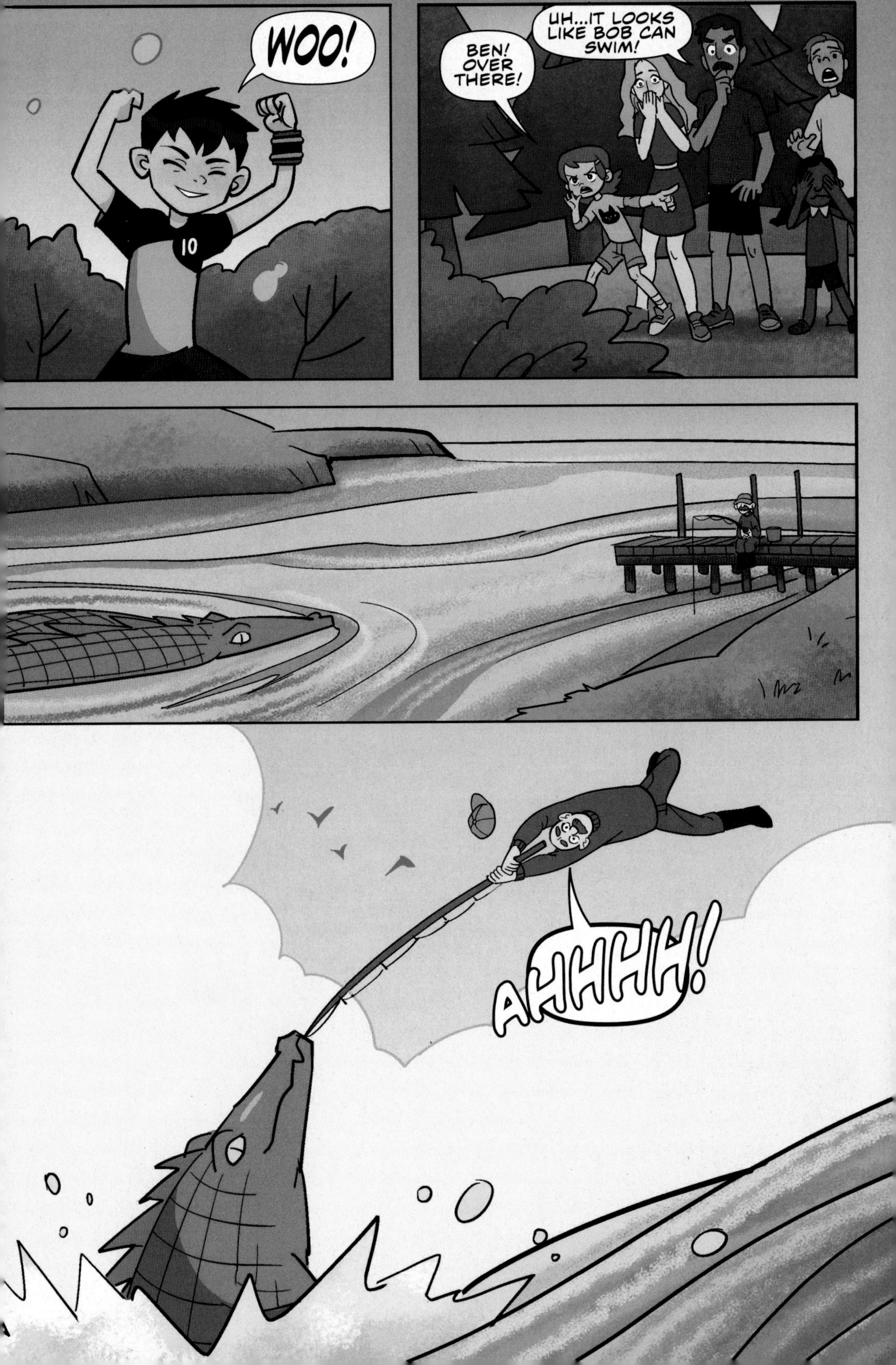
WOO!
BEN! OVER THERE!
UH...IT LOOKS LIKE BOB CAN SWIM!
AHHHH!

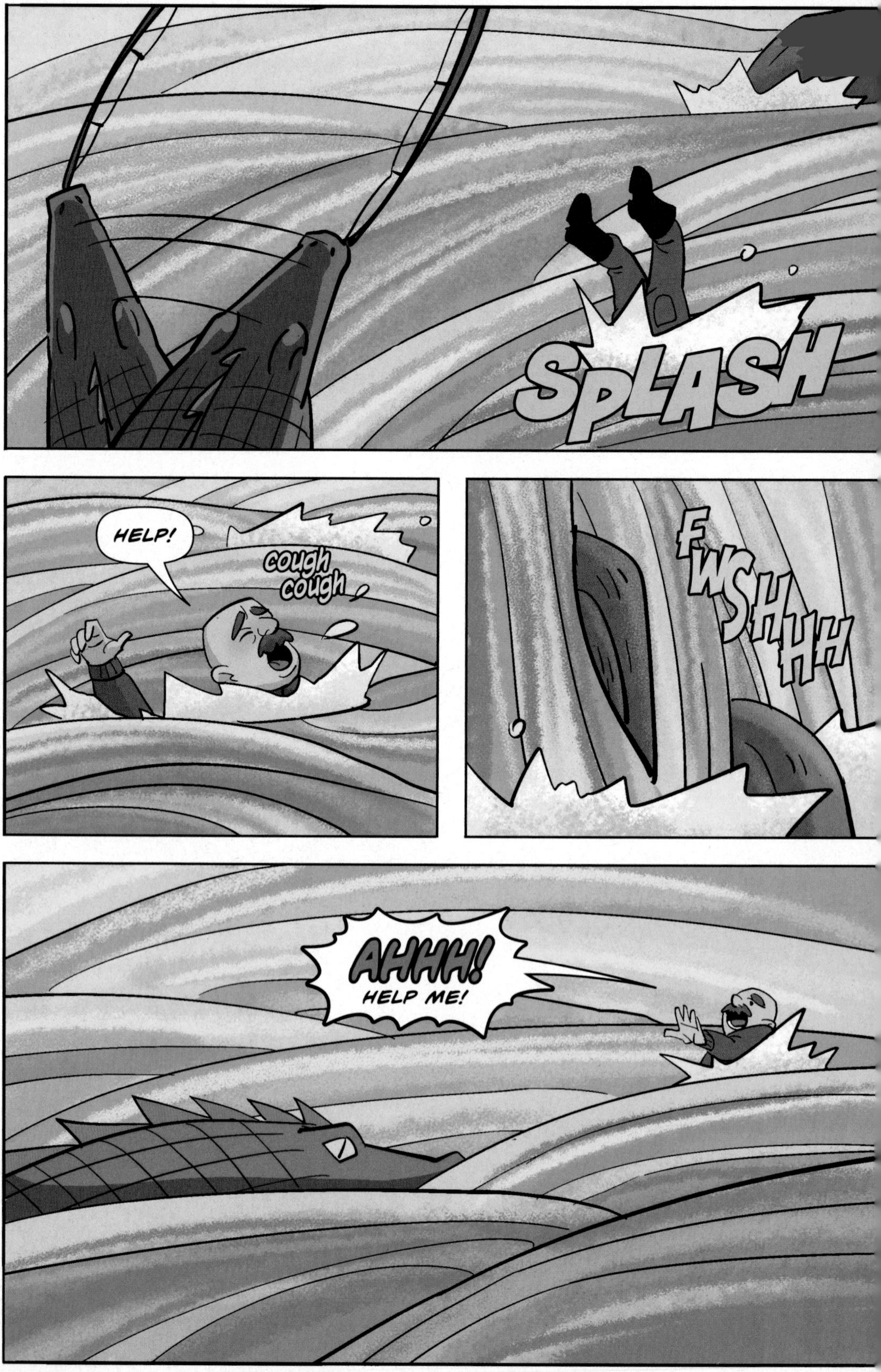
SPLASH
HELP!
cough cough
FWSHHHH
AHHH!
HELP ME!

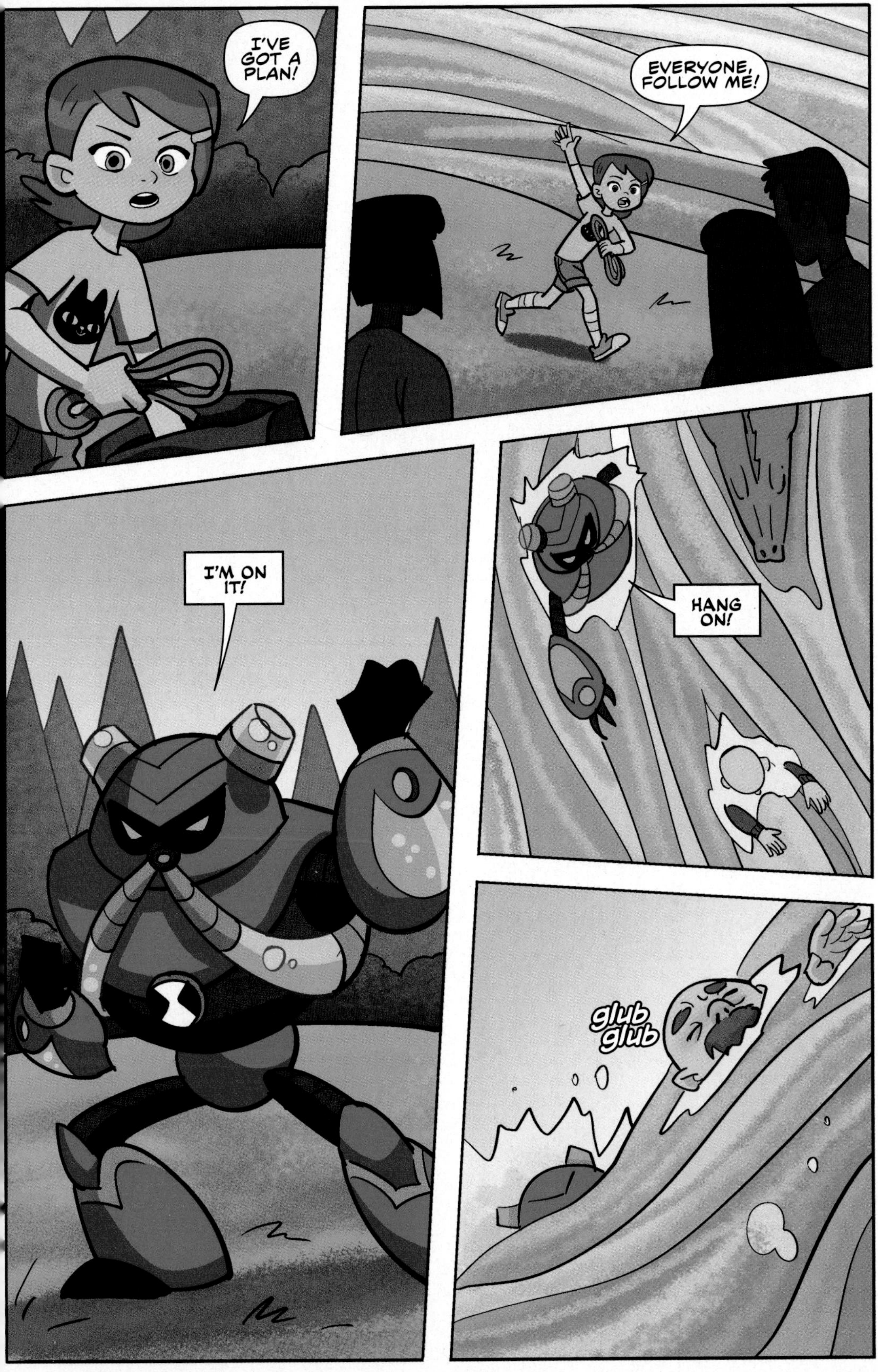
I'VE GOT A PLAN!
EVERYONE, FOLLOW ME!
I'M ON IT!
HANG ON!
glub glub

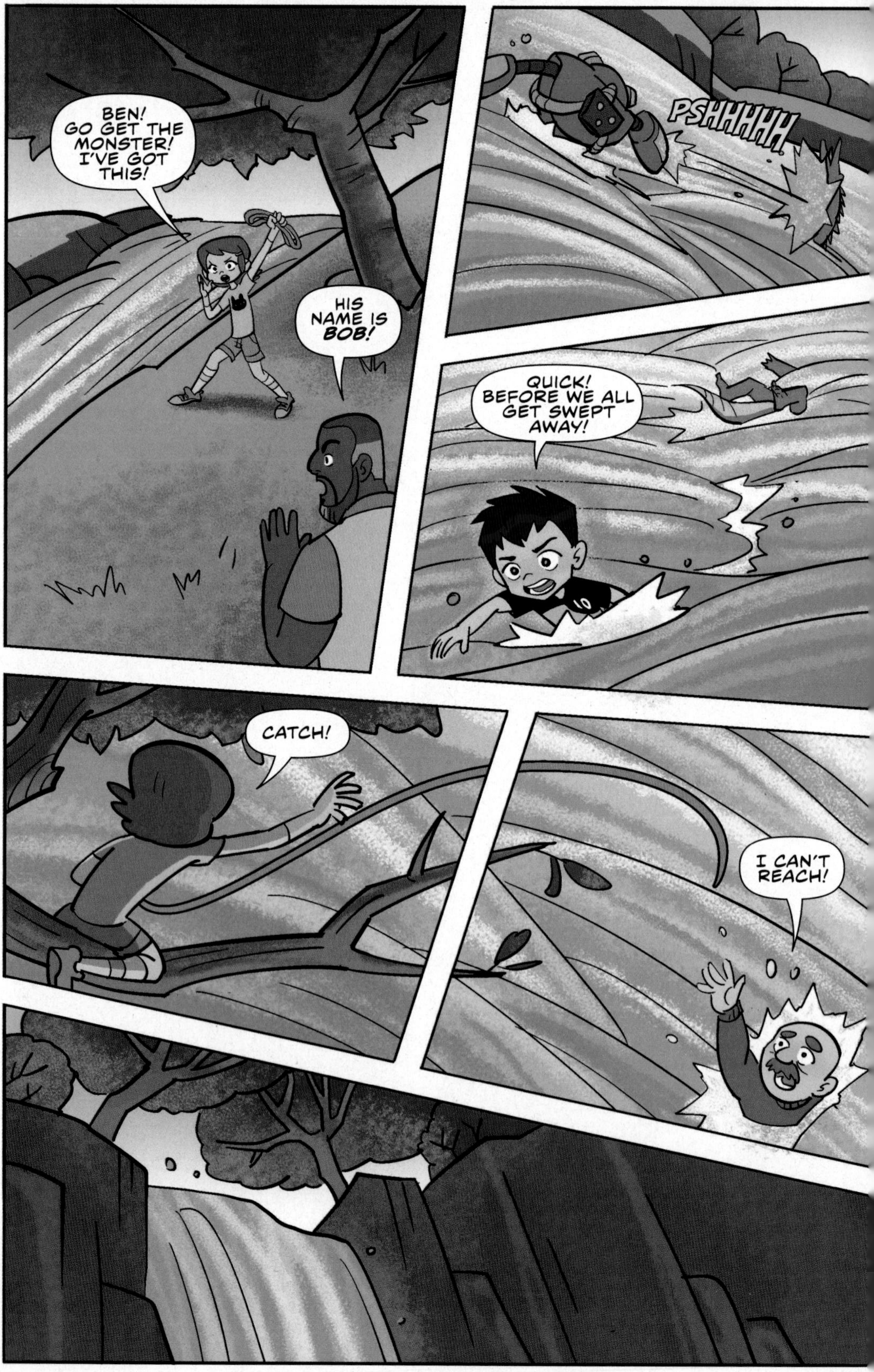
BEN! GO GET THE MONSTER! I'VE GOT THIS!
HIS NAME IS BOB!
PSHHHHH
QUICK! BEFORE WE ALL GET SWEPT AWAY!
CATCH!
I CAN'T REACH!

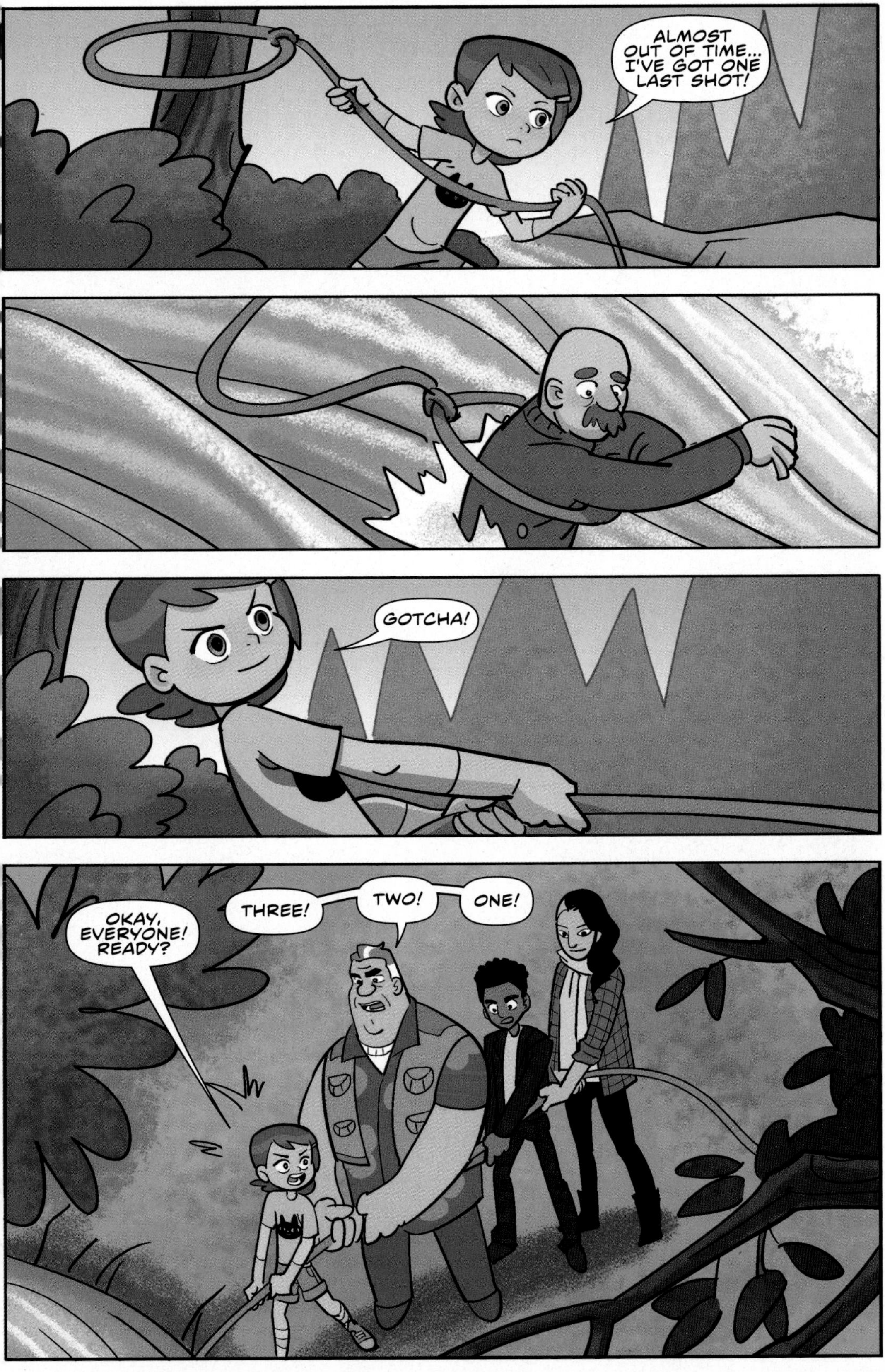
ALMOST OUT OF TIME... I'VE GOT ONE LAST SHOT!
GOTCHA!
OKAY, EVERYONE! READY?
THREE!
TWO!
ONE!

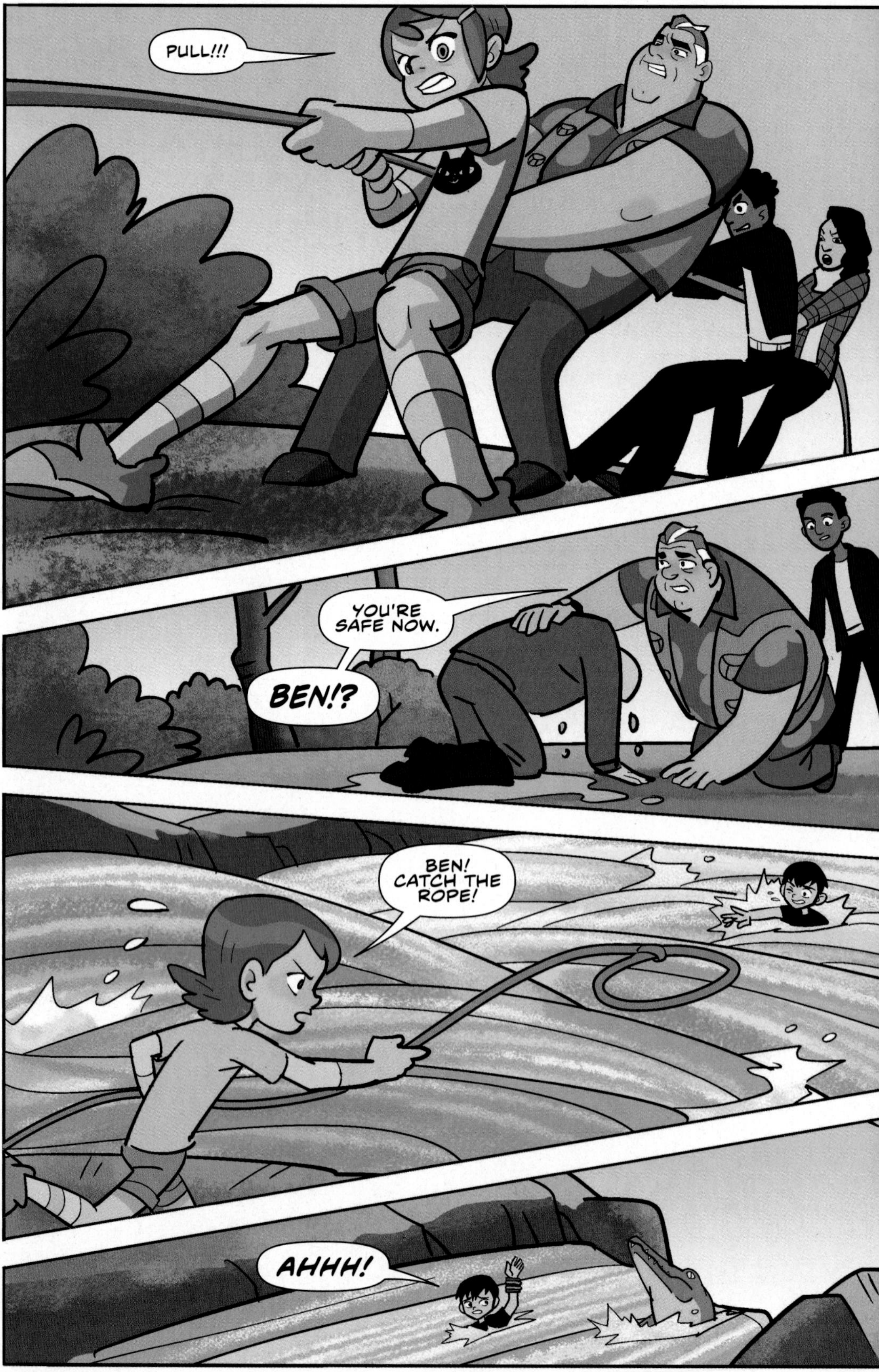
PULL!!!
YOU'RE SAFE NOW.
BEN!?
BEN! CATCH THE ROPE!
AHHH!

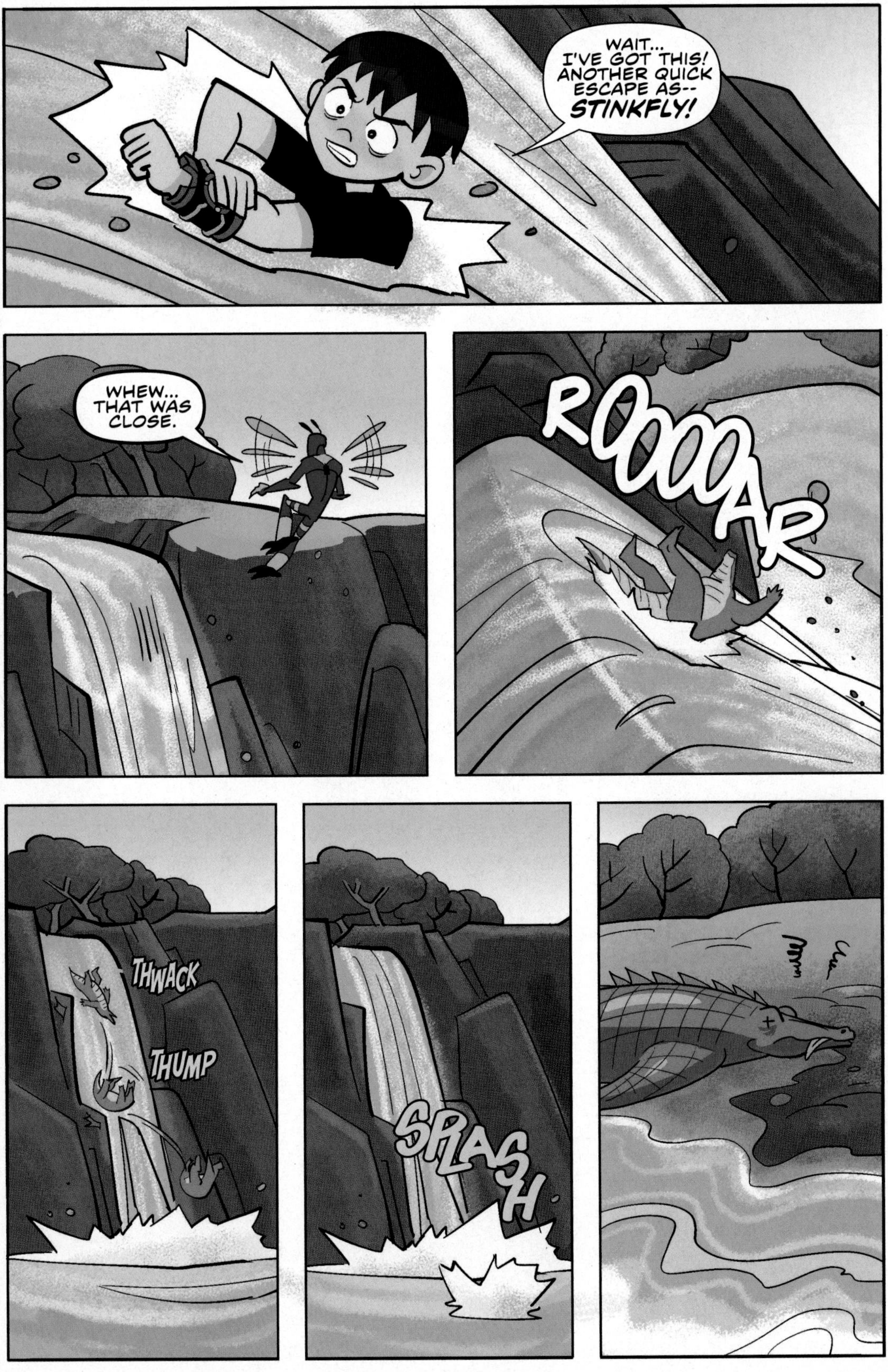
WAIT... I'VE GOT THIS! ANOTHER QUICK ESCAPE AS-- STINKFLY!
WHEW... THAT WAS CLOSE.
ROOOOAR
THWACK
THUMP
SPLASH

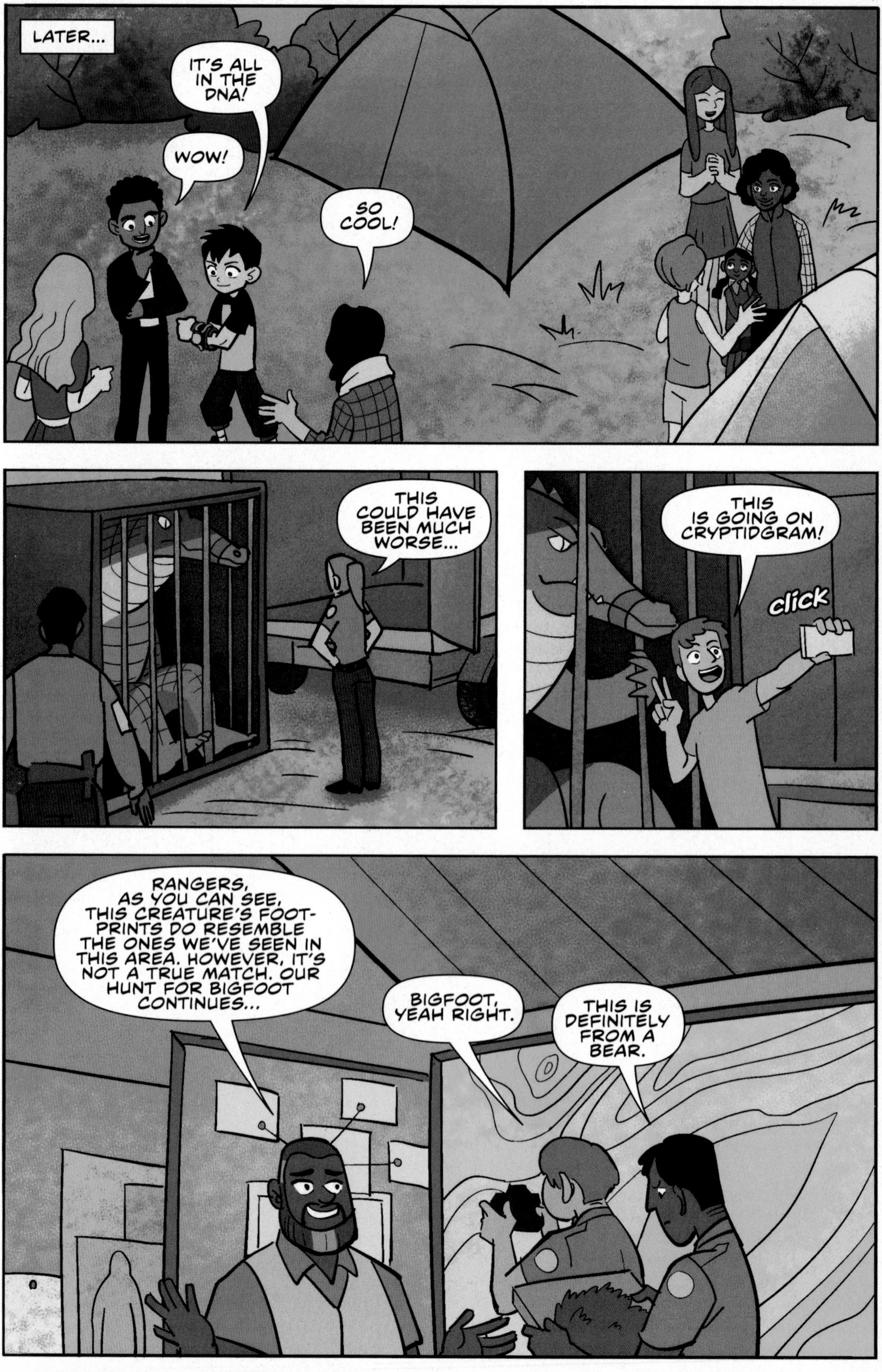
LATER...
IT'S ALL IN THE DNA!
WOW!
SO COOL!
THIS COULD HAVE BEEN MUCH WORSE...
THIS IS GOING ON CRYPTIDGRAM!
click
RANGERS, AS YOU CAN SEE, THIS CREATURE'S FOOT-PRINTS DO RESEMBLE THE ONES WE'VE SEEN IN THIS AREA. HOWEVER, IT'S NOT A TRUE MATCH. OUR HUNT FOR BIGFOOT CONTINUES...
BIGFOOT, YEAH RIGHT.
THIS IS DEFINITELY FROM A BEAR.

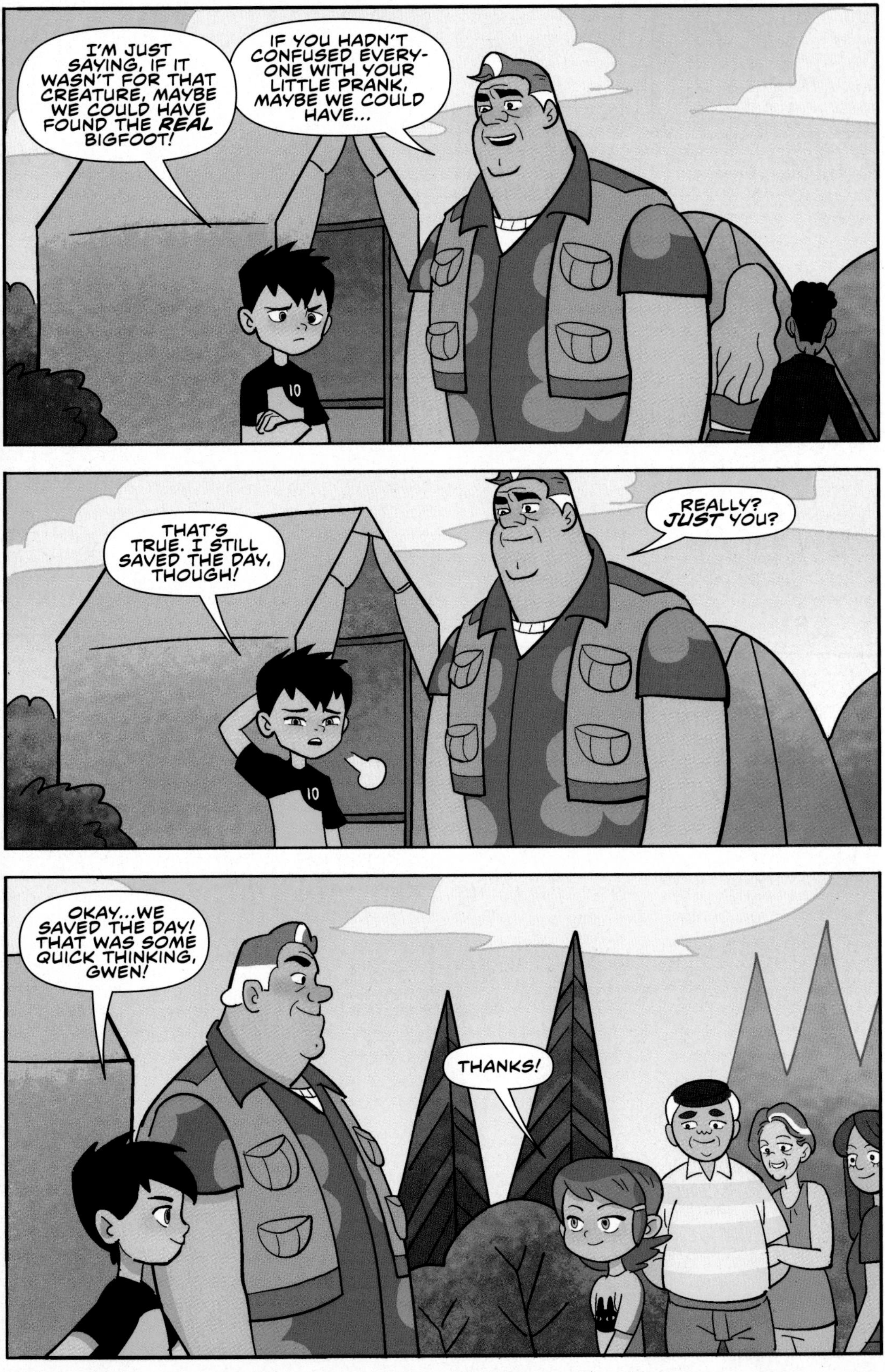
I'M JUST SAYING, IF IT WASN'T FOR THAT CREATURE, MAYBE WE COULD HAVE FOUND THE *REAL* BIGFOOT!
IF YOU HADN'T CONFUSED EVERY-ONE WITH YOUR LITTLE PRANK, MAYBE WE COULD HAVE...
THAT'S TRUE. I STILL SAVED THE DAY, THOUGH!
REALLY? *JUST* YOU?
OKAY...WE SAVED THE DAY! THAT WAS SOME QUICK THINKING, GWEN!
THANKS!

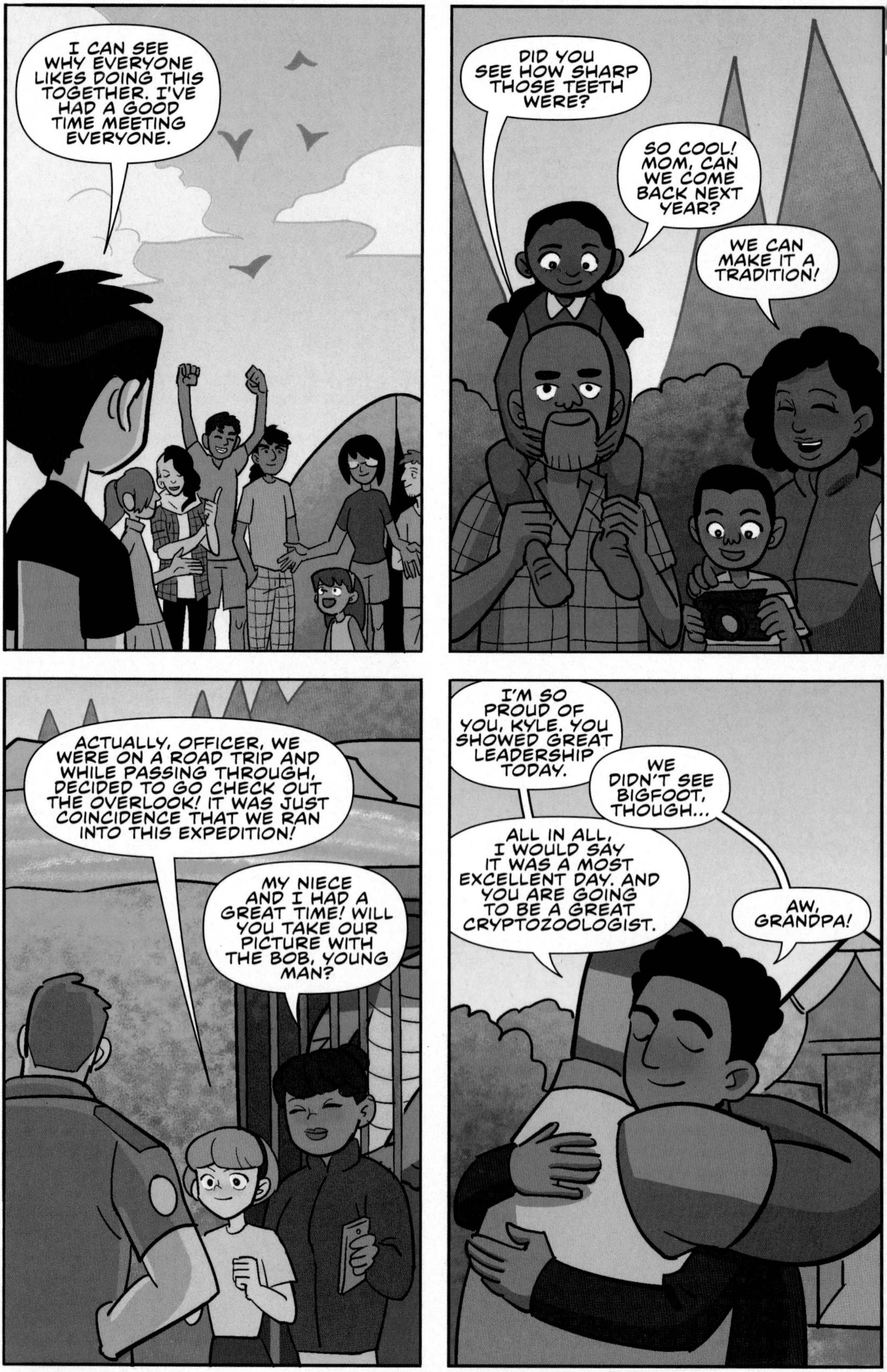
I CAN SEE WHY EVERYONE LIKES DOING THIS TOGETHER. I'VE HAD A GOOD TIME MEETING EVERYONE.
DID YOU SEE HOW SHARP THOSE TEETH WERE?
SO COOL! MOM, CAN WE COME BACK NEXT YEAR?
WE CAN MAKE IT A TRADITION!
ACTUALLY, OFFICER, WE WERE ON A ROAD TRIP AND WHILE PASSING THROUGH, DECIDED TO GO CHECK OUT THE OVERLOOK! IT WAS JUST COINCIDENCE THAT WE RAN INTO THIS EXPEDITION!
MY NIECE AND I HAD A GREAT TIME! WILL YOU TAKE OUR PICTURE WITH THE BOB, YOUNG MAN?
I'M SO PROUD OF YOU, KYLE. YOU SHOWED GREAT LEADERSHIP TODAY.
WE DIDN'T SEE BIGFOOT, THOUGH...
ALL IN ALL, I WOULD SAY IT WAS A MOST EXCELLENT DAY. AND YOU ARE GOING TO BE A GREAT CRYPTOZOOLOGIST.
AW, GRANDPA!

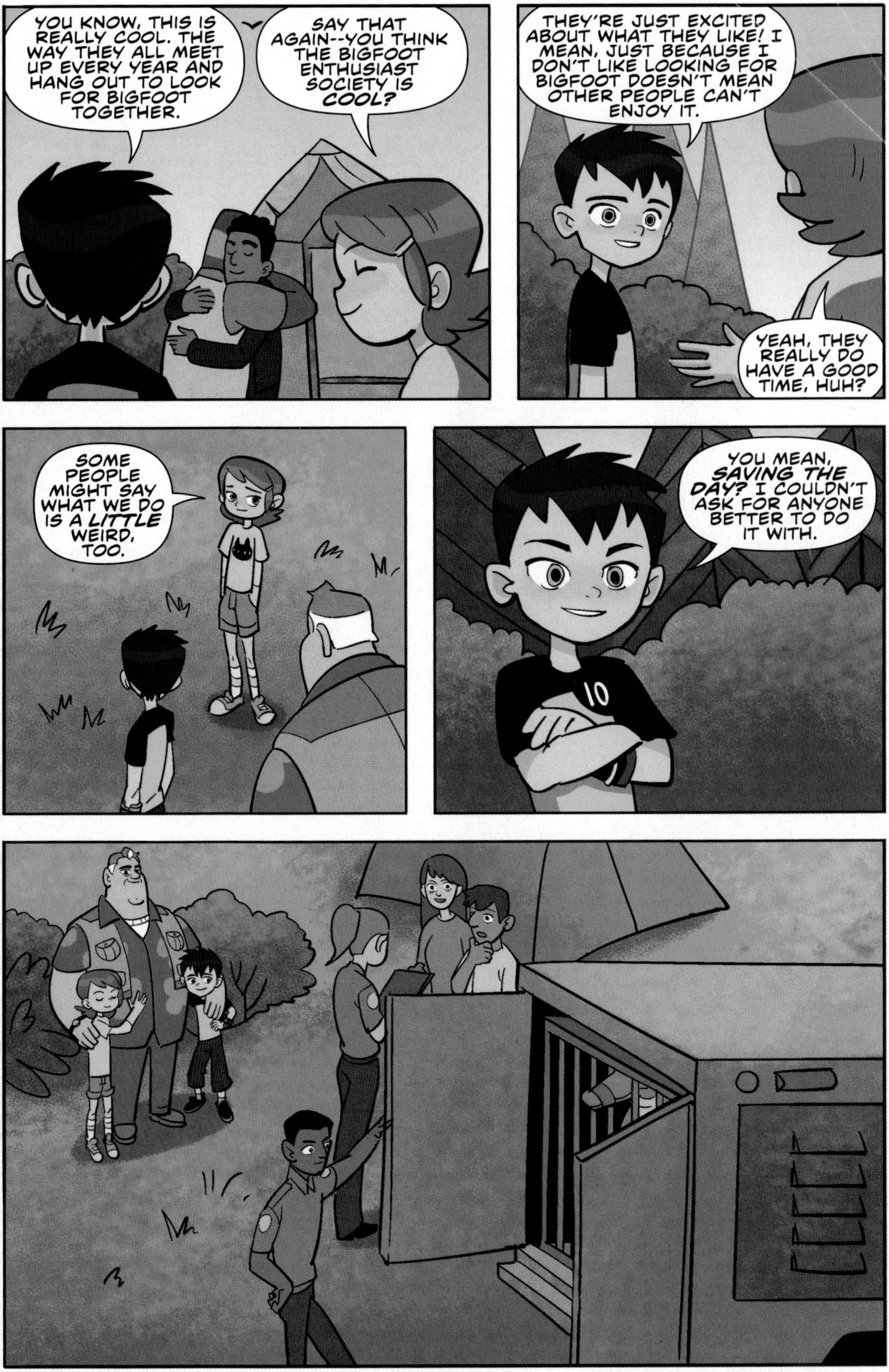
YOU KNOW, THIS IS REALLY COOL. THE WAY THEY ALL MEET UP EVERY YEAR AND HANG OUT TO LOOK FOR BIGFOOT TOGETHER.
SAY THAT AGAIN--YOU THINK THE BIGFOOT ENTHUSIAST SOCIETY IS *COOL?*
THEY'RE JUST EXCITED ABOUT WHAT THEY LIKE! I MEAN, JUST BECAUSE I DON'T LIKE LOOKING FOR BIGFOOT DOESN'T MEAN OTHER PEOPLE CAN'T ENJOY IT.
YEAH, THEY REALLY DO HAVE A GOOD TIME, HUH?
SOME PEOPLE MIGHT SAY WHAT WE DO IS A *LITTLE* WEIRD, TOO.
YOU MEAN, ***SAVING THE DAY?*** I COULDN'T ASK FOR ANYONE BETTER TO DO IT WITH.

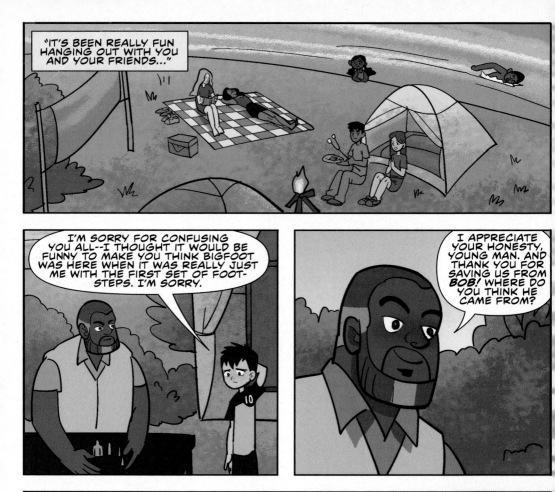

"IT'S BEEN REALLY FUN HANGING OUT WITH YOU AND YOUR FRIENDS..."

I'M SORRY FOR CONFUSING YOU ALL--I THOUGHT IT WOULD BE FUNNY TO MAKE YOU THINK BIGFOOT WAS HERE WHEN IT WAS REALLY JUST ME WITH THE FIRST SET OF FOOT-STEPS. I'M SORRY.

I APPRECIATE YOUR HONESTY, YOUNG MAN. AND THANK YOU FOR SAVING US FROM *BOB!* WHERE DO YOU THINK HE CAME FROM?

I THINK BOB MUST BE ONE OF DR. ANIMO'S ESCAPED EXPERIMENTS.

WHOA! DO YOU THINK THERE ARE ANY MORE OUT THERE?

IF THERE ARE, WE'LL GET THEM!

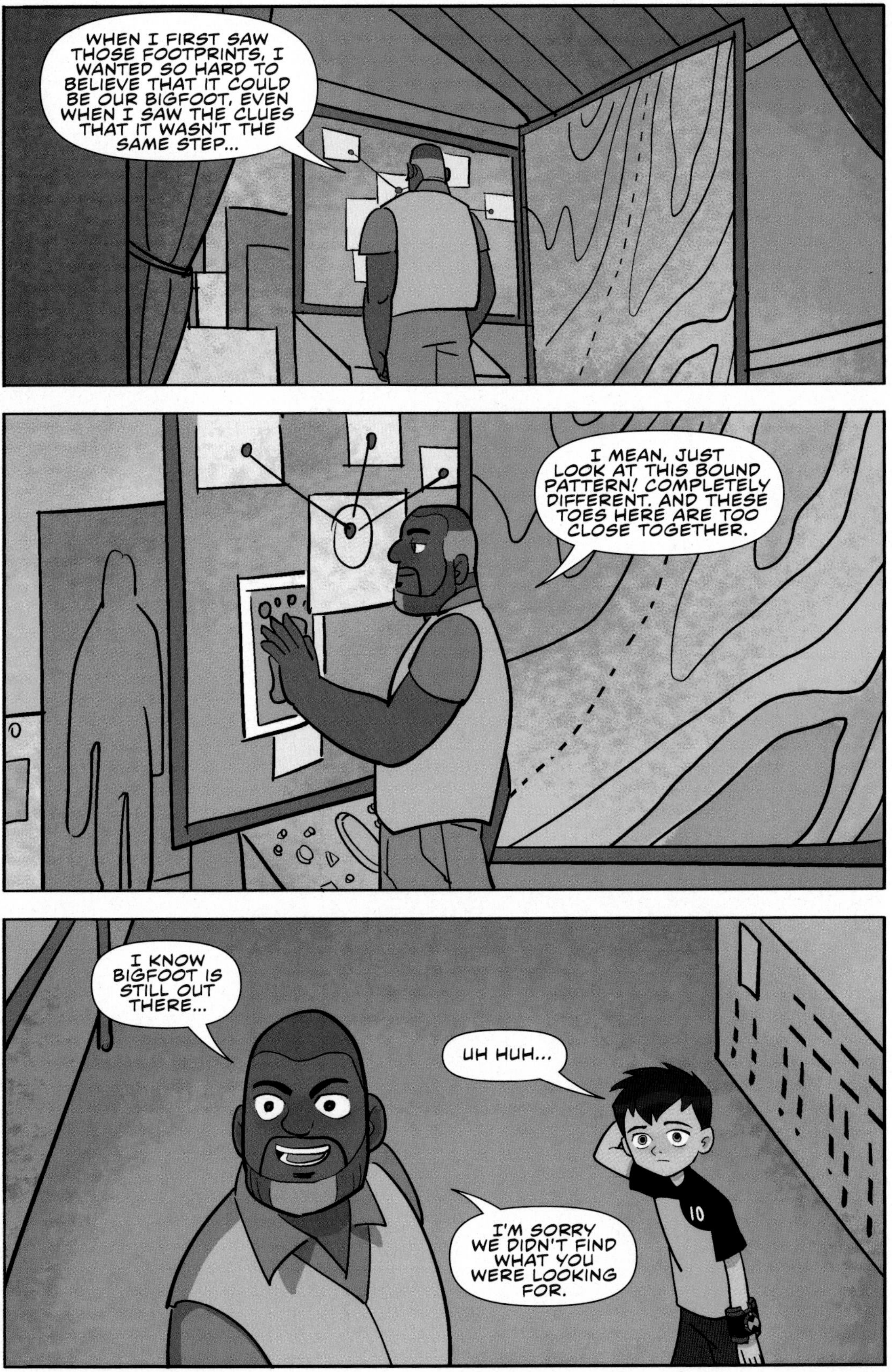
WHEN I FIRST SAW THOSE FOOTPRINTS, I WANTED SO HARD TO BELIEVE THAT IT COULD BE OUR BIGFOOT, EVEN WHEN I SAW THE CLUES THAT IT WASN'T THE SAME STEP...
I MEAN, JUST LOOK AT THIS BOUND PATTERN! COMPLETELY DIFFERENT. AND THESE TOES HERE ARE TOO CLOSE TOGETHER.
I KNOW BIGFOOT IS STILL OUT THERE...
UH HUH...
I'M SORRY WE DIDN'T FIND WHAT YOU WERE LOOKING FOR.

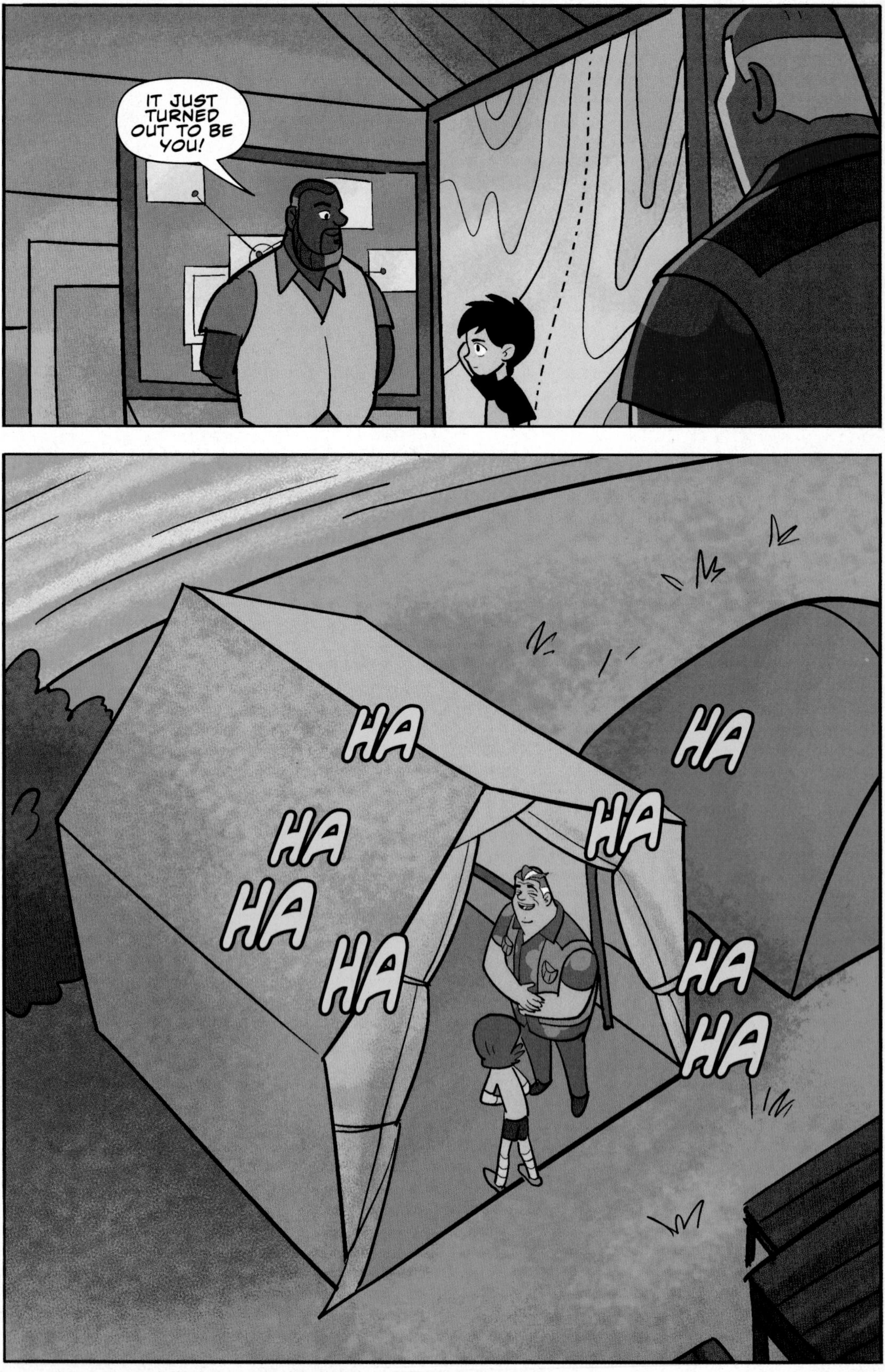
IT JUST TURNED OUT TO BE YOU!
HA
HA
HA
HA
HA
HA
HA
HA

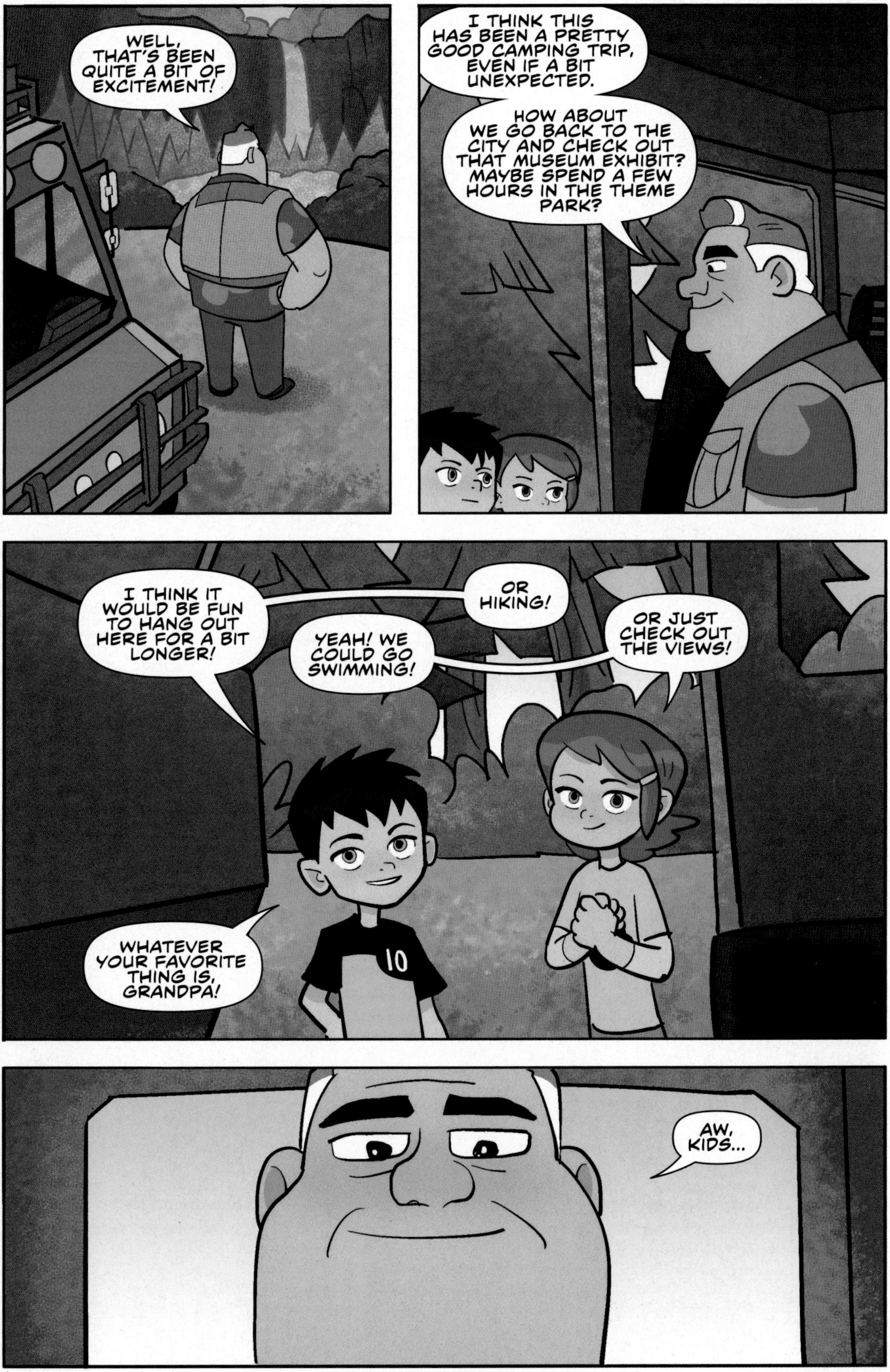

WELL, THAT'S BEEN QUITE A BIT OF EXCITEMENT!
I THINK THIS HAS BEEN A PRETTY GOOD CAMPING TRIP, EVEN IF A BIT UNEXPECTED.
HOW ABOUT WE GO BACK TO THE CITY AND CHECK OUT THAT MUSEUM EXHIBIT? MAYBE SPEND A FEW HOURS IN THE THEME PARK?
I THINK IT WOULD BE FUN TO HANG OUT HERE FOR A BIT LONGER!
OR HIKING!
YEAH! WE COULD GO SWIMMING!
OR JUST CHECK OUT THE VIEWS!
WHATEVER YOUR FAVORITE THING IS, GRANDPA!
10
AW, KIDS...

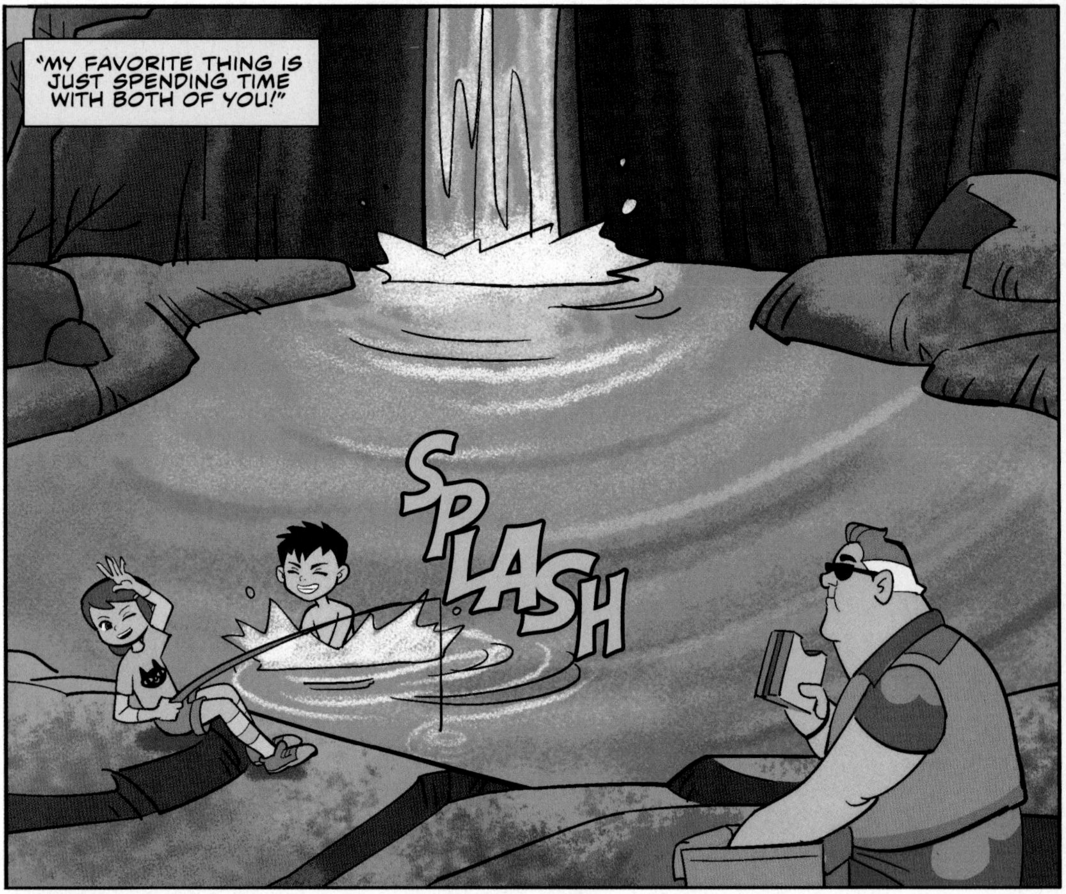
"MY FAVORITE THING IS JUST SPENDING TIME WITH BOTH OF YOU!"
SPLASH

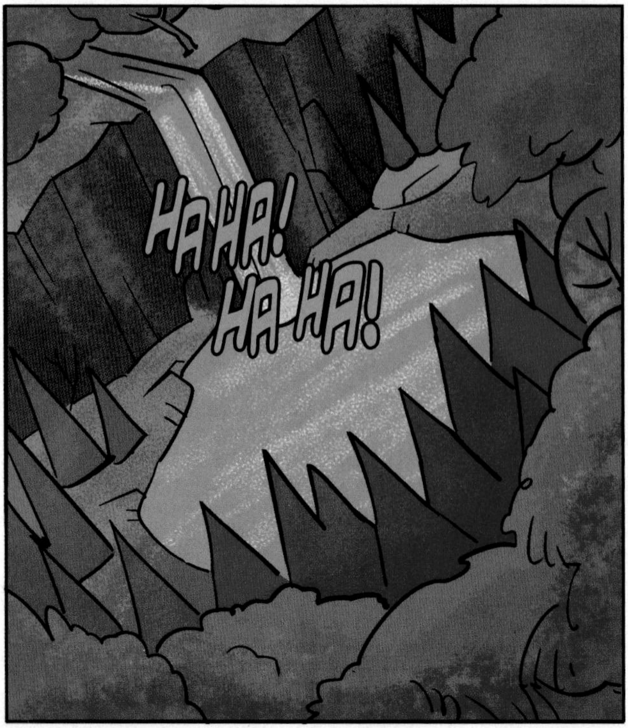
HA HA!
HA HA!

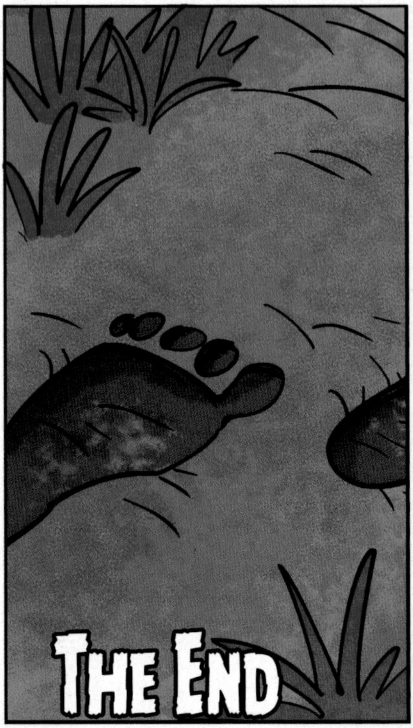
THE END

AN EPIC NEW BEN 10™ GAME
SUMMER 2019

BEN'S ADVENTURES IN THE RUSTBUCKET CONTINUE IN...

"FOR SCIENCE!"

AVAILABLE FALL 2019

CN
BEN 10
FOR SCIENCE!
BEN 10™ FOR SCIENCE! C.B. LEE MATTIA DI MEO
kaboom!

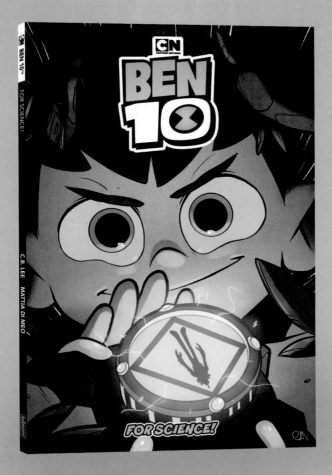

WRITTEN BY
C.B. LEE

ILLUSTRATED BY
MATTIA DI MEO

For Science!

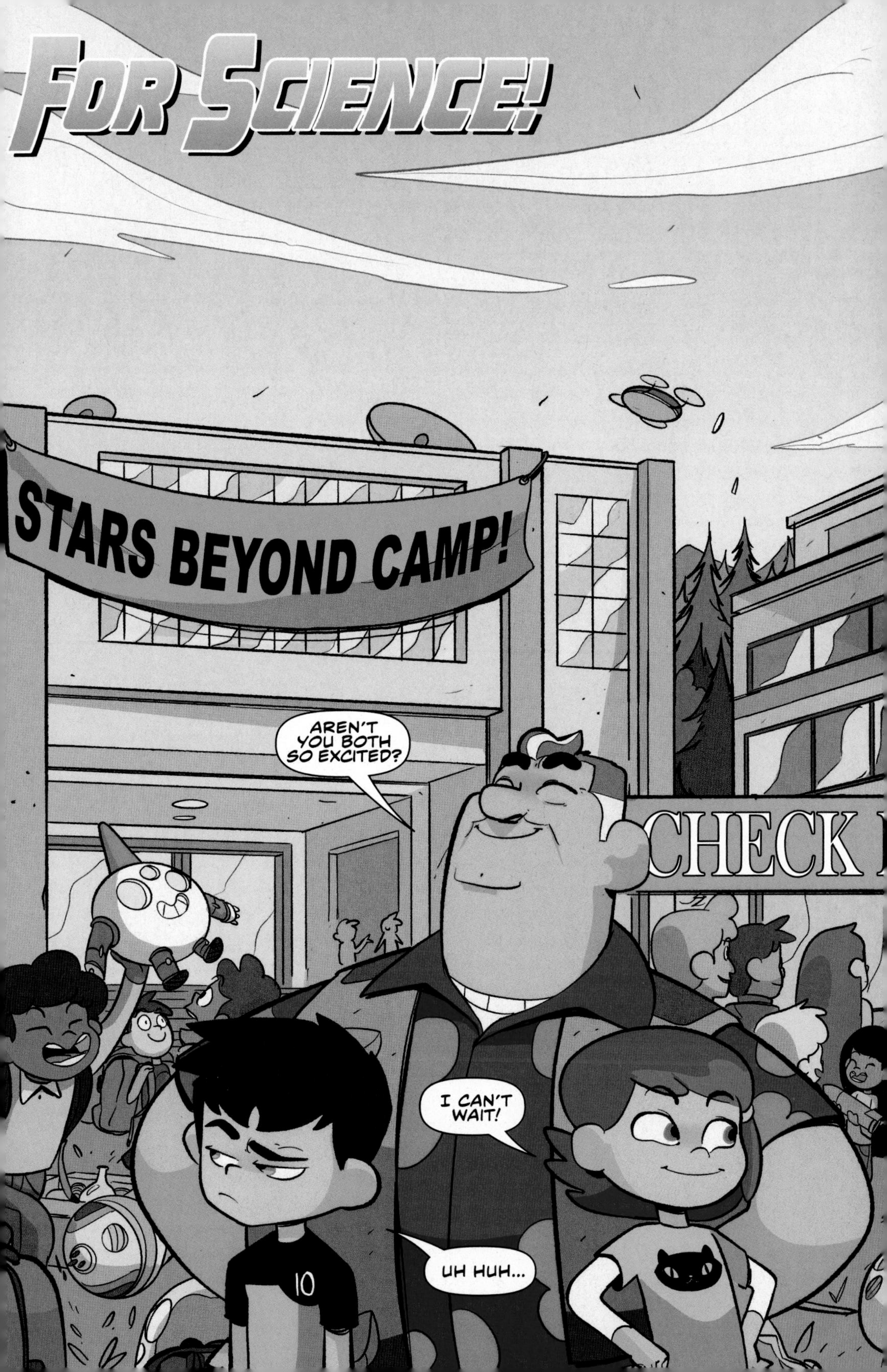
STARS BEYOND CAMP!
AREN'T YOU BOTH SO EXCITED?
CHECK
I CAN'T WAIT!
UH HUH...

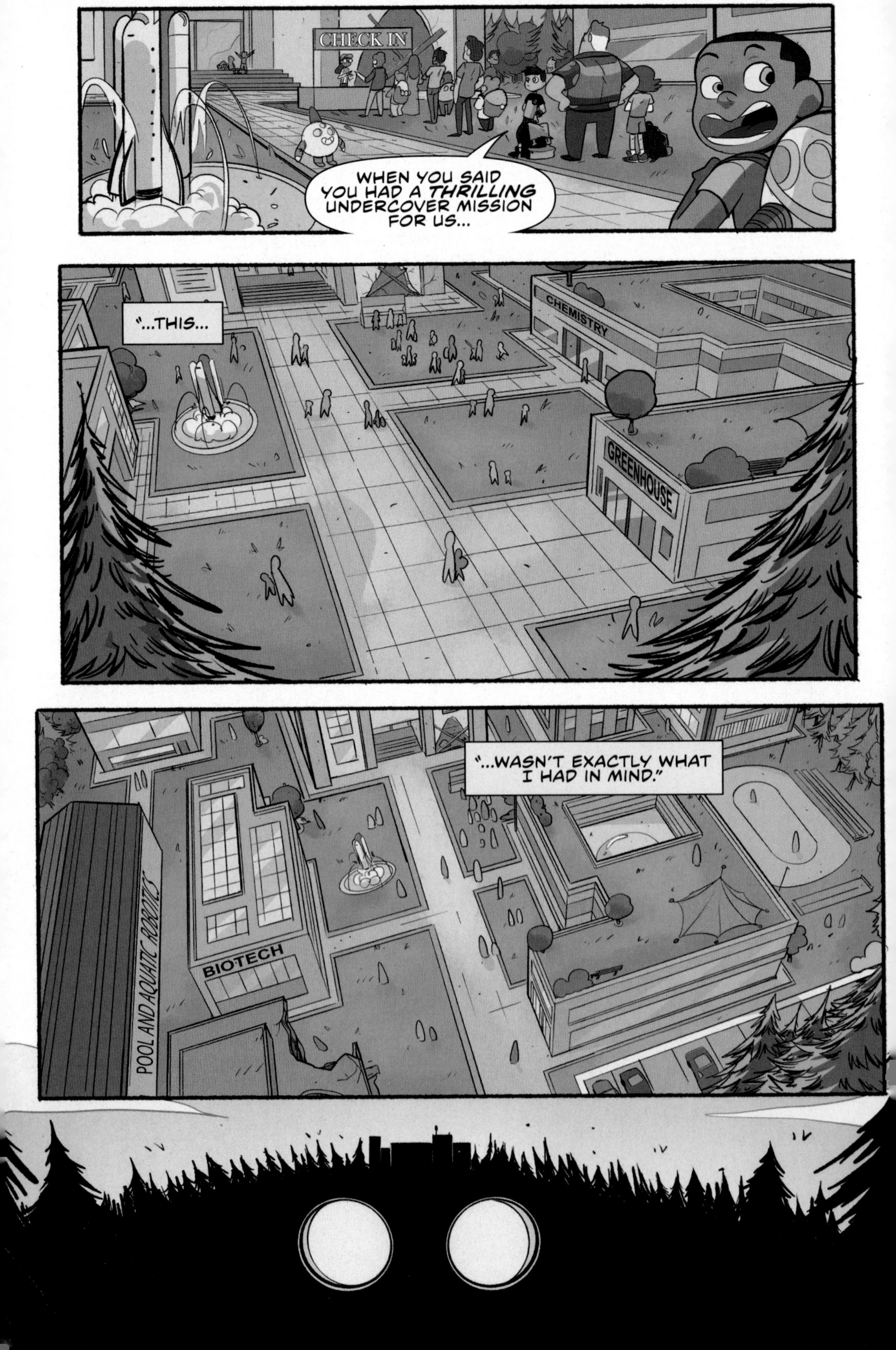
CHECK IN
WHEN YOU SAID YOU HAD A *THRILLING* UNDERCOVER MISSION FOR US...
"...THIS...
CHEMISTRY
GREENHOUSE
"...WASN'T EXACTLY WHAT I HAD IN MIND."
POOL AND AQUATIC ROBOTICS
BIOTECH

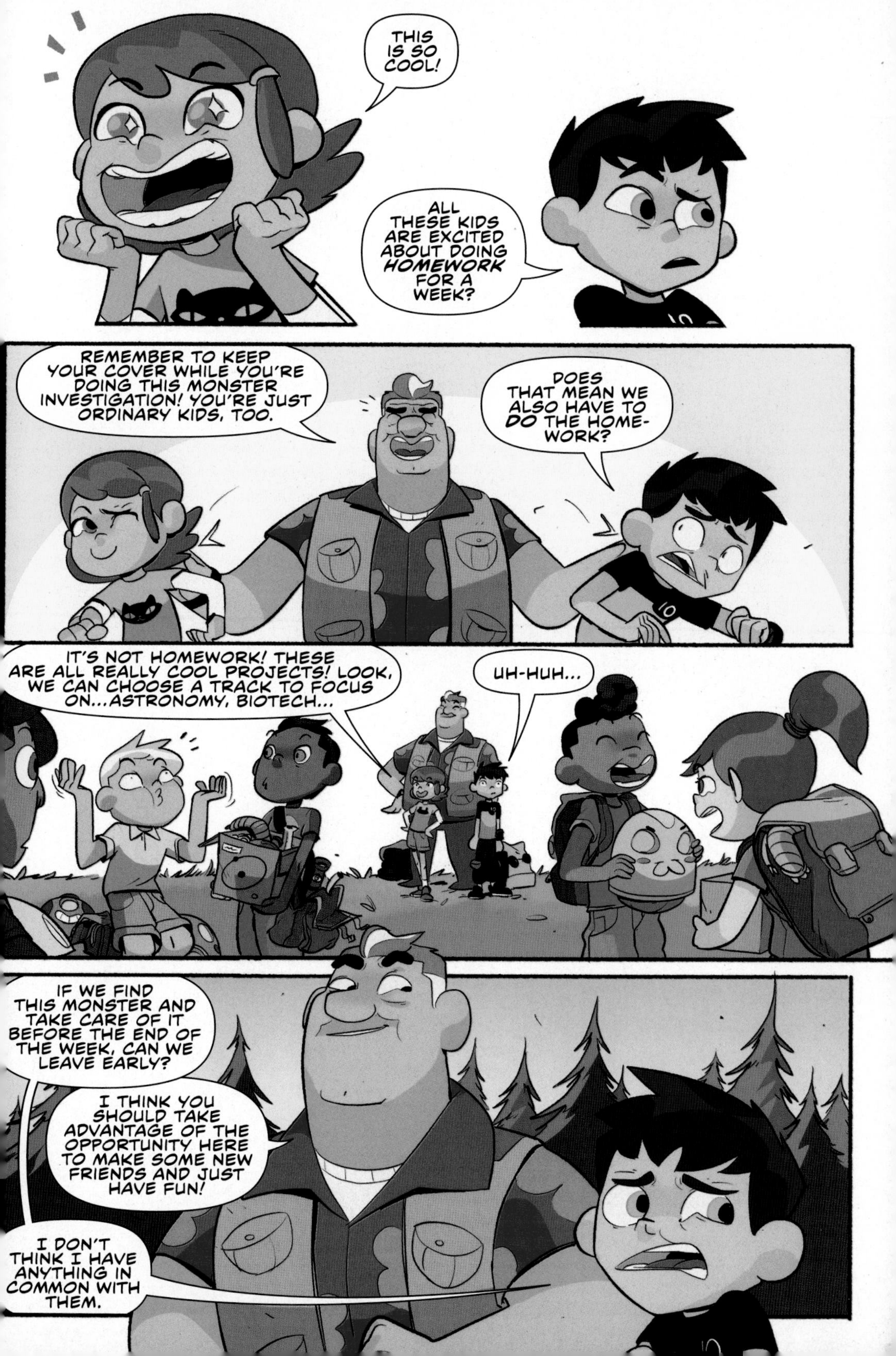
THIS IS SO COOL!
ALL THESE KIDS ARE EXCITED ABOUT DOING *HOMEWORK* FOR A WEEK?
REMEMBER TO KEEP YOUR COVER WHILE YOU'RE DOING THIS MONSTER INVESTIGATION! YOU'RE JUST ORDINARY KIDS, TOO.
DOES THAT MEAN WE ALSO HAVE TO *DO* THE HOME-WORK?
IT'S NOT HOMEWORK! THESE ARE ALL REALLY COOL PROJECTS! LOOK, WE CAN CHOOSE A TRACK TO FOCUS ON...ASTRONOMY, BIOTECH...
UH-HUH...
IF WE FIND THIS MONSTER AND TAKE CARE OF IT BEFORE THE END OF THE WEEK, CAN WE LEAVE EARLY?
I THINK YOU SHOULD TAKE ADVANTAGE OF THE OPPORTUNITY HERE TO MAKE SOME NEW FRIENDS AND JUST HAVE FUN!
I DON'T THINK I HAVE ANYTHING IN COMMON WITH THEM.

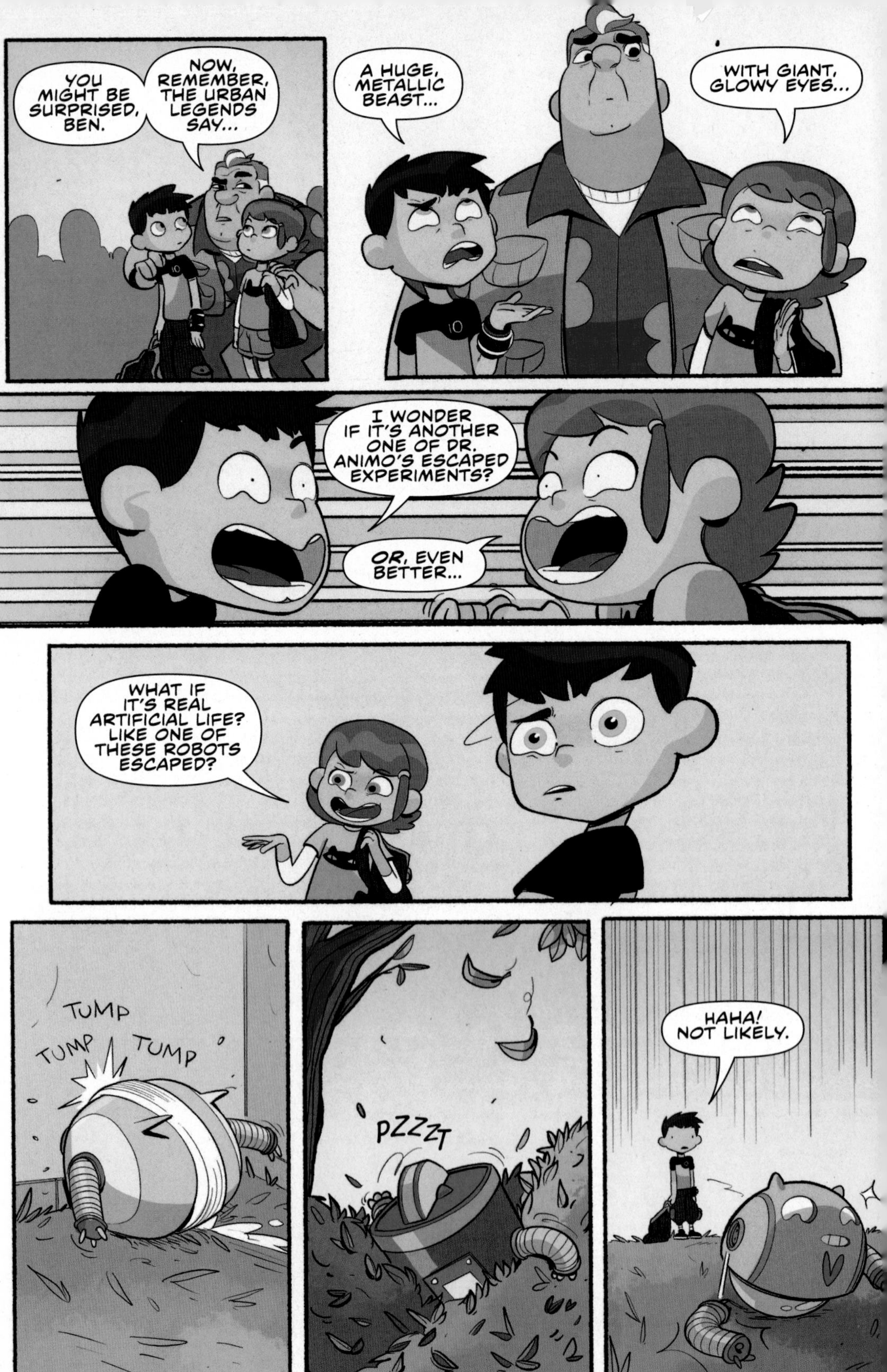
YOU MIGHT BE SURPRISED, BEN.
NOW, REMEMBER, THE URBAN LEGENDS SAY...
A HUGE, METALLIC BEAST...
WITH GIANT, GLOWY EYES...
I WONDER IF IT'S ANOTHER ONE OF DR. ANIMO'S ESCAPED EXPERIMENTS?
OR, EVEN BETTER...
WHAT IF IT'S REAL ARTIFICIAL LIFE? LIKE ONE OF THESE ROBOTS ESCAPED?
TUMP
TUMP
TUMP
PZZZT
HAHA! NOT LIKELY.

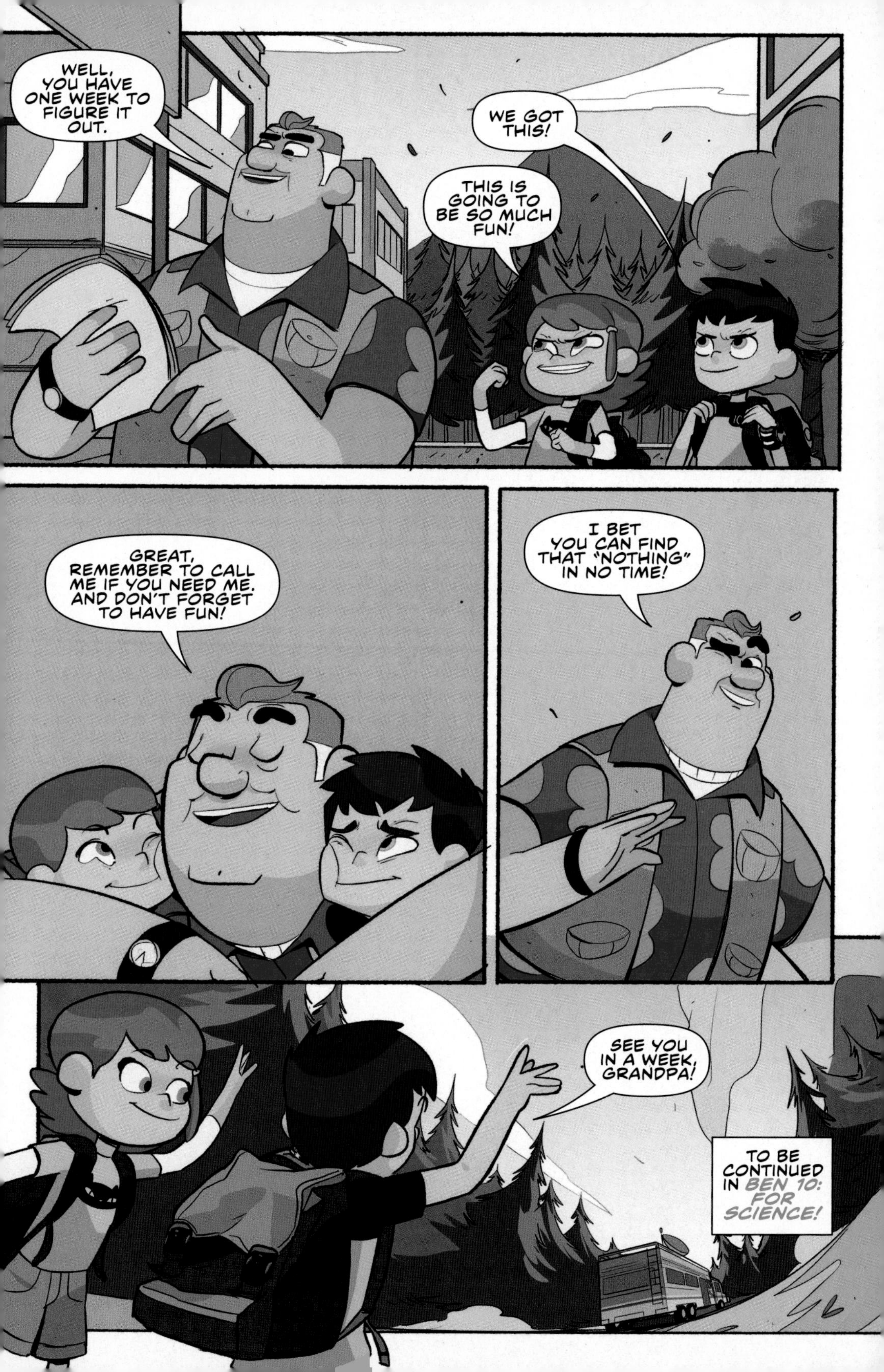
WELL, YOU HAVE ONE WEEK TO FIGURE IT OUT.
WE GOT THIS!
THIS IS GOING TO BE SO MUCH FUN!
GREAT, REMEMBER TO CALL ME IF YOU NEED ME. AND DON'T FORGET TO HAVE FUN!
I BET YOU CAN FIND THAT "NOTHING" IN NO TIME!
SEE YOU IN A WEEK, GRANDPA!
TO BE CONTINUED IN BEN 10: FOR SCIENCE!

DISCOVER
EXPLOSIVE NEW WORLDS

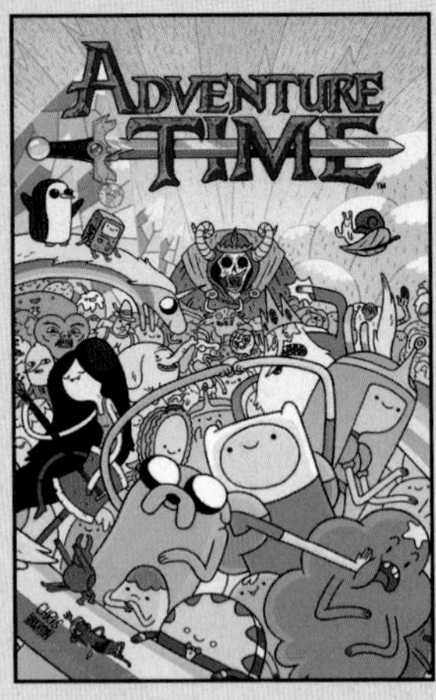
ADVENTURE TIME

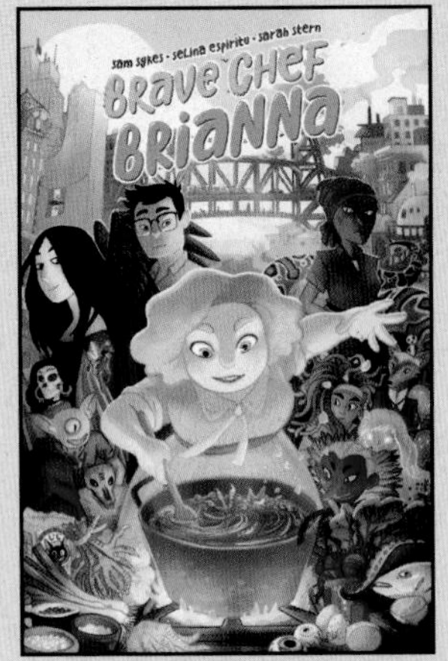
Sam Sykes · Selina Espiritu · Sarah Stern
Brave Chef Brianna

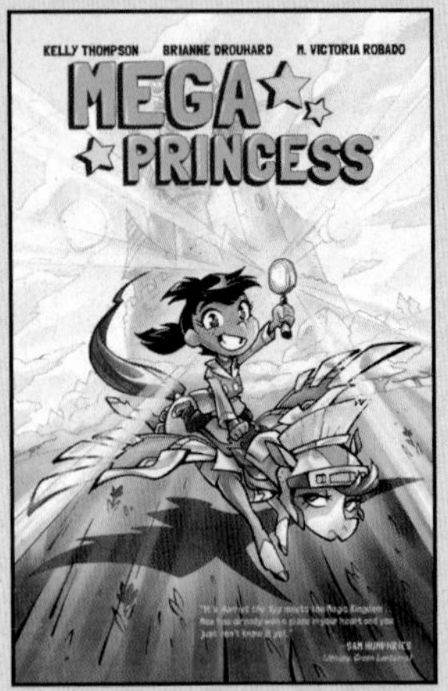
KELLY THOMPSON   BRIANNE DROUHARD   M. VICTORIA ROBADO
MEGA PRINCESS

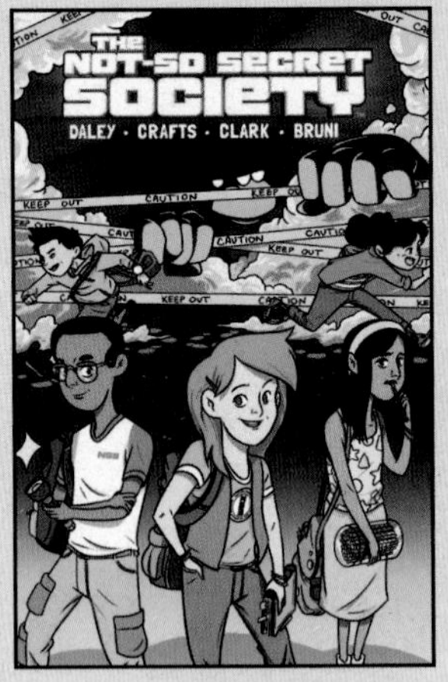
THE NOT-SO SECRET SOCIETY
DALEY · CRAFTS · CLARK · BRUNI
KEEP OUT
CAUTION

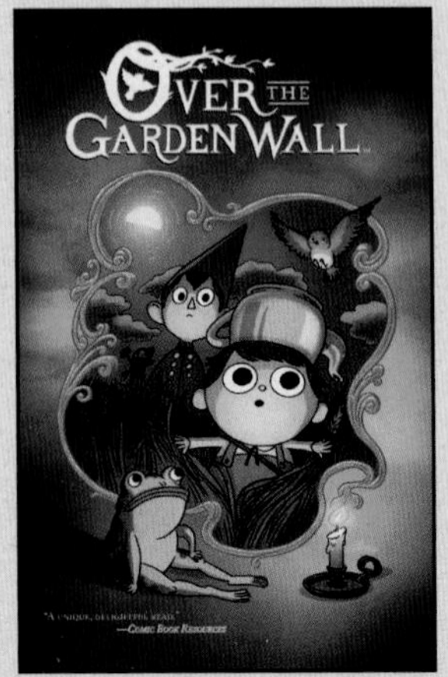
OVER THE GARDEN WALL

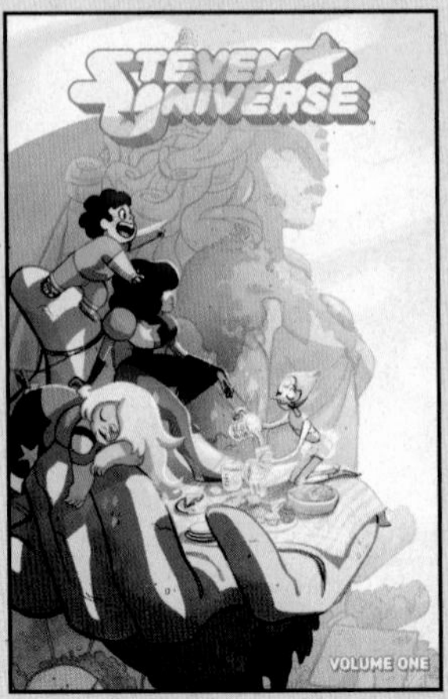
STEVEN UNIVERSE
VOLUME ONE

Adventure Time
Pendleton Ward and Others
Volume 1
ISBN: 978-1-60886-280-1 | $14.99 US
Volume 2
ISBN: 978-1-60886-323-5 | $14.99 US
Adventure Time: Islands
ISBN: 978-1-60886-972-5 | $9.99 US

The Amazing World of Gumball
Ben Bocquelet and Others
Volume 1
ISBN: 978-1-60886-488-1 | $14.99 US
Volume 2
ISBN: 978-1-60886-793-6 | $14.99 US

Brave Chef Brianna
Sam Sykes, Selina Espiritu
ISBN: 978-1-68415-050-2 | $14.99 US

Mega Princess
Kelly Thompson, Brianne Drouhard
ISBN: 978-1-68415-007-6 | $14.99 US

The Not-So Secret Society
Matthew Daley, Arlene Daley, Wook Jin Clark
ISBN: 978-1-60886-997-8 | $9.99 US

Over the Garden Wall
Patrick McHale, Jim Campbell and Others
Volume 1
ISBN: 978-1-60886-940-4 | $14.99 US
Volume 2
ISBN: 978-1-68415-006-9 | $14.99 US

Steven Universe
Rebecca Sugar and Others
Volume 1
ISBN: 978-1-60886-706-6 | $14.99 US
Volume 2
ISBN: 978-1-60886-796-7 | $14.99 US

Steven Universe & The Crystal Gems
ISBN: 978-1-60886-921-3 | $14.99 US

Steven Universe: Too Cool for School
ISBN: 978-1-60886-771-4 | $14.99 US

kaboom!™

AVAILABLE AT YOUR LOCAL COMICS SHOP AND BOOKSTORE
To find a comics shop in your area, visit www.comicshoplocator.com
WWW.**BOOM-STUDIOS**.COM

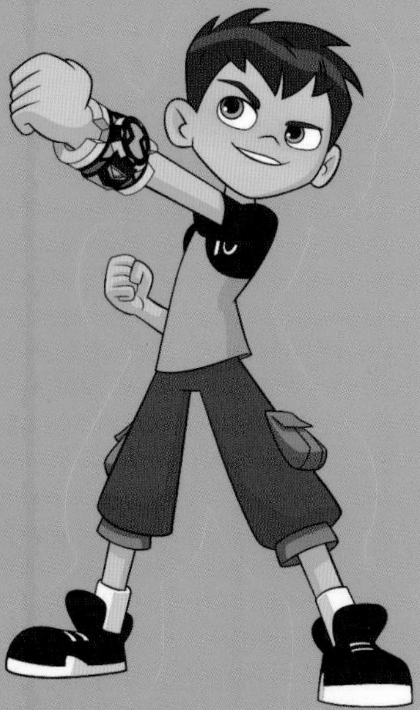
10

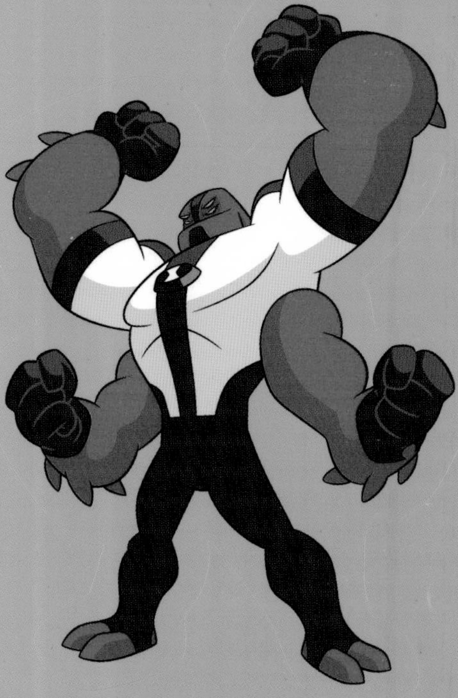

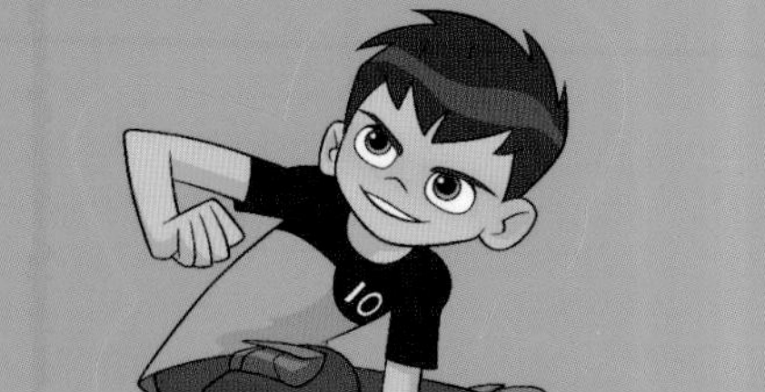
10

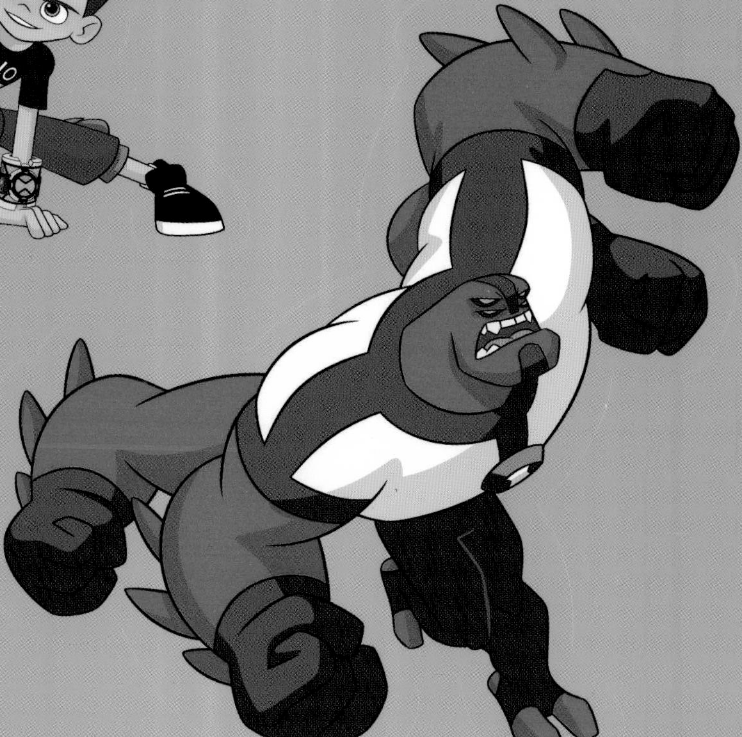

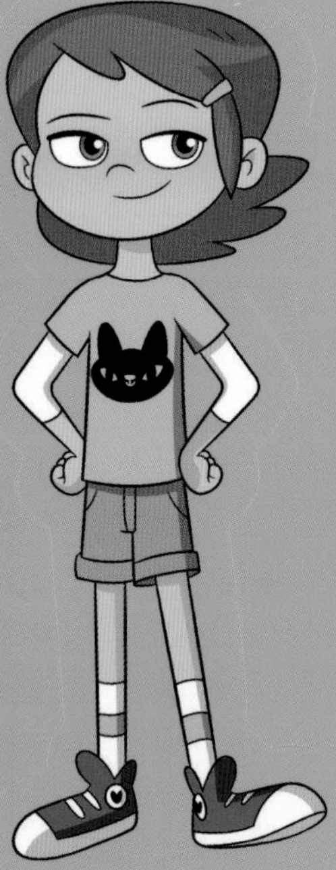

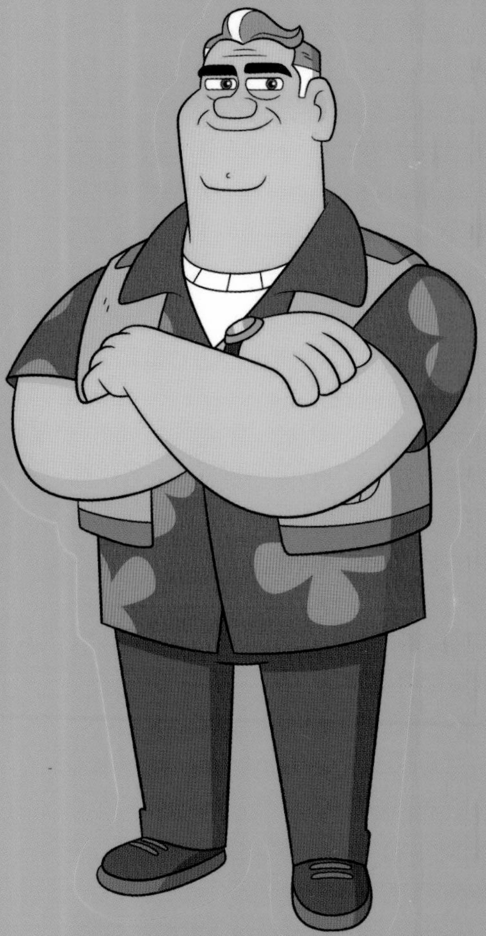

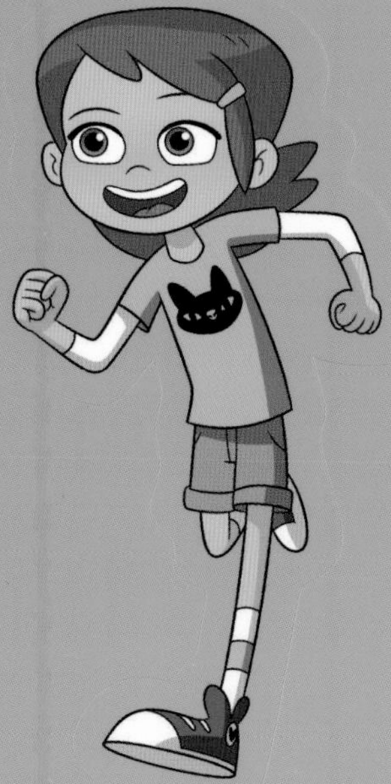

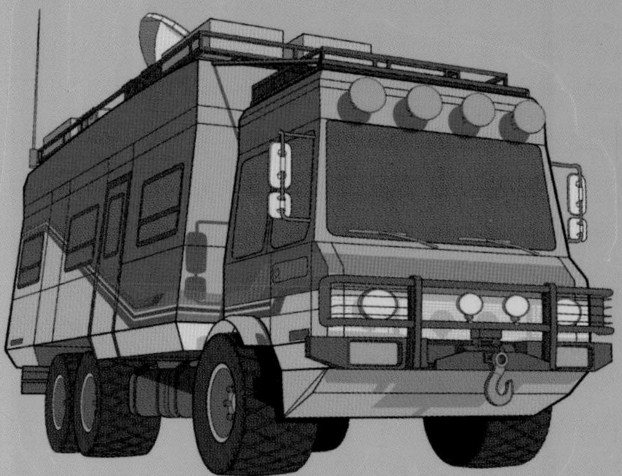